The Settlement

ALSO BY JOCK SERONG

Quota
The Rules of Backyard Cricket
On the Java Ridge
Preservation
The Burning Island

Jock Serong's novels have received the ARA Historical Novel Prize, the Colin Roderick Award, the Ned Kelly Award for First Fiction and, internationally, the inaugural Staunch Prize (UK) and the Historia Award for Historical Crime Fiction (France). He lives with his family on Victoria's far west coast.
@JockSerong

The Settlement

Jock Serong

TEXT PUBLISHING MELBOURNE AUSTRALIA

The Text Publishing Company acknowledges the Traditional Owners of the country on which we work, the Wurundjeri people of the Kulin Nation, and pays respect to their Elders past and present.

textpublishing.com.au

The Text Publishing Company
Wurundjeri Country, Level 6, Royal Bank Chambers, 287 Collins Street, Melbourne Victoria 3000 Australia

The Text Publishing Company (UK) Ltd
130 Wood Street, London EC2V 6DL, United Kingdom

Copyright © Jock Serong, 2022

The moral right of Jock Serong to be identified as the author of this work has been asserted.

All rights reserved. Without limiting the rights under copyright above, no part of this publication shall be reproduced, stored in or introduced into a retrieval system, or transmitted in any form or by any means (electronic, mechanical, photocopying, recording or otherwise), without the prior permission of both the copyright owner and the publisher of this book.

Published by The Text Publishing Company, 2022
Reprinted 2022

Cover design by Jessica Horrocks
Cover image by Catherine MacBride/Stocksy
Page design by Text
Typeset in Adobe Caslon Pro 12.5/17.5 by J&M Typesetting

Portraits of Truganini, Woorady and Mannalargenna by Thomas Bock from the collection of the British Museum

Printed and bound in Australia by Griffin Press, an accredited ISO/NZS 14001:2004 Environmental Management System printer.

ISBN: 9781922458797 (paperback)
ISBN: 9781922791009 (ebook)

A catalogue record for this book is available from the National Library of Australia.

 This book is printed on paper certified against the Forest Stewardship Council® Standards. Griffin Press holds FSC chain-of-custody certification SGSHK-COC-005088. FSC promotes environmentally responsible, socially beneficial and economically viable management of the world's forests.

Once it was taught that their death was somehow to our credit. We would come, in the name of the dead, to admire ourselves. That was a long time ago. Now all we understand is that we don't understand. But we come in humility, and in guilt, knowing that in some way we are all murderers, we are all cannibals, and the dead have been our victims.

Randolph Stow, Tourmaline

Statement Regarding First Nations Cultural Knowledge

This story did not only arise from my thoughts, and it belongs in significant ways to others. I have been generously supported. I pay my respects to the Tasmanian Aboriginal Nations whose rights, culture and land are represented in this novel. I acknowledge their authority to have custodianship of appropriate cultural knowledge and history in relation to their unceded lands. I acknowledge the importance of respect for all Indigenous people of Australia in the owning and holding of stories and cultural knowledge from their own nations and clans.

Multiple First Nations organisations and individuals have been contacted for consultation. I have read and applied the Australia Council's Protocols for Using First Nations Cultural and Intellectual Property in the Arts.

A donation has been made to the Indigenous Literacy Foundation, to be applied to the First Nations children of the Furneaux Islands, in recognition of the knowledge that has been shared with me.

J. S.

Foreword

This morning I developed my plans to the chief Mannalargenna and explained to him...that, if the natives would desist from wonted outrages upon the whites they would be allowed to remain in their respective districts and would have flour, tea and sugar, and clothes etc. given to them; that a good white man would dwell with them who would take care of them and would not allow any bad white man to shoot them, and he would go with them about the bush like myself and they then could hunt. He was much delighted.

George Augustus Robinson, Journals

George Augustus Robinson (1791–1866) was a builder of no great reputation, and later an evangelist.

In that latter role he walked the wilds of Tasmania between 1830 and 1834, negotiating a series of truces, or 'conciliations', with the decimated First Nations of Tasmania, as their asymmetrical war against the settlers collapsed into genocide. God would protect his 'Friendly Mission', Robinson believed, and He would protect the Indigenous peoples.

It was others who established 'Wybalenna' at Pea Jacket Point on Flinders Island in eastern Bass Strait, as a place to relocate the survivors. The name was said to have been plucked from the language of an unknown tribe. It has never been traced to one, and the survivors never used it.

Although Robinson is closely associated with the settlement, its stated purposes—to 'Christianise and civilise' those survivors—were in truth other people's goals. But he had made promises. Those who became its residents, or inmates, or captives—each label is freighted with judgments—invested their faith in him to deliver them from slaughter and to return them to safety on their country at some future date.

He did not return that faith. Tasmania's Aboriginal peoples suffered and died in large numbers at the settlement. They never went home.

Robinson himself took charge of the settlement between 1835 and '39. During that period he kept minutely detailed journals containing his thoughts and aspirations, his rages against perceived injustices, written with a propagandist's eye to posterity. Every day, no matter the monotony, he made an entry. In the main, they were copious, and they stand as one of history's most remarkable real-time records of an indigenous society under the onslaught of colonisation.

During the 1960s and '80s, the historian N. J. B. Plomley collected and transcribed the journals, alongside the diaries from Robinson's time in mainland Tasmania. He added annotations and supplementary documents, and called the massive books he'd created *Friendly Mission* and *Weep in Silence*. To read them from one end to the other, especially *Weep in Silence*, with its personal asides and grim tallies of burials and mortuary reports, is a bleak odyssey; an immersion in the pitiless logic of religious colonialism.

There is clear evidence—some of it written in his own hand—that during his time in charge of the settlement, Robinson was taking cultural artefacts, sacred amulets and even human remains from the people in his care. The most benign explanation for this behaviour is that he wished to discourage traditional practices and therefore confiscated any evidence of them that he found. Perhaps he wished to style himself as a man of science, or to ingratiate himself with his superiors, or with the anatomists of London.

As with every other event in those dark days, Robinson diarised the suffering and death in 1835 of the great Pairrebeenne chief, Mannalargenna. For the preceding five years the two men had been collaborators, rivals and reluctant political allies. Yet Robinson's journal barely mentions the final hours of this towering figure. From many hundreds of carefully compiled pages, those describing Mannalargenna's funeral are missing.

They appear to have been torn from the diary.

All of that appears in the historical record. However the passages in this novel attributed to the Commandant's journal and correspondence are in some cases taken from Robinson's actual journals (as transcribed by N. J. B. Plomley) and in some cases created for dramatic purposes. The reader should be aware that no reliance can be placed upon anything in the text that purports to be a historical document unless it is verified against archival sources.

PART ONE

~

Van Diemen's Land
October 1831

Embers

When he came to the clearing where the child had gone, the bad feeling was already well ahead of him.

The boy, Whelk, was there in the open, looking back over his shoulder at his own small footprints in the ash. Tiny whirls where the air was hot and escaping.

He had walked into the centre of the clearing, high trees all around him. A little smoke still rose from the place where the fire had been, and even several yards back the Surveyor could feel the warmth of it on his face. The ground must be glowing hot under the boy's feet, but he was paying no heed, and seemed unaware of the Surveyor watching him. He reached his fingers into the gloom, seeking balance. A misplaced step could crush through the powdery surface. A burnt foot would slow everybody down. The Man would be displeased. The Man was often displeased.

The charred timbers splayed outwards: the Surveyor saw now

that Whelk was standing in the ghost of a hut. The air was thick with menace: no birds, no breeze. The rest of the party were out in the bush around them but there were no voices. The world was dumb and blurred as he watched the boy, and he felt as though he had been struck over the head. In the white powdered ash he saw an iron door latch, sooted black. The barrel and breech of a rifle. Bottles standing in a crate now burnt away.

The smell of it was powerful, recent. Not the smell of a cooking fire, of the burning grasses, of the pyres he'd seen that these people made for their dead. This one was just timbers, but it hadn't started of its own accord. There would be people.

He called Whelk back from the clearing, and the boy looked up at him, returning from wherever his mind had gone to.

~

They'd watched from a high bluff earlier in the day as the smoke rose from the far side of the plain. It was far away, where the forest resumed beyond the grassland. The Man believed it was the news they'd been waiting for: the Big River tribe, signalling that they were willing to talk. When he'd seen enough he started making orders, bustling about in high excitement, sending advance parties to flank around the place, ensure it wasn't an ambush. That meant sending white men with black men, so that a trap set either by stockkeepers or by the Big River warriors might be averted.

Once the parties were provisioned and another group selected to watch over the supplies, the Man turned to Mannalargenna, the old chief.

'I want you to come down there with me. Be my emissary among these people.'

The chief watched him, his face unmoved under the ochred hair.

'Emiss—'

'Emissary. I want you to talk to them. In place of me.'

The chief frowned. He looked at the Man, then at the sky. 'Good day to hunt,' he said, as though he'd been asked something else.

The Man took off his cloth hat and crushed it in one hand, and the Surveyor saw his frustration.

'Plenty *tara-na* that way.' The chief waved a casual hand to the east. 'Good hunting.' The men had already brought out the blocks of ochre they had been keeping. The chief wandered off to gather his tools for the hunt, leaving the Man fuming.

His gaze fell upon the Surveyor, taller than him but unthreatening. His long cheeks and poking bones obscured his nature somehow; he knew this. His was a face in clouds. It meant his inner thoughts were concealed, and he preferred it that way.

'You will come with me,' said the Man, and the Surveyor, accustomed to these sudden demands, looked for the satchel that contained his maps of their route. He would be able to sketch the valley floor, he supposed. All of it was useful work. Useful work for an honest wage, and an honest wage drew a man closer to financial comfort. Closer to asking for the hand of a woman.

Whelk appeared with the satchel slung in hope over his small shoulder. The Surveyor thought to tell him off, then relented. There was no one else for the boy to follow. Mannalargenna would not hunt with a child, and if Whelk stayed with the older ones who were guarding the camp, they would make him fetch for them. The Surveyor rested a hand on the boy's head and smiled back at him.

The people were naked now, glowing in the sun, bodies rubbed with grease and draped in strings, necklaces and bracelets. They stroked and murmured over scarifications. The Surveyor watched this transformation, watched the bold streaks of ochre striping their flanks, and he saw that the Man had noticed it too and, in his bottomless pride, had made no comment.

So they set off together; the Surveyor, Whelk and the Man, down from the high rocks that had been their lookout. The land levelled at a narrow creek and they waded through, and the Surveyor saw in Whelk's eager motion the pride he took in being this person, chosen to accompany the Man.

They had walked the flat, weaving between tussocks and saplings as the sun went high then started to fall in the west, and all that time they could see the top of the smoke plume where it faded into the blue sky. Sometimes the Surveyor imagined stockkeepers crouching in the shadowed distance with their guns levelled—the country was crawling with them, intent on slaughter—but when he looked at the Man and the small boy he saw no sign of fear. The whole party thought the Man was a fool, that he was pompous and possibly mad. But no one questioned his bravery.

They did not talk as they travelled. The Man appeared triumphant, marching faster and faster so that at times Whelk had to skip into a run to keep up. Small creatures burst out of the grasses. Barefooted, the boy stayed directly behind the Surveyor's thumping boots.

It was late afternoon when they reached the clearing, when it became apparent that this was not the moment they had hoped for, but a cruel mistake. The Man broke through the thick scrub first, so that the Surveyor had to swing his arms through the clouds of swirling insects he'd raised. The air was hazed with smoke as the Man surged forward, surely by now suspicious at having heard no voices. Whelk saw him slump, saw the loss of all that energy. This was no signal fire; it was no gathering of the Big River elders and their chief, come to offer their submission to the Man and his great Conciliation.

Something terrible had happened here.

~

The Surveyor watched the boy standing at the centre of the clearing, and for a long moment he could not decide what to do or say. He hated this indecision in himself, and the boy felt important to him in ways he couldn't fathom.

Whelk was apparently transfixed, or waiting for his senses to guide him. It was a white man's hut: it would have been a stockman's, like the ones they had seen many times in the three weeks they'd walked the high country. But there was nothing to say who had burnt it, or why.

Just as the Surveyor determined that he should walk through the ash and retrieve the boy, his small body seemed to remember itself, and he walked out the far side of the clearing. The Man remained where he stood, watching, but the Surveyor went after him. Whelk was moving into the trees, picking his way through the dry twigs of the undergrowth, as though following the scent of some dark suspicion.

When they found her, it was not a surprise.

Face down, her hair thrown forward, she wore a possum coat and a large kangaroo skin over her shoulder. It had been full of pups: they had spilled near her outflung arm, fawn bodies entangled and sleeping peacefully on the dry leaves. Whelk had stopped and was staring at them, entranced again. The Surveyor was still gathering his breath from the headlong plunge through the scrub. As his gaze rested on the warm mass of the pups he saw movement and briefly thought the woman was alive. But it wasn't that, he realised. There was another pup trapped under her.

Whelk had noticed it too: and together they knelt and lifted the poor woman's shoulder. Her flesh was cold and the twigs and leaves stuck to it. They felt underneath the shoulder for the pup's legs, and the boy pulled them free. There was some blood stuck in the fur of the hind legs he had in his fist. The tiny dog yelped as its body stretched, and once it was free it circled about, confused, then sat in the waves of the woman's hair, pawing at the strands.

Whelk squatted and clutched his knees. The Surveyor sat on his haunches and waited. He was a patient man, not given to rushed decisions. The sun came down to him in shades through the canopy, angular now and nearly gone. He didn't know what the Man would want him to do. He had no spade to bury the woman, and it would be hours of work: the boy was too small to assist him. But presently his dilemma was solved for him. The Man appeared out of the undergrowth: his eyes fell on the boy and the woman and the pups, and the sadness pierced him.

'Ah,' he said. 'Oh dear Lord.'

He came over, ignoring the Surveyor, and placed a hand on Whelk's shoulder, and the other one on the woman's neck. His fingers searched her throat gently, then reached down her back and shifted the possum cloak away to reveal a circular scar on her skin.

'Big River,' he said to himself. 'Such a shame.'

The Surveyor could not tell what was the shame, the fact that the woman had been killed or the fact that she was Big River. He said nothing. The boy was crying, the Man looking at him, looking at his tears, and suddenly Whelk got up and stormed off into the trees. Finally the two men locked eyes, and the Surveyor saw only bewilderment in the Man's face. No one knew where Whelk's country was, what his true name was, or how these sights affected him. He was an orphan in more ways than the word had means to carry. He had been assigned to the Man for so long that he had more of the Man's language than his own.

There was another sound in the bush, apart from the cries of the butcher birds and the tapping leaves. The Surveyor listened intently. Sometimes the squeak of a split tree could sound that way, but no—it was steady and did not come and go with the wind.

They started to move towards it. The brush was thick and tangled—it had not been burnt—but it was veined with slender paths under the low boughs. A fat orb spider was creating its web for the coming night, running threads across a gap in the faint track: Whelk darted below without heed, but the web draped itself over the Man's chest as he passed.

He stopped then, flicked the spider from his coat and listened. A ledge of rock towards the setting sun. There. An overhang.

The rocks had formed a hollow and it had been barricaded with snapped boughs. The Man bent down and pulled them away, crouching to look in. Whelk and the Surveyor peered in too. The air inside was cool, the space lined with flat sand, and on the sand sat a little girl, fat and naked and crying.

She stopped when she saw them. Her body jerked with the echoes of lost sobs. There was some substance, perhaps dried food, on her chest. She assessed them, saw no threat and began to study Whelk's skin. The Surveyor understood it was white men who had done the thing, whatever it was. Whelk must have appeared safe with these white men—by extension they were not murderers.

The wall of stone behind her offered no retreat. They were blocking the entrance, and without discussion they sat back, pulled away to each side and the Man made a soft sound of encouragement. The girl eyed the opening they had created but at first she did not move.

A single shaft of light cut through the leaves of the canopy and down between all the timber, over the Surveyor's shoulder and into the hollow, and it found the girl's eye, wide and wounded and sad beyond measure. Deep in her eye was hidden the evidence of all she had endured. There in the forest, on the high country that belonged to the Big River mob, they had come under a responsibility. She gazed at the boy and he was tied to her immediately.

Her breath shuddered and her face moved out of the light, was lost in shadow then crossed into the light again. She stood and bent low, came forward out of the crowding space and took hold of Whelk's hand.

A Circle on High Ground

It had been eight days since the woman and the pups, eight days Whelk had spent caring for the girl. The other parties had come in from their separate travels: Mannalargenna and Umarrah from their hunts, Kickerterpoller and Little Jemmy from their careful search for stockmen. The women were there, the convicts, all of them. And nobody had any idea who the little girl was.

They guessed she was Big River, but only because they had found her out here. Some of them thought she was the daughter of the fallen woman, the one near the burnt hut, but only because she'd been found nearby and the woman was clearly Big River by the designs on her skin. They thought maybe the mother had stuffed her under the overhang and hidden her with the branches when she'd heard the marauders coming.

The girl could tell them nothing. She had words for simple things: food, fire, water. But they were not words anyone recognised, and she refused to speak her own name.

Stansfield the convict poked eagerly at her, grinning with his gums so that the whiskers of his cheeks spread like a stretching echidna. When he'd seen that same leer directed at Whelk, the Surveyor understood that the boy hated and feared it. Instinct would drive Whelk nearer the girl to protect her, which would get Stansfield laughing and nudging his friend McGeary.

'Whelky got hisself a missus!' In the absence of an inn this passed for entertainment. 'Now whatayer call a missus for shell boy?' and Stansfield scratched at his head until the scratching turned to picking at a scab.

Dawn was spreading over the hills. The air was thin and cold and the fire held them close. The Man was already working in his journal, and it was clear from the movement of his nearer eyebrow that he was half-listening.

Stansfield's face lit up. 'Pipi! Nuther kind o shell.'

The Man closed the book over his pen and frowned. 'Now then, gentlemen,' he rumbled in the voice that was too big for him. 'I think we might wait until we can identify the child by its correct tribal name.'

Stansfield adopted a look of childish mischief. 'Not enough of em left for identifyin.'

'The tribe is still out there,' the Man replied calmly. 'There can be no doubt.'

'Seem pretty sure of it,' Stansfield smirked. 'Whyn't you git the chief there to ask his devil?'

'Mind your tone, Stansfield.'

Across the fire Mannalargenna raised his chin slightly, aware that Stansfield was drawing him into the conversation. He was sitting cross-legged by the coals, heating a length of ti-tree for a spear, concentrating. Only a year earlier, he had been out in the bush of the northeast, a fighter and a fugitive of the very kind they were seeking. Now he turned an irritable gaze towards the convict. The eyes, ringed by remnant ash, rested heavily on him.

Stansfield chuckled nervously and looked away. 'Tryin a git his devil on me now!' He swallowed, got up and took himself away from the fire to piss on the scrub. *Pipi*, he grunted over the hissing, and he laughed to himself.

The Man turned to Mannalargenna. 'You will come with me and have a look up the valley, then?'

The look of irritation now turned upon the Man. 'Said I would, mister. Told you yesterday.'

The Man took a deep swig from the mug beside him and threw the dregs on the fire. 'Well, come on then.'

Their bodies disappeared into the dark scrub, heads and shoulders silhouetted against the orange sky. The sound of them retreated. The Surveyor had his own work to do: notes to assemble, equipment to be cleaned and repacked. He thought about following the two men: he was curious about everything the two of them did, that unlikely pair, but now the party had the extra girl to think about. She was asleep, curled in a bundle of possum skins by the boy's side. She adored him: that much was clear. But Whelk was watching the departing men also, and then looking down at her, indecisive.

'Go along.' The voice came from behind the fire. Pagerly, Kickerterpoller's wife, smiling gently. 'Go chase em, boy. I watch this one here.'

A grateful flash of the eyes and he was gone. The Surveyor climbed to his feet.

'I might, um, might be best I go keep an eye on the boy, then.'

~

They were easy enough to follow. In the distance he could see the boy making his way over the dawn-lit landscape, and by keeping him in sight he knew he would be led to the other two.

His mind drifted as he trailed after them. The Big River mob: the Man talked about nothing else but them, and how he might meet them and persuade them to come in from the bush. The old people said nothing, but they made clear they wanted no part of it. There were dark mutterings: *Bad people. Killers.* When Mannalargenna said he was going out hunting, he was going out lighting fires to warn the Big River mob to stay away. He had his own history with them, and he had no intention of meeting them. Everyone knew it. The Man had to be aware of it, but he grimaced and pressed on.

Ahead of him Whelk stopped and yawned, placed a hand on a tree and lifted a foot to pull something from the sole. The boy knew the Surveyor was there behind him, but he was unconcerned. His feet must be hurting. It had been weeks of this, over stones, under branches. Now the land was sloping upwards, just slightly. Beyond them was the sound of murmuring voices. He looked at the sky and it felt like it was changing shape, like the land was about to end and let the sky take over.

And when he cleared the last of the trees, he found this was so. There was a sharp edge, and beyond it the vast open air, hills in soft colours in the distance. Mannalargenna and the Man lay on their bellies looking over, the boy kneeling beside them. The chief's body was long and spare; the Man's short and clumsy. Where the Man's dusted black coat and trousered legs made him look like a fallen crow, the chief was nearly naked and his limbs were sleek and brown. Both heads—hat and piped hair—were raised, alert, as the two of them looked over the edge. The boy, on the other hand, looked back at him as he approached.

Mannalargenna turned and motioned for him to be silent. He pointed to the ground next to himself and went back to his vigil. The Surveyor crept silently to the indicated place, lay down and peered over.

The world below was huge: a plain that extended almost to the horizons where steep forested hills rose in a darker green. He knew from the shape of the plain that a river skirted around it on his left. There might be another one, a lesser one, to his right. He was practised at these observations. The clouds seemed to build from the far end of the valley—the sun was behind them and the weather in front.

And there in the south, a long way off, he could see the sharp white outlines of a house. There were lurid greens around it, English trees that the settlers had planted to remake their homes in this incorrect landscape. The owner of the white house in the south had been the topic of campfire discussion for three nights now. *Mister Cameron*, the Man had said, feigning business but revealing worry. *We will give him a wide berth.*

'Do not tell me again, please,' the Man was saying now. It sounded as though he and the old chief had been engaged in some sort of argument before the Surveyor's arrival. 'I have heard this nonsense many times now.'

Mannalargenna looked at him quizzically.

'This talk of devils, your *personal* devil. You must know that it is unhelpful in teaching the others the way of the Lord—*ah!*—There!'

He looked down his eyeglass. 'Three men. Coming this way down the plain.'

The Surveyor could just make out the shape of a strong, dark horse, being led by the men. Something circled around the horse and the men. After a moment he saw by the pattern of movement that it was a large dog, tethered somehow, maybe tied to the horse. A single agitated bark drifted up on the air. He looked down and saw that there was a small stockyard below them, where the plain ended at the forested wall of the cliff. The men and their animals were headed towards it.

'What he doing?' asked Mannalargenna.

The Man squinted, baring his teeth again, and rotated the barrel of the eyeglass. 'The one on the right is a servant—a prisoner, I would say. That's Cameron on the left, his son with him, with the horse.'

'Got musket?'

'No. But the mare is loaded up. Not sure with what.'

'You know, maybe we go other way, get away from this lot. Round back way.'

The Man lowered the eyeglass slightly. He sighed.

'So many times now I have asked you to put your interests aside and assist me, Mannalargenna. I cannot divest myself of the feeling that if you wanted to you could walk into this scrub behind us and return with the entirety of the Big River tribe.'

The Man always strained to keep his face neutral when he addressed the old chief, but now his frustration was plain. 'This was your promise, you may recall. You would guide us. You would conciliate on my behalf.' He huffed, his impatience released.

The Surveyor had heard these exchanges for weeks now. Mannalargenna would listen. He would seem puzzled, as if he was trying to keep up with the strange language the Man used: not only a different tongue, but as complicated as possible on top of that. It was a game, he was fairly sure. The Man would become angry and the anger would tangle his words ever more grotesquely. The chief would play at confusion, and it would make the Man even more bellicose. He didn't understand why the chief tormented the Man like this, but he thought there must be reasons. The chief didn't do anything without reason. The boy, he saw, read all of this drama in some private way. It did not perturb him so much as fascinate him.

Below, the men and the black horse and the dog had reached the stockyard and the Surveyor could see the agitation in their bodies, in their movements. They were arguing. Tiny fragments of their voices rose up the escarpment to where they lay. Cameron's movements betrayed his greater age. He had taken the load off the mare now, and with a flick of a whip he drove the dog into the stockyard, where its rapid barking signalled its displeasure.

Cameron and his son were doing something to the stockyard fence while the dog barked furiously at them. The servant was sitting on the grass, some distance away. *Odd*, thought the Surveyor. Normally the servant would be the one doing the work.

The Man put the eyeglass down and rolled onto his back. He looked at the sky, then lowered his cloth hat over his eyes. It was rare that the Surveyor saw the Man unoccupied, yielding to the tiredness of his body. But he was tired. He did everything, *everything*, that he expected of the guides, and of the prisoners. He worked nearly as hard as the packhorse. And he did it in those heavy clothes, the coat and the hat and the necktie, the shoes with their silver buckles.

In the early days of these expeditions, back at Port Davey in the south, he had thought the Man misunderstood how to travel in the bush, that it was all a matter of learning the right way to do it: lightweight and quiet, more like the natives. But the Man had made clear that God wanted it this way. And his little ruddy face would go pink with the heat and his knuckles would mottle white with mosquito bites because he would not rub grease on them. This was the way he wanted things to be.

Mannalargenna rolled onto one hip so that he faced the Man, regarding him with something like pity, or mere patience. Watching him there as a body, and not as the great chief, the Surveyor found him fascinating. Old wounds all over him, but he still flowed over the land like water, long and thin like the younger men but imbued with a singular power. His words could stop everything.

The Man had no such power. The prisoners and the soldiers would snigger or talk over him and his words were frequently wasted. He would raise his voice and make it worse. It was possible, in those moments when he watched the chief so intently, that the Man was wishing he had Mannalargenna's power to persuade.

A faint echo of hammering from the valley below.

'What happen…' Mannalargenna's voice suddenly cut through the Surveyor's thoughts. 'What happen when all them people gone?'

'Who?' answered the Man from under his hat.

'Big River mob. What about all this country?'

There was a long silence then, and the Surveyor imagined the Man's thoughts coming and going from under the hat in humming spirals like bees at a hive. The Man tipped the brim back.

'The land will be empty for a time.' He paused. 'The settlers will move their livestock through, I imagine.'

Mannalargenna's puzzlement now looked perfectly real. 'Then we come back,' he said, or perhaps asked.

'Well, not immediately,' replied the Man, plainly wanting to close off the discussion. 'If I bring you back too soon, the trouble will start again. I cannot have that on my conscience, you understand. And besides'—his tone became brighter—'you might like the islands. Plenty of hunting there.'

'You be bringin us back.'

'Yes, of course. Just as soon as that becomes possible.' The Man rolled over onto his belly and took up the eyeglass. 'Good Lord.'

The Surveyor shuffled himself to the edge again and looked over. The scene in the stockyard below was so bizarre that at first he doubted his eyes. The servant was in the stockyard now, running, darting, flailing wildly, his face contorted by terror. He had removed his shirt and wrapped it around his right arm. There was a possum-skin cloak over his shoulders and in his left hand he held a spear.

The stockman's dog was lunging at the poor man, trying in a frenzy to bite at his legs and bring him down. As Whelk watched, the dog got its huge paws on the man's chest and pushed him over: he tumbled onto his back and jabbed frantically at the dog with the end of the spear, but he would not use the spear to its proper effect and kill it.

The dog had no such qualms. It snarled and took hold of the bundled shirt with the arm inside, and shook its massive head. Even so high above, the bands of muscle were visible, bulging over the dog's eyes and locking the jaws on the servant's arm. Cameron and his son sat on the rail of the yard, laughing uproariously. They yelled encouragement at the dog, and when the servant veered towards them, seeking the sanctuary of the rails, the older man swung a boot at the side of his head.

'Tell me why you come here,' the chief said, his voice sad and steady. The dog set up a frantic, furious baying and lunged again at the servant.

'Here? We needed to find out if Cameron is in residence at his property.'

'No, *here*. All of you. All this.'

The Man rolled over and sighed. 'We have had this conversation before,' he replied. He looked up at the sky like the answer was there. '*We*—Englishmen—pursue a duty to bring light to darkness. Civilisation.'

The four of them edged back from the lip of the escarpment and sat upright. Mannalargenna looked at the Man, and his eyes made clear what he thought of that.

~

They moved on after returning from the cliff, to the northeast and then the east, making a wide circle in the high country. By nightfall they were many miles from Cameron's stockyard and the Man felt comfortable allowing a fire. He had spoken often of his concern about the bands of settlers that roamed the bush, looking to discharge their grudges.

It was a strange game: travelling across country, looking for a tribe that seemed to be hiding, while at the same time hiding themselves from the settlers. At nights when the Surveyor lay vulnerable in his bed-roll he wondered if his white skin afforded him any sanctuary. Couldn't the likes of Cameron see that this work—the work of emptying the land peaceably—was in their interests? He guessed that Cameron would see them as sympathisers, impediments to clearing the place by force, without all this cumbersome negotiating.

Oddly enough, this particular night—the night the attack finally happened—the Surveyor had had no such thoughts. The people lay about in the grass, in the groups that accorded with their unseen ways, arranging their hides and blankets as the night cooled. They had finished eating when they heard the sound of hoofbeats approaching. Kickerterpoller sat alert, listening. *Heavy one*, he muttered.

The horse was coming from upwind. There was no stealth in it, and for a long moment they all mistook the audacity of it for harmlessness. Nobody stood, nobody skirted away from the fire to take up a position in the bush. Nobody hid from what was approaching. But when it arrived, it did so with shocking violence.

The Surveyor realised that it was the great black mare from earlier in the day and for a terrified second he thought the huge dog was alongside it. The mare came crashing into the clearing and the horseman on its back hauled it broadside so that its hooves stamped among the remains of the meal.

Whelk darted to the far side of the fire, taking the terrified girl with him. The man on the horse was heavy and skilful, and his face under a broad hat was burnt deep red. He wore a horseman's trousers and long boots, and the Surveyor glimpsed in the flicker of firelight the rifle slung under the saddle, the whip. The mare's eyes were wild: maybe panic at being run into this crowd of people, maybe an animal poorly trained to begin with.

There were cries of fear from the people on the ground. The Man was raising his voice towards the horseman, but no word came in return. His mouth was pressed into a determined line, and he worked his arms, elbows high, to circle the horse. As people scattered, a hoof struck the fire and a shower of embers leapt up: the horse wheeled in fright and twisted into a low turn that nearly threw the rider off.

So fast, so great and heavy, the bellows of its ribs and the mighty wall of its chest. The Surveyor saw to his relief that Whelk was safely out wide, clutching the girl. The stink and the noise, the muscle of a black flank. Its fur was worked into a glowing sheen in the dim light: it had been driven over distance, and at speed.

The women were screaming, the men shouting, waving arms and weapons at the horse and its rider. The fire gleamed on the steel bit in the animal's mouth. The rider's face showed no strain or surprise and, having recovered the animal from its stagger, his control was total. The mare reared onto its hind legs, and the rider worked the reins so that its flank swung at the men on the ground and the last thing the Surveyor saw was the flare of its tail and it was gone.

~

The Man tried to control the talk afterwards, but it got away from him. Although nobody could tell who the rider was or why he had come, the old people were convinced it was Cameron, come in warning. The Surveyor thought they were right: it appeared, after all, to be the same horse they had seen at the stockyard that afternoon.

The Man urged them not to leap to conclusions. The rider had come alone; he had not discharged his rifle. Perhaps it was all a misunderstanding. He appealed to the Surveyor.

'Surely you would agree, Loftus—he could not have come all this way, up the escarpment and across country.'

He actually thought that was exactly what the rider had done, and he remembered how slowly they had travelled through the afternoon. It was entirely possible that Cameron had tracked them. But he hated to agree or disagree in front of all of them. They waited for his answer: he nodded equably and looked at his feet.

No one was convinced by the Man's reassurances. Mannalargenna said they should leave before something worse happened. He took the incident as a clear message: 'This Big River lot,' he said, 'this mob killed more white men than white men kill them. No one else done that. Fightin us, too, years and years. Bad people, dangerous people.'

The old ones nodded their agreement. Only Kickerterpoller seemed to demur: among the senior people he was the only one who had friendly links to these people and their terrifying leader, Tongerlongeter.

'Now this bloke on his horse,' Mannalargenna continued, 'he can't get the Big River mob. Too quick, runnin on their own country. But he can get *us*, see? Make his message with *us*.'

There were murmurings among the people. Even the prisoners were stirred: they now saw themselves in as much danger as the rest. Any shooting would be imprecise. If fire was used it would not discriminate. Talk turned to the landscape and the dangers of gullies, visions of the whole party caught in a bowl in the land, fire sweeping in and the stockmen propped on the rim, firing down. They'd done it before.

Mannalargenna turned on the Man. 'How you gonna protect all these people?' He pointed his finger around the gathering as he said it.

'It is too late for such assessments,' said the Man from where he sat on top of a sleeping roll. 'We are here now. If you try going back to Campbell Town without me they will surely shoot you all. And I will leave neither you nor the Big River people out here without my protection.'

The Surveyor understood this. It was only the Man's presence that constituted protection: there was nothing he could do or say. And the older people like Woorady and Kickerterpoller could follow enough of the Man's tortured language to accept his logic. All of them looked jittery, spooked by the thought of pressing higher into this country, towards Lake Sorrell and away from the stock runs. Mannalargenna was deep in conversation with Woorady and Dick and Lacklay. They closed themselves in with their turned shoulders, excluding the Man.

Whelk had gone to Pagerly, who was lying with the little girl in her arms. He nestled in beside the two of them. He was still small enough that the women would let him do it, and Pagerly was big and warm: to Pipi and Whelk she would stand for everything that was kind and safe. She was not one for agitated talk. Even as the Surveyor watched them, the boy was cupping his hand very carefully behind the little girl's head and stroking her fine hair with his fingertips while Pagerly smiled at him with a warm kind of gruffness. Pipi, *Pipi*. He would have to think about that. The prisoner meant it as an insult, he thought, but it suited the girl all the same.

Where had she really come from? Where had the boy come from? This long march left behind a leaf litter of memories, scraps and fragments of people's pasts, falling away from them all the time as the Man strove each day to invent their future. It was disturbing, and the Surveyor began to wonder if he had lost any of *his* past in the trampled grass behind their procession. There, there were the eyes of his parents, and his sister, and there was a childhood home in Kent. All secure in their places. He should practise them, recite their names each morning lest they vanish.

He looked down again at the boy in Pagerly's lap: he was asleep now, adrift on some tide, a body that may or may not have ever known the ocean.

~

When he woke it was the middle of the night and the moon was up, casting blue shadows from the skeleton trees.

He had dreamed about the black horse, and the fear was thick all over him. The dream horse writhed and bucked in and out of the lines of contour he had been drawing, an animal as tortured as the land itself. There was no sound but a mopoke and a slender rustle of breeze, the breathing and snoring around him. He lay there alert, watching the night, thinking he could never return to sleep. The slightest pulsation in the darkness, even the harmless thuds of the wallabies, could be the return of the dreaded hooves. He sighed and drew back the blanket that had covered him: he would walk the horse-dream out of his body and replace it with something calmer. As he rolled onto his front and knelt up, he saw the whites of the little girl's eyes in the darkness of Pagerly's lap: unafraid, watchful, almost iridescent in the moon's glow. She stirred and settled. A watch had been set, and the watchers would be on higher ground downwind, if the prisoners had sense enough to listen to the native guides. He would walk upwind so as not to alarm them. He climbed from his bedding and started away from the camp, feet bare and gentle on the ground.

Before long he had left the protective glow of the fire behind as the ground rose gently before him. Away from the smoke, the bush smelled alive and new, and now the air carried something else: a sound, coming faintly to him. He stopped, held his breath, rested his hands on his knees there in the strange light.

A voice. Not a conversation but one voice, soft and murmuring, sometimes spiking louder.

Fear surged in the Surveyor's belly and for a moment he was paralysed by it. Insects alighted on his ears and neck, and the tips of the grasses brushed his trousers. The mopoke sounded again. The murmuring went on and he briefly imagined that Mannalargenna heard his devil this way: a devil that came to people in the trees and commanded them to do things. Soft persuasion, something tempting. The Man had scoffed at such talk, but he wasn't here now, was he? Things easily dismissed when the sun shone bright stuck firm under a full moon.

The voice had not grown louder. It was not approaching. A wild thrill coursed through him as though he was a boy again, engaged in some transgression. Another memory he must protect. He walked towards the sound, compelled and reluctant.

Bright places, low trees that straggled in no particular way, neither forest nor grassland. There was enough space between the trees for the moon to work its light over the grasses and there, over there, behind a handful of gnarled trunks, was the source of the sound: a human shape, a man bent low. The voice rumbled on, and now he could see the pale reflection of the moonlight on an uplifted face. He crept closer, through a low wallaby tunnel in the grasses. Now when he peered out he saw, and he understood.

It was the Man, on his knees. His hands were pressed together in front of his chest and his face was upturned to the heavens so he was eerily bathed in starlight. He was talking to his god, begging him, perhaps; but his features were transformed by joy, a powerful rapture that the Surveyor had never seen in him. He was at one, now, with the dusted, fathomless sky. The words were nonsensical and had no shape but found structure as a chant: rhythmic and so familiar to the speaker that he never once hesitated. His body swayed with it. His hands would occasionally part from each other and he would raise one of them before his eyes, as though to emphasise something. Just once he raised them both, making a cup with his arms, and as he did so he dropped his head and hung there: a devotional image of Calvary. Jesus, thrashed and limp.

The Surveyor was transfixed. The language the Man was using was not English, maybe not an earthly language at all. It had curls and babbles and lumps in it, a stream working frantically over stones. He sat on one hip and listened carefully, his own head bowed, and he remained in that position for a long time, a time that was hard to measure.

Away in the distance, much later, a bush creature barked and the spell was broken. The Man stopped and cocked his head, listening. Deep in the grasses, the Surveyor held his breath again and waited until the Man relaxed and rose slowly, pushing to one knee, then stood. Calm now, he looked up once more at the moon and began to walk back towards the camp.

Staying low over the grasses, the Surveyor followed him in silence.

Led Deeper by the Big River People

For three more days they pressed on in a great curve around the lands claimed by the settler Cameron.

The Big River people, fierce and fleeting, existed only as maddening hints. Warm ashes, a marked tree, distant smoke. Everyone understood that these people must be approached, must be warned that their survival depended on them coming in with the Man. And they also knew that only Kickerterpoller could make the approach. Whatever they thought of Mannalargenna's devils and his agendas, they recognised that it was Kickerterpoller who had the authority over these hills and valleys, more land than they could see or even walk over, and he had the trust of Tongerlongeter. Mannalargenna was senior, but it would not be him who put himself in the way of a spearing by making the final approach.

Mannalargenna was playing games again: going off hunting, coming back with only a wombat or a possum. Engaging in long discussions with his devil, who would speak to him by making his muscles twitch, tugging at his chest while he made motions as though to resist.

It convinced many of the people; Woorady and Umarrah and his wife, Tanleboneyer. When the devil started working his convulsions on the old chief everything else—all walking or gathering or even discussion—had to cease immediately.

The prisoners, for whom this expedition was a forced march, had long ago decided that the only possible end to it was to find the Big River people and drag them in. They had no way of measuring Kickerterpoller's credibility and they doubted that Mannalargenna was being guided by a spirit, though the Catholics among them were wary of disregarding something that so resembled the workings of the Holy Ghost.

The Man, for his part, was forced to respect Mannalargenna: his temper threatened to get away from him but he held his tongue. He would grit his teeth and ask politely what the devil wanted them to do, and Mannalargenna would frown and incline his head, apparently listening for guidance. But the Man also had to assert that he, not Mannalargenna, was in charge. So he'd try ordering the chief to do something—*go climb that hill and tell me which way the river turns*. The chief would either glare at him or ignore him altogether. The Man dared not insist because the stand-off would confirm his lack of authority beyond doubt. So he'd divert the order to the Surveyor, or pretend something else had suddenly arisen and rush off. The Surveyor saw a poorly hidden glee in the chief's eyes at such times.

On the third day after the horse, they were scrambling up a rock face when there were shouts from the people in front and the column halted: someone called that there was a snake. The Man sighed down his nose to signal his displeasure and strode forward. Tibb and Lacklay were standing back from a heavy tiger snake, threaded along the track and watching them with its glittering black eye.

'Oh, for God's sake,' sighed the Man. 'Is that it?'

No one answered him. They backed further away. Mannalargenna had now pressed forward and was watching the snake, speaking quietly to Tanleboneyer. 'He very bad one,' he said aloud. 'No good.'

The party began to file around the snake.

'What's the trouble?' the Man asked loudly. 'As with so many things,' he answered himself, 'you must never let the animal know you are afraid. Would you not agree, chief?' Locking eyes with Mannalargenna, the Man took the snake by its tail. It swerved drowsily at his hand but did not strike. The strong coils poured themselves over the ground in an effort to be rid of him, but the Man lifted the whole body of the snake until it dangled nearly to the ground, twisting his hand so that the tail was wrapped over it, improving his grip. And suddenly, he thrust downward and whipped the long body in the air. There was a snapping sound and the snake hung limp. The Man dropped it on the ground at Mannalargenna's feet, upturned and yellowy-white, apparently dead.

'We must dispense with superstitions,' said the Man, bringing his face close to the chief's. He stared at all of them now. 'We must do away with small fears if we are to succeed.'

The Surveyor watched all of this closely, and later he would wonder if the chief had indeed been frightened, or if he knew something about the snake and its place in the world that the Man could never fathom.

~

The people were uneasy as they moved across the southern shore of the Great Lake, with the slopes of the Western Tiers now looming above. Mannalargenna gestured at the furrowed rocks and said the Big River people would be up there, pushing higher out of reach of the stockmen. Kickerterpoller nodded in mute agreement: his time was coming. The announcement made the Man more determined: he drove them to pick up the pace.

They stopped to drink at a hoof-muddied creek. Dick and Trugernana studied the crushed ground, making small sounds of sadness. The Man sat in the shade, removed his cloth hat, wiped the sweat from his forehead and said that it was now December. That meant the changing of the seasons, he explained: the coming of summer. It struck a chime of nostalgia in the Surveyor, a thing he felt about his old home. But here the seasons did what they wanted with no regard for calendar dates. Trees decided the turn of the season by flowering, grasses by bolting to seed. Neither thing had happened.

Mannalargenna pointed to the trees and announced that the weather was *coming no good*, which felt like a deliberate contradiction of the Man's seasonal announcement. The Man carried no glass with him to test the chief's assertion, but he looked up at the clear blue skies and declared him wrong.

Always this choice between two poles of belief: the Man and the chief. The Surveyor looked down at Whelk, who hovered nearby. The boy's eyes were on the cold and angry-looking rocks of the Tiers. The girl walked beside him, as she had done since the moment he had found her in the hollow. She held his hand. She looked where he looked.

Soon, she said to the boy quietly, and the Surveyor overheard it. Had she already learnt English words? Had she always known them? The word did not feel like a guess, but more as if she *knew*. She was not bold, and she had no answer to danger, but somehow, he thought, she was made the same way as the old chief.

~

The afternoon sun lit the towering rocks and a breeze came off the lake by their side. The forest broke open into tumbling rivers of scree. And now a thread of smoke caught the light.

Some of the party were tiring of this game. Another false lead? Another killing? Parties were sent out: they were schooled in a set of signals so that one ambivalent message might not be compounded by more of them. The rest of them would wait for word.

The Man now arranged his writing materials and pushed the cloth hat down low. Knowing these indications, a prisoner brought him tea. The insects hovered over him and a great clumsy blowfly inspected the mug but he did not look up. *One day this will become a book*, he had said to Trugernana at the beginning of the journey, when he noticed her studying the heavy journal. He patted the leather cover and smiled. *And it shall be the toast of London.*

While he frowned and wrote, the women busied themselves weaving. Whelk took the pups from the burlap sack the Overseer had given him and spilled them onto the ground between himself and the girl. She squealed with delight at the tails and noses, the sleepy confusion. They were eight nights older and already bigger. Pipi took them by twos and threes into her arms and buried her face in their warm fur. They nipped at her with their needle teeth and pulled at her hair and she corrected them and repositioned them in ways that the Surveyor thought were quite expert for such a small child.

The scene at the burnt hut reappeared in his mind: maybe she'd known these pups before the fire. Before they'd found the dead woman whose hair stayed with him; the way it spilled, motion stopped forever. They were a distance apart when they'd found them, the dead woman with the pups, and the girl. He'd never know. Perhaps it didn't matter now.

How d'you do, how d'you do, she was saying to each pup in turn. The Man's young son had been teaching the phrase to the natives. He sat nearby, unoccupied. A gentle soul; not yet a man, lost in the uncertain space beforehand. There was down on his cheeks and his lip, and he was bulky and strong but not hardened. He looked to his father with uncomplicated respect, seeking to please. But he had no stamina, little courage and a sad way of turning up empty-handed, or turning back, apologising. Any change in the food made him sick. Sudden noises made him jump. Insects troubled him and the leeches, constantly appearing between toes and in his armpits and groin, filled him with panic and horror. He could not speak sternly to the convicts, who responded only to severity and so took liberties in his presence. Yet he continued to present himself for assignments. He would gather wood, stand sentry, shoot fowl. Anything, *anything*, begged his eyes. The Man's hardness wasn't personal: he was hard on everyone, himself included. There were orphans here: the boy and the girl and probably others, who could not imagine how it felt to have a father. The Surveyor saw the sadness in having one who could not be pleased.

The pups rolled in the sun and yawned and slept. So much of this eight-week journey had been waiting, as had the journeys before it. Around him the natives slept or wove or fashioned tools.

The prisoners were playing cards, singing fragments of ballads. Whelk practised counting with Pipi. *Five*, on her fingers, and a triumphant squeal.

Late in the day there was a whoop from Tibb, who had climbed a tree to act as lookout. Two more smokes, and they were the right signals. The prisoners cheered at the prospect of their long slog ending, and their broken faces lifted to the sky as though they saw it for the first time. The women laughed and chattered and stood to gather their things. The Man carefully closed his journal and replaced his pencil in its slender wooden box and calmly inspected his watch.

'I believe we have finally located the Big River people.'

~

The optimism made the outcome even more bitter.

It was not the Big River people who had been found, but a solitary woman and a dog. She stood like a dead tree in the plain, the dog circling manically, barking at the women who went to greet her.

When they brought her closer and sat her down she seemed confused and frail. Her eyes were dull and she stared at the grass at her feet. The Man questioned her gently in a pidgin of all the tongues he knew. Kickerterpoller contributed, at times cutting across the Man's voice. She confirmed that she was Big River. The Man leaned around her, peered at her exposed flanks and found the characteristic circles on her lower back. But the mystical status they ascribed to these people made her seem a fraud. She was supposed to be a member of the proudest, fiercest tribe of them all, the final holdout over the six punishing years since the colony strung up Musquito and Black Jack.

Why would they leave behind a woman? The killings had reduced their numbers dramatically across all of the nations, and that in turn had made children a rarity, and it had driven conflicts between bands for the handful of women who remained. The reason was clear: she had been left behind as a messenger, too sick to go on. They had told her to say they would meet, very soon. They knew the Man and his party were looking for them, but the times had been unsuitable. They would talk to Kickerterpoller. Cameron and his men were out night after night, scouring their trails. The Big River people were watching the roving parties. No one was sleeping.

'Harassment,' the Man declared. 'He wishes to wear them down.' Sometimes he said such things for his own satisfaction: the woman did not react. He shooed the others away and told a prisoner to make tea. As he paced anxiously around, she watched him, eyes dull, and Mannalargenna watched her. 'Lookit what you got,' he said.

The Man came back to her now, as the convict lifted the tin off the fire and poured the tea. 'You will take us to meet your people,' he said to the woman, again working his words through a tortuous jumble of gestures. It was not clear whether the Man meant this as a question or an order, but the woman mimed that she would. Mannalargenna was immediately against following her. These people were known to set traps, he argued, and they would all be speared. He himself had speared their chief, he reminded them, and they had long wanted payback.

'I will go with her,' the Man said abruptly. 'I will take with me whoever is willing to come.' He went to the pack horse and took water, some bread and a pistol, along with its cartridges and powder flask. Woorady offered to accompany the Man, as he sometimes did when Mannalargenna had set himself in opposition to an idea. It was not that Woorady and the chief were rivals: Woorady just liked to be agreeable.

The Surveyor could see that Whelk was torn: his darting eyes, his skipping feet. He wanted desperately to go with them. But not even Woorady was going to allow it. Whelk was too small, and he was more use looking after the girl. *She sweet on you*, laughed Woorady. *Lookit her.* Whelk looked down: Pipi was staring at him with undisguised adoration.

The party that went—the Man, his son, Woorady and two prisoners led by the Big River woman—were not gone for long. They returned as the troubled sun was setting, and they were loaded down with bark-wrapped bundles. The Man grunted under the weight of the one he carried, but he wore a look of grim satisfaction. The bundles were placed beside the fire and as the prisoners and the old people gathered around they were unwrapped to reveal an arsenal of guns. The Man wrote the lines carefully in his journal: *Eight fowling pieces, four muskets. Spears—four dozen, sundry balls, powder flasks.*

The two children squatted in close. The gleaming steel of the barrels was shaped perfectly, in a way that nothing made from the land ever was. Forever things, hard and cold, that could not be un-made. The boy bent lower now, smelling the metal, and ran his fingers over the breech of a long gun. They traced an inscribed word. The Man's son had also been watching, and he crouched beside Whelk and smiled.

'Can you read that? It says *London*.'

The boy looked back at him, polite but uncomprehending. What was a *London*?

Mannalargenna towered over the bystanders, glaring at the woman. He began to question her sharply and she answered with her eyes averted. 'She say no more gun out there,' the chief announced. 'They runnin from Cameron. Now they got no gun. This fella ben took em all.' He waved a long finger in the direction of the Man, who was still busy writing down the details of the weapons. 'How you gonna save em, eh?' The heavy ochred cords of his hair shook in anger.

The Man looked up but did not move. 'These were not their guns to begin with,' he said evenly. 'By taking possession of them I am helping to broker the peace.'

'You leavin em no defence.'

These were the contradictions the Surveyor could not resolve. The Big River mob were meant to be Mannalargenna's enemies. He was meant to be helping the Man to bring them in. Why was he so angry that they'd been disarmed?

He looked at Pipi, who sat solemnly alongside the boy, within touching distance of him as always. The look on her face wasn't happiness or sadness, but something much harder to grasp. Nothing was a shock; nothing tore at her. No one else looked that way. Even the Man looked shaken, and he was supposed to be in charge. Kickerterpoller stood at a distance, as always, awaiting his time.

~

The night was deep and still. They ate in disagreeable silence except for the prisoners, who sat apart as always, muttering and swearing. Their salt rations stank in the cooking, and worse in the digesting.

The Surveyor squinted over the tiny book of Wordsworth his beloved had given him. The print was so faint by firelight that he began to wonder if it too was escaping, along with everyone's memories, lifting off the delicate paper and away like smoke into the night. He would commit the words to memory, damn it. He would carry the book in his head until he returned to her.

When the meal was done, Woorady tried to interest the people in dancing and song, the ways they would ordinarily pass the evening. But they had walked so many miles, and the weight of disappointment had left them tired and sore. One by one they moved themselves further back from the fires and found places to sleep. Mannalargenna sat up last of all, and the Surveyor watched him out of one open eye. He was studying the big whirring bugs that swarmed the firelight, slapping at one as it landed on him. He examined it more closely. Stood; felt at the air with his hands, as if it had become heavy. The world compressing itself, coiling.

The Man slept in a thin bed-roll, fully clothed but for his cloth hat, which was crushed in a ball beneath his head. Mannalargenna had wandered out into the night and returned with three large sheets of bark. He shook them to remove the ants and spiders, then lay them over himself on the ground. He had murmured to the others about the coming downpour: each now made their own preparations. Animal skins, bark, little hollows in the ground. No one told the prisoners or the Man and his son.

An hour after they all settled, the wind died entirely and the first drops smacked straight down onto the bark sheets. A cold breeze prickled the Surveyor's skin. The night sky had clouded over and the glow of the fires had dimmed, embers hissing and popping under the first impacts. He was restless. The drops felt like a release, like the start of something, but they did not build. The night was an itch he couldn't identify to scratch. He sat up, careful not to wake the sleepers nearby.

Between two tussocks he saw Mannalargenna's head, a faint

orange glow on the clumped hair. He was alert, fixed upon something. His eyes swivelled across the camp and found him. He beckoned. The Surveyor hesitated—he was rarely brought into the chief's schemes—and the crooked finger sought him again. He disentangled himself from the bed-roll, yanked his boots on and slipped between the bodies until he reached the chief.

'Listen,' the chief said; the faintest whisper. 'Listen good.'

The Surveyor held his breath, closed his eyes and concentrated on the night. He heard nothing but the isolated raindrops and the silences between them.

'Something,' breathed the chief.

Why was the chief trusting him? There would be a logic to it, if only he could think it through. The chief's eyes continued their search. The camp was on open ground: the margins of the bush well back and the dark bulk of the trees rising uphill, out in the night. Beyond that, the great mass of the Western Tiers.

'Come.' Mannalargenna began moving away, low and supple. The Surveyor mimicked his stance as they headed towards the tree line and he found himself plunging again into the secrecy of the night-bound world. The ground changed from grasses to wiry scrub, and the rain came down, surging from its ticking and popping to a great drenching rush. There was no hope of either man hearing the other speak. He shaped himself to Mannalargenna's movements: the darkness so thick that the Surveyor feared he'd be left behind and lost if he slipped out of sight. The rain-slicked ground began to slide under his feet. He was trapped in the small moment of the present, following this man through the darkness and the downpour. The water ran under the thin shirt he'd intended to sleep in. It ran into his trousers, down his legs. It was in his eyes and he had to flick them dry to see the flashes of Mannalargenna's feet ahead. How was he hearing? What was he tracking, in this onslaught?

They came to a creek bed and watched the water come down in a tiny wall. Here Mannalargenna stopped. He turned to his left along the near bank of the creek and pushed through the foliage that crowded the edge of the water. Soon enough it opened at a tumble of boulders, and he moved among them, the Surveyor following, until they came to a dead tree, cracked open by the seasons. A dark mouth in the pale timber.

The chief pushed his body halfway into the hollow. When he wriggled back out, he was clutching a bark bundle like the one the party had retrieved from the Big River mob. This one revealed not metal but half a dozen spears. He rolled the thin shafts between his fingers, selected two and stood them against the great trunk, rewrapped the bundle and replaced it in the cavity. He did not look back at the Surveyor.

Onward, onward, the Surveyor tiring now and the trees closing in. The darkness more complete, the rain heavier and the sound a pitiless roar. He was desperate to sleep now, no longer sure this wasn't a dream. Sometimes he staggered because his eyes had closed.

Without warning the chief stopped and splayed a hand behind himself, a signal to do likewise. A slight rise in the ground ahead, and the light was different. Another fire. Someone else's fire.

Men there. One, two, three, four. Cameron and his lad, two others. Heads down in concentration, glittering wet. One making cartridges, another cleaning a gun. The son, with a pistol barrel broken over his knee, picking it up now, squinting through the barrel, rubbing with a cloth to keep the moisture at bay. Cameron ramming the barrel of a long musket. As the Surveyor looked on in horror, Cameron set aside the ramrod and worked the breech: once, twice. The sound of the steel a hungry crunching.

Their faces were grimly confident. The teeming rain did not dent their sense of purpose. One of the unknown men had laid down the weapon he was working upon and stuck a pipe in the slit of his mouth. He had both hands over a tinderbox that would not spark, though he struck it again and again. Water ran off the brim of his hat and off the tip of his fleshy nose. He cursed and put the tinderbox down, reached over from where he sat and stuck the pipe in the embers of the fire. Swore again, loudly, as his fingers scorched. The others were looking at him now: he stuffed the pipe back in an unseen pocket. They were so ordinary, the Surveyor thought. *Ordinary men in the rain, and they intend to murder us all.*

He suddenly wished he hadn't left the boy and the girl back at the camp. The urge came over him to go back and wake them, tell them all to flee back to Campbell Town and give up this ridiculous pursuit of the Big River people. The Man would come to his senses when he realised the danger they were in. He would thank the Surveyor for saving them, and it would all redound to his credit and bolster his prospects of matrimony, and…

He gathered himself to turn and run.

Just as the thought stirred in his mind, Mannalargenna took a step forward. He stood tall on the rise they had been hiding behind, a spear held loosely at his side, not pointed but resting there, level. Two more lengths of the spear was all the distance between him and the men who wanted him dead. Lost in their small tasks, they took a moment to realise he was there. It was only when Cameron himself looked up and said *shit* that the other three reacted. The Surveyor froze, torn between watching the men and looking up at Mannalargenna, who towered into the night as the fire-flecked raindrops fell. He had never seemed so tall.

The moment hung there while they made their decisions. An apparition from the storm stood before them, impassive and calm: the ambush had been turned on its head. Cameron stood and the rain sloshed from his hat. He said nothing as he raised the musket to his eye, the long barrel extending almost to Mannalargenna's breastbone.

You evil man, thought the Surveyor, *you are not even going to hesitate*, and Cameron pulled the trigger.

With a soft *whump*, a cloud of smoke enveloped Cameron's grimacing head. The rain had done its work. The son, watching it happen, snapped the pistol shut and jabbed a frantic hand into his coat pocket, fumbling with a cartridge. His eyes had gone huge. The cartridge skipped from his hand, bounced near his knee and fell on the wet grass at his feet. All four of the men began to edge backwards, eyes never leaving the chief.

Mannalargenna, through all of this, had neither moved nor spoken. He knew about fear, the Surveyor thought, and about how it weakened an enemy. Four men and their guns against a spear, and terror. He knew how he looked to them in the night.

He took two steps forward, down the small incline to the campsite. The spear was raised but in a vague way, neither aimed nor cocked to throw. Cameron dropped the useless musket and pointed a finger at Mannalargenna. *Take yer damned useless self an begone*, he spat. The black horse whinnied in the darkness away behind the fire, and Cameron backed in that direction. The others kept close by him. The chief moved around the fire, the spear tip leading like it knew each of them and all their thoughts.

Time'll come, Cameron was saying. *Mebbe not tonight*.

He reached the horse and swung himself onto it, heedless of the other men fleeing in different directions into the bush.

Mannalargenna stood loose and easy. He still had not spoken. When the last sounds of their departure had vanished into the rain, the chief wandered around the fire, picking things up and examining them. He took up the gun and the powder cartridge the men had dropped. He lifted a heavy canvas, tipping water away and revealing the gleaming barrels of rifles, muskets and long pistols. He tore open a cartridge and shook the powder over the fire so that the flames roared and spat coloured sparks in scribbling lines, and he watched the beautiful light for a moment, then broke open a tin canister. Forgetting himself for a moment, the Surveyor reached into the canister and took out one of the lead balls meant for them. He rolled it in his fingers; saw it tearing through warm flesh.

~

It took a long time to return to camp with the guns and ammunition. There was sugar, too, but most of the murderers' food must have been in the panniers on the black horse. The chief was particularly disappointed to find there was no tobacco.

The haul of guns and the weapons from the previous day had been sent off to Campbell Town to keep the expedition light. Nobody had wanted the job—they would be a slow-moving target for brigands and disgruntled settlers—and in the end, as with many unwelcome tasks, it fell to the Man's son, leading the prisoners McGeary and Platt.

Now the Man turned on Mannalargenna. How remarkable, he said, that the chief had known Cameron and his men were there, lying in wait. *In all this rain.* Had he perhaps spent his 'hunting trips' following their progress so that he could flaunt this victory at a time of his choosing? If the chief was angered by this, it did not show. His devil had told him, he said simply. He held one arm at an odd angle: the hand shook like it was not his. *Sometime tell me, sometime not.*

There wasn't room for some people to have devils and for everyone to have Jesus. The Surveyor knew that he was expected to fall into line with the Man, with his discordant combination of Holy Ghost and rationality. But then there was Mannalargenna's unerring sense of where the white men were hiding. The fearless assurance with which he had stood before the gun.

Across the camp, Pipi sat beside Whelk as the eastern sky began to redden and the people built the fire up again. Her eyes were upturned towards him, fearful, and the Surveyor wondered if it was not the fear of what had just happened, or nearly happened, but a dread of something wider and deeper, something worse than the night.

They had to find the Big River people soon, he thought. They had to end this journey, and not just because his soul was frayed by the demands of it. The Man and the chief could not work together for much longer.

From the Bitterest Snows

With the new day they covered the same sloping ground past Cameron's abandoned campsite. In the daylight it felt closer than it had in the dark: dangerously close. The Man was interested in the camp, and he pored over everything that remained.

The ground was boggy and the heavy rain of the night before had settled back to a mean drizzle, and with it a cold southwest wind that clawed at the ribs. Despite the possum skin on her shoulders, Pipi's lips were blue and her chin wobbled with the chattering of her teeth.

Under the leaden sky, the trees made no shadows and the birds were down. The thumping of the pademelons had gone silent and the air was emptied of insects. The land rose ahead of them: the strange woman led them on a twisting path through trees and along channels of exposed rock.

Unable to walk abreast in the close country, they formed

a long, snaking procession: the Man staying close behind the stranger, followed by a small party of prisoners. Next came the people, who had ordered themselves by seniority and other unspoken rules of clan and kin. The Surveyor walked near the front of the procession to note the terrain and take bearings. Pipi and Whelk were near the back, unable to push forward through the larger bodies, and Whelk carried Pipi when she tired.

As they gained height above the plain and looked out over the grey expanse under a blur of drizzle, he could make out the camps of the previous nights, the creek where he and Mannalargenna had found the spears, the gully where the would-be killers had prepared their ambush. Before long the path had risen far enough that there were hundreds of feet of open air to their left and only scree and twisted shrubs to their right. Most of the time he walked alone with his thoughts, but late in the morning the boy came alongside him.

'Where's Pipi?' the Surveyor asked him, offering a companionable smile.

'Aunty Pagerly got er,' the boy replied. 'She happy.' He seemed to consider something as they walked. Then the words came abruptly.

'Mister, where did I live?'

'What do you mean, boy? When?'

'Before we been out here. Was I livin in a house?'

The Surveyor was taken aback for a moment. 'Well, I can't say for sure, because I was hired for this mission and that's where we met, you remember? In Campbell Town.' *Why didn't the lad remember?* 'But I think you were living at the Man's house in Hobart Town along with the other'—the word caught, but he said it anyway—'the other orphans.'

The boy poked his lip, considering this. 'Where before that?'

The Surveyor sighed and shuffled his pack. 'Couldn't say for sure, lad.'

Someone must want this boy back, he thought. How could it be that no one remembered who, or where? All of these people had such a firm idea where their home was. They named country, animals, with a deep familiarity. Their songs, their dances—the Surveyor could feel the fullness of meaning in them. How was it possible to have none of these things?

And it was clear that the boy was not only asking for his own sake. The girl would grow up the same.

~

When the path stopped climbing and the country lay open below them, the Man said they should rest. It was clear by then that some were struggling more than others. Kickerterpoller had been sick for a while now and had to edge into the bush to blast the muck out of his backside. At first there had been stifled laughter when he did this; now there was nervous silence. Whatever afflicted him was getting steadily worse.

Kickerterpoller was the link between worlds: with the Oyster Bay and Big River peoples, between Mannalargenna and the Big River chief, Tongerlongeter, and even between the Man and Mannalargenna. He joined in with the Man's prayers but saw no contradiction in Mannalargenna's talk of devils and ancestors. When he was well enough, he spent his time harassing the Man about writing to the Governor. He said he had been promised a whaleboat: he could not understand why such a promise would not be honoured.

McGeary, the most outspoken of the prisoners, had thought this was hilarious. *Whit would ye do wi' a boot out here?* he'd asked, his voice all gums and whiskers. He never used the name Kickerterpoller, but called him Black Tom. He had a gift for insult.

Trugernana and Woorady had been arguing, apparently about the Man's insistence that they keep going. Woorady had had enough. Trugernana had accompanied the Man so many times now, over so much ground, that her belief in him was unshakeable. Peevay, who was about the same age as Trugernana, hovered around the two of them like a little brother might, teasing and trying to lift their mood, but there were signs that even he was tired of the endless slog.

They slumped about, trying irritably to get themselves out of the wind. Whelk curled around Pipi and she nosed her way into his armpit. They had taken every skin the women would spare them.

The Man sat alone, writing again, upright and tense.

Mannalargenna had cupped his firestick through all of the wind and the sleet and now, crouched and breathing words over a nest of crushed twigs, he opened his fingers to reveal a flame. Before long there was tea. The Surveyor saw that Whelk had managed to snatch a mug of it for Pipi, and they curled their hands around it. She was eating better now, he thought, although he could not shake the fear that the girl was enduring, rather than living. Maybe she was a person who would always be that way. Maybe she would live to a great age, at every moment threatening to sicken and die. Her face spoke of a mistrust for which she did not yet have words, only shadows of fear as she watched the prisoners heckling and cursing.

The rain whipped in stinging flurries across the ground and upwards from the plain below. The weather was closing them in, towering over them. Even the Big River woman eyed the clouds fearfully. The horizon it came from grew darker and darker like it could send squalls forever. This would not blow through.

The Man was talking to his son about model villages, about the West Indies and the colonies of the Cape, as though the weather was irrelevant. '...European clothes and labour apportioned by sex. Men learning to build, women to cook and clean.' He began to write furiously in the journal on his knees, as though the idea had tried to make a bolt for freedom.

The lad watched him avidly, water running off his chin. He was trying so hard. 'And then?' he asked. 'What then, Father?'

The Man bridled as though the boy had sworn. 'What do you mean *and then*? Are you suggesting that taking natives from slaughter and Christianising and civilising them is somehow not sufficient?'

'Why no.' He shook his head and the droplets swung. 'Not at all, sir. I...I will make us tea.' And he fled the conversation with obvious relief. The Surveyor watched him pouring the water, face shifting with emotion. It must have been lonely in there, in his heart.

After the break, the Big River woman said they should walk north. But again, again, Mannalargenna spoke up. She knew nothing, he said. These people could not be trusted. The weather was coming *from* them. He pointed upwind: they could be found by walking into the weather. The Man rolled his eyes and for once he spoke for all of them. *Must you take us by the hardest route?*

Mannalargenna glared at him. *Not me*, he said quietly, for that was when he was most forbidding. *Devil say it. Only way.* He swivelled the glare around the whole party, seeking dissent. People looked down; the convicts sneered, but with lowered faces. Kickerterpoller shrugged. No one was going to challenge him.

This way. We go.

He marched off, striding upright with the long, fine shafts of the spears balanced in one hand and the firestick in the other. When the Surveyor stood, the wind howled in his ears and he wondered how much more he could take. Pipi and Whelk shifted in behind Pagerly, and in that procession they beat their way windward in a wide line across a meadow made of scrub. It would be kinder under the children's feet than the uphill scree had been, but Pipi was disappearing nearly up to her waist in the undergrowth with each new step. No one but the Surveyor noticed her constant battle to stay upright: the faces around them were preoccupied with their own struggles.

Mannalargenna had got his way. The Man must have been seething, but there was no sign of it on his face. He had fallen back now and he walked alone, deep in thought. The air plunged again and then the rain changed its nature, swirling around them in delicate flakes of pure white, and Whelk looked up at the Man for some explanation.

December, then, he muttered. *Bloody snow.*

The flurries came at them steadily, driven by the harsh wind. All twenty-nine of them were trudging now, slower and slower, bare faces and bare feet burning. Sounds were muffled by the snowfall, and the morning dragged on forever. The Surveyor had to turn his face to one side to stop his eyes stinging, and from that angle he saw the Man's face, set grim, snow hanging in shelves on his brow and his cheeks. It had stiffened his hair into silver icicles either side of his ears. He had never seen a man in such misery as this. Under the black cloth hat, his head was English still, but his body, wrapped in kangaroo hide, was surrendering to the demands of this place.

Mannalargenna walked stooped as well, although he could

not show his suffering, because it was he who had chosen this way. The prisoners carried the snow about their shoulders and on the brims of their hats. And all of them were in pursuit of the broken remnants of a nation, driven higher and higher off their hunting grounds and into the home of the wind, clad in little more than grease and ochre. Their suffering, thought the Surveyor, must be far greater.

The women staggered under their burdens. Their bird-chatter had been stilled, and they no longer checked on Whelk or Pipi. Time let go of them at some point and the procession stopped. Mannalargenna had managed to keep his firestick alight, and once again they scooped twigs and scraps of cloth to make a fire in a depression. Above them an outcrop of ancient rock wore a coating of lichen against the weather.

'Loftus,' said the Man, appearing above the Surveyor as he sat with his head bowed in exhaustion.

'Sir.'

'May I borrow your mapping for a moment, please.' He had his hand out, as though expecting resistance. The Surveyor retrieved the roll of papers from his pack. In a hollowed voice the Man then told Mannalargenna to come sit with him. The chief pursed his lips, but did so. The Surveyor sat unnoticed only yards away. Their conversations always interested him: never more so than now, when everyone's fate seemed to perch on a wire between their eyes.

The Man opened the maps on his knee. He leafed through the pages of swirls and dots and names with theatrical amazement.

'Everywhere,' he said tightly. 'You have dragged us everywhere.'

Faint lines squiggled all over the pages, and over it all, the Surveyor's thick pen line wandered back and forth, doubling over itself and making strange shapes. There was no pattern to this line: it went where it pleased. They had not made a great crossing of the land, nor evenly covered the ground. They had merely gone over and over themselves, a lost dog trailing a string.

'You are torturing these poor people,' the Man was saying. 'For reasons best known to you alone.'

Mannalargenna had a faraway look in his eyes, like the matters at hand were more complex than the Man understood. The muscles of his hard breast were twitching. The Surveyor had thought they were following the Big River woman, but the Man was right: all of this had been at the chief's behest until now.

'Must we do this until someone dies in the snow? Until Cameron returns?'

In the line of the Surveyor's vision, past the two men, the woman who was supposed to be guiding them was sitting alone. She had no clan, no family to bind her to anyone. It was unclear what purpose she served anymore, or who would sit with her when the night came.

'You never take me Guv'nor,' the chief was saying now. He said it quietly, and for a moment the Man's face betrayed confusion, as though he'd heard wrong.

'I beg your pardon?'

'You never take me Guv'nor.' Snow dusted the heavy locks of his hair. 'You promise.'

Now the Man looked disgusted. 'All of this'—he waved an arm in a wide circle—'all of this *nonsense* is some kind of tit for tat because I wouldn't arrange an audience with the Governor? You appal me! You're as bad as Kickerterpoller and his boat!'

Mannalargenna did not react.

'You would place all of these people at risk,' the Man

continued. 'You would frustrate my purposes, endanger the Big River people...all because of your precious meeting with the *Governor?*' His voice had risen. His eyes roved over the whole party now, beseeching their support. 'You would truly do that to us?'

'Come on now.' The chief had folded his arms. 'We talk like this, then? All these people listen? We get this lot. Lairmairermener, Big River. Bring em in. Then all of us'—he ran the words together so the sound was *alluvus*—'mebbe we go with you for while, eh.'

Mannalargenna leaned a hand in the snow and pushed himself upright. He stood over the Man.

'But you bring us back, put us on our country again. No more spearin *raytji* fella, no more shootin blackfella—'

The Man was nodding eagerly; writing, nodding.

'This is what I want from Guvnor! Why I not seen him?'

When he had first heard Mannalargenna talking with the Man, the Surveyor had thought Mannalargenna didn't understand English, he chopped his words so hard. But time had taught him that Mannalargenna followed English, and he understood the Man perfectly. He simply could not be bothered with words that bumbled aimlessly around.

The Man closed the book in his lap now, and his face returned to an expression of patience. 'My friend, I have the delegation of his excellency the Governor. Everything that you agree with me, you are, in legal effect, agreeing with the Governor.' He looked around, smiling, at the gathering. But it was clear that he had not impressed the chief.

'You jus work for im,' he said dismissively. He waved the backs of his fingers at the Man. 'Be like this fella, or this fella'—he pointed at Woorady and Kickerterpoller in turn—'maybe deal with you. But *me*...' He placed a hand on his own chest. 'I deal with the Guv'nor.'

Away from where the Surveyor sat, the girl shivered in Whelk's arms. The fire was dying, reflected in the pools of her eyes. They had been still too long now and the cold was regaining its grip. But the chief wasn't done. 'I wanna tell him: I want tea, blankets. Sugar. And he send a good white man to watch over us. No fella be shootin at us then, see? Kickin his horse round...'

'That veers close to hostage-keeping,' muttered the Man. Now in the grey light, he couldn't conceal his exhaustion. He was clutching the journal against the front of his coat.

Mannalargenna jabbed his chin upwards, wanting the words repeated, but the Man was silent.

Then he said, 'It will be me. I will come and watch over your country with you. I am devoted to you all. I will bring my family and we will live among you.'

Mannalargenna watched him sceptically.

'I told you I would return your wife to you'—he gestured towards Tanleboneyer—'and I was good to my word.'

Please stop, the Surveyor silently begged. *Stop talking, bury the embers and let us finish this thing.*

'Gonna promise again?' The chief's eyes were shrewd.

The Man sighed. 'Promise what, this time?'

'Same again. Promise our country back. All them things we need. Tucker...baccy. And you come live with us. Look after us.'

'I have already given my word about these things.'

But Mannalargenna wasn't satisfied; or at least he was clever enough to create that impression. 'Them Lairmairermener my enemies, see.' He looked out at the banked cloud as if the Big River people would materialise through it. He frowned. 'Now you say these ones only ones left on country.'

'I am quite convinced that is the case.'

Mannalargenna poked his lip out dubiously. 'Not so good, lookin round for your enemy.'

Another sigh from the Man. 'We have been over this many times. You knew about these things when you agreed to come. Now you admit that all the hunting and the devil nonsense, all of *this*'—he jabbed an angry finger at the tangled lines on the maps—'has been a charade. You never wanted to find these people in the first place.'

'Devil nonsense…' muttered the chief.

He looked at the strange woman in their midst and raised his voice, trying some sequence of words on her. If she understood him she gave no sign of it. He shook his head and in the dead air of the snowfall the Surveyor heard him snort down his nose.

'Harder now, see. All this.' He gestured at the snow. 'No tracks.'

He approached the woman and sat next to her, murmuring as his fingers attended to the heavy locks of his hair. Her face became animated and their hands began to move as she explained something to him and he added his own understanding. A final nod of assent, and he stood.

The Man dried his journal with a cloth and replaced it in his satchel. He adjusted the pack on the horse and issued orders to the prisoners, who gave no sign of having heard him. And among the dull noises of cleaning and packing and loading, the party re-formed itself and began to crawl northward again, across the face of the wind.

~

They ground on that way for several hours, the woman walking beside Mannalargenna, remarking upon a tree or the run of a gully. Her eyes were down, words escaping from the corner of her mouth. Something between them, the Surveyor thought. Kin, or old problems. Tanleboneyer walked just behind them, carrying the chief's spears and string bags for them both. If the closeness between her husband and the strange woman bothered her, she did not let it show.

When they came to a long, low cliff that extended across their path, they smelled smoke. Mannalargenna muttered something to Kickerterpoller, who nodded in agreement. He was well enough, and without a word to anyone else he went up first, the two women following after him. Mannalargenna ambled away from the rise, across its face for a distance, the little curl of blue from his firestick disappearing after him. Soon the bush had concealed any sign of his quiet retreat.

The others waited at the foot of the cliff at the Man's insistence. Standing still invited the cold back into the bones. The Surveyor stamped his feet: Whelk was rubbing his hands, and Pipi pressed close to him though she had the ample flanks of Pagerly there to shelter against.

When he stood over Whelk and spread his fingers to warm them on the fur of the horse's shoulder, the delight returned to Pipi's eyes and she did the same, standing beside them both and reaching only as far as the underside of the animal's chest. The Surveyor looked down at her, at the glittering snowflakes on her lashes. She was calm. Her restless muttering was stilled, and she smiled faintly.

They began to move again. The snow had stopped; the world was clean and the clouds were low and black against the brilliance. A piercing whistle cut the gloom: Kickerterpoller.

The Man's eyes darted among the natives and saw no anxiety that might indicate a warning in the sound. He called for them to start up the cliff. The women hefted their burdens; the men started off in their order of authority and clan, all of them bare-footed in the snow. The prisoners pushed their way up, a sense among them that this might finally be the end of their torments.

When the Surveyor reached the top of the rise, he saw the natives ahead of him, gathered tight against the cold. He wove through them, with Pipi in his wake. There was still no sign of Mannalargenna but Kickerterpoller stood out in the clear, alone, and the Surveyor would remember the image years later: the warrior with a kangaroo mantle over his shoulders, seeming bigger on his lean body. Tall and graceful, his hands speaking low, his head tilted loosely so that he appeared as neither aggressor nor supplicant. The spears were on the ground by his feet and the firestick pointed downwards, smoke threading up his arm. His back was turned to them all because they were not his concern. His concern was ahead of him, there in the snow.

Their bodies were different, as different as the prisoners'. They wore their hair differently. Their markings—the scarred circles—were unlike anyone's. Their faces were set in weariness and caution but not resistance.

Their leader, Tongerlongeter, stood at the apex of the group, only a yard from Kickerterpoller. He was older, as raw as the earth, battered and pitiless. His body was a mass of old scars, one arm severed at the elbow, shot away by raiders. Somewhere in the dark, months before in the deep forest, the Big River people had tended to the terrible wound, stemming the bleeding and grinding down the shattered bone so a bearable stump would form. Cold and hungry and living in fear, the last few dozen of the fugitive nation had expertly tended to their chief until he could lead them again.

They spoke quietly, the young warrior and the old chief, so that even if the Surveyor had known how to understand their speech, he would not have been able to overhear it.

Gradually, calmly, the people behind Tongerlongeter were picking up their belongings and coming forward across the empty snow. Sixteen men, nine women and a child.

The journey was over. The Lairmairermener were leaving their land.

The Day of the
Great Parade

Then came the months of waiting in Hobart Town, seasons bathing the docks and the mountain in cloud and sun, snow and haze. Roads that were dust, then mud, then dust again. The months became years. The Surveyor found work from time to time, measuring out the bones of the city, documenting the ever-expanding settlements in the midlands and the myriad harbours and bays.

He filled his days with reading and walking and writing to his beloved. She could not yet come to Hobart, she wrote, not until his patchwork of assignments had firmed into a living. He had waited for an appointment with the Man, he told her, but the Man was preoccupied with weighty matters: expeditions into the northwest, then to Macquarie Harbour, and the weather-beaten west coast. But he had no use for a surveyor.

When he finally received an audience at the Hobart house he was told that there would be no further missions into the bush. He received the news with relief: no more leeches, no more cold, confusion and disharmony. No more Camerons in the night. But he knew it also meant there were no more tribes to search out. The Man was bound to this obsession of his and, it seemed, increasingly fond of the Governor's money. If there was another nation out there refusing to come in—even just another clan—the Man would have assembled a party and gone after them.

The Man assured him he was valued and trusted, and he offered an alternative. The search would begin immediately for an isolated site where all of the gathered tribes could be housed safely, away from the depredations of the city and the settled districts. There he, the Man, would be charged with ensuring they were Christianised and civilised. He would need good people. He could offer no work that was cartographic in nature, but would the Surveyor consider a role as storekeeper?

The Surveyor took his leave and thought it over. He wrote to his beloved, and to his great joy she told him she would join him if he could secure such a posting. She believed their prospects would be better in Van Diemen's Land than in Sydney. The Surveyor looked out on the grey Derwent as he read her words, and he wondered how that could be so. But it did not dim his happiness.

Their future was settled. All that remained was to find out where the Man intended to send them.

~

The day of the great Hobart Town parade started early.

The people of all the nations and clans were shepherded by smiling strangers from the Man's house to a park, where they were assembled. The Surveyor went along in his best coat, whether out of loyalty or some long-dormant sense of duty, he couldn't tell. He knew some of them well—Pagerly and Trugernana and Woorady. Others he remembered dimly from earlier expeditions, and some he had never seen at all. Some of the children had grown and changed: some of the adults had weakened, and now hovered at the edge of recognition. Some were gone altogether: when he fell into conversation with the Man's son he learned that Kickerterpoller had succumbed to the flux two winters ago; yet the older and more damaged Tongerlongeter continued to grow in power.

Not knowing whether his proper place was with the crowd on the roadside or in among the marchers, the Surveyor stood idly by the trough, where the children were being instructed to clean their teeth and brush their hair. They wore smocks, so he failed at first to recognise Pipi in a bright, clean dress and with ribbons in her hair. She was older now but still a child, and she had not cast off that hunted look that he remembered from the Western Tiers. The boy Whelk hovered nearby, and this reassured him: they had somehow remained together. Pipi looked at him fleetingly and he thought she smiled with her eyes. Then the crowd swept them along.

The Man's wife moved through the crowd, giving out fans of grasses and flowers and telling the children they should wave at the crowd to make them clap and cheer.

Ahead of the group, beyond the low picket fence that bounded the park, stretched a long wide road made of dead earth. The horses had shat on it here and there, and it slumped down at the edges to stone gutters pooled with old water. This was to be their route, and the Surveyor saw the old familiarity of the families and clans arranging themselves for a day's walking:

the calls, the laughter, the sharp correction of children. They were all brought together and inspected once again: hair and clothes, skin and fingernails. The buildings of the city awaited them further down, where the land tilted towards the sea. The sea was invisible between the buildings, but the masts of ships poked among the rooftops, as though they were stranded in the streets.

They waited while more people arrived: the adults, among them the Overseer who had been in charge of the convicts when they were out in the bush, and the senior people like Tanleboneyer and Umarrah—and last of all the chief, Mannalargenna. The Surveyor wondered why. Had the Man arranged it or was it his own sense of theatre? Perhaps he was simply late to arrive.

The Big River people were among them, painted and scarred, in the shade of a great tree at the edge of the park. As they flowed into the crowd their dogs poured around them, all ribs and tails. The people from Arthur River and the ones from Oyster Bay moved around each other. The costumes, the fans and the smocks and the cleaning and brushing were meant to make them into something the townspeople could behold in comfort. *Here are the savages you once feared, stripped of their terrors and set to become Christians.*

Mannalargenna moved through the crowd, fierce and solemn. He was draped in possum cloaks, a fistful of spears in his left hand, the smouldering firestick in his right. He had ochred his face and his hair was distinctively clumped. He wore an amulet on his arm above the elbow, tied on with a strip of hide. He looked careworn, troubled. Set deep in the ochre, his eyes were bright specks of worry.

It wasn't just the children who'd been bundled up. The women's bodies were hidden under stiff clothing; the first time the Surveyor had seen them that way. Their wide, clever feet that had felt the earth were laced into boots and their dinted shinbones poked out between boot and dress. The music of their laughter was gone; in its place was coughing.

Gradually now, the crowd was moving off and he was taken along with them. The spaces between people grew larger, and there were short bursts of singing that failed before they could spread. In the distance he saw the Man, dressed in a new black coat but with the old cloth hat on his head. The pageantry was infusing him with energy: he was smiling broadly and had surrounded himself with children. He swept down among them every so often to encourage them to smile, taking their wrists to guide their waving.

They were saved, that was the message. They were leaving for an island where they would live as free people, and could devote themselves to thanking God and learning European ways. The old people had fallen quiet, perhaps because they explained everything in stories and they simply had no story for this preposterous idea.

Among the spectators, women clapped politely in gloved hands that made no sound. Men held parasols over their wives and hoisted their children onto their shoulders for a better view. A mother stood holding her daughter's hand, watching as Pipi walked past them. The little girl wore a bonnet: she was about the same age as Pipi; the mother's lips twisted as if she had eaten something bitter. She held the Surveyor's gaze for just long enough that he started to turn his neck as he went past her. Then she looked down and pretended to fuss over the child.

~

They were due to arrive at the Government House at precisely four o'clock, but when the walking was done and they gathered there, the crowd was already tailing off.

The Governor came out onto the steps at the front of the building, a cold man with a long narrow nose and silver hair that left the corners of his forehead bare. To counter this he had combed his remaining hair forward as if a great wind blew from behind his head. He stood at a timber lectern and spoke, his voice barely audible over the murmurs and coughing. The Man was standing behind the Governor's left shoulder, beaming and applauding each sentence with his hands up high in front of his face. He had removed his cloth hat, and the clapping required him to stuff it in his armpit.

When the Governor was done, he turned his back and disappeared into the building through a grand doorway behind him. The door slammed. The Man was left awkwardly rushing forward to say something in reply to the speech. He looked back over his shoulder, smiled desperately at the crowd. For a moment it was unclear what would happen next: the Man put his hands up to beg their patience, then darted backwards to knock on the grand door with his baton. The soldier who stood sentry by the doorway told him to stop and they began arguing. The afternoon sun mocked it all. At the front, people started to walk off.

But the Man lingered there, raising his voice now, scolding and pleading. He wanted tea with the Governor: he wanted his family admitted. His voice was shrill, he thought it all *rude, terribly rude*, and he was no longer the man the Surveyor recalled drinking tea, seated on a boulder among the tussocks of the lake country, reading from his journal, in charge of his own small world.

The day was over. The Man stormed off and the crowd

dispersed. The Surveyor felt a longing to speak to the two children, to satisfy himself that they were, if not happy, at least looked after.

He found them sitting on the short grass by the podium where the speech had taken place. They looked up at his approach, neither welcoming nor shy. He squatted down on his haunches, suddenly intensely moved yet unsure what he wanted to say to them. Before he could compose his thoughts, a shadow crossed the afternoon sun.

A huge man stood over them.

He was so tall that he seemed to come from far away when he bent towards the children. A crunching sound passed through his knees as he did it. His coat was black, of a fine material that shimmered in the light. He wore a suit under the coat, and a high collar. His hat was not the large shapeless kind that the Man wore; nor was it tall and well formed like the ones on the town's men. It was flat and very wide, casting the man's entire shoulders in shade. He had come to them from the side where the sunset flared in a gap between two buildings. The light burned red behind him; darkness purred under the hat's brim.

The dark man ignored him. He had eyes only for the children: eyes of a horrible intensity. The Surveyor felt he should intervene somehow but he was transfixed.

There was something wrong with the man's face. His chin and jaw were strong, faintly whiskered with a sheen of silver. He was old. The flesh hung a little loose into the part of his throat that was visible above the collar. His mouth was wide and firm but it hung open slightly, and the teeth were peculiar, bright and too large for the man's mouth, as if they were not his teeth at all.

But it was what happened above there that tightened the

knot in the Surveyor's stomach. The man's nose was crushed and turned severely to one side, so that a nostril opened wide and black, straight ahead like an eye that had been eaten from a socket. He held his mouth open to breathe, giving the impression that he was about to say something.

The injury was an old one, that was clear. Hairs grew from strange parts of the nose as though they believed themselves to be back where they belonged. And the sun had long since cooked all of the displaced parts into a colour darker than the pale pink of the town's other men.

Above the nose there was a long, raw furrow that ploughed from the corner of one eye across the brow and disappeared under the hat. This scar was newer than the smashed nose: deep and wide and not the dent of having been struck by something. Only a musket ball could cause such damage.

The moving eye calculated, and the mouth hung ajar. The other eye, the one under the scar, did not move. Pipi began edging uncomfortably away.

'Who are you, sir?' the Surveyor blurted, and wondered why he had done it.

The stranger looked up at him, disregarded him completely and fixed his gaze back on the children.

'Now,' he said finally, and his voice was pleasant. 'Let me see if I have this right. You'—he placed a huge hand on Whelk's shoulder—'you'd be the one they call Whelk. And *you*'—his other hand drew her in from behind the small of her back—'must be Pipi.' He smiled now. 'I was told you would be inseparable, and here you are.'

Neither of them said a word in response. The Surveyor could not take his eyes off the scars, not even to look at the children.

'The Bible says I must not separate what God has joined.'

He hesitated, inhaled over the teeth. 'So we will have to work out whether it was God who joined you.'

'Sir,' mumbled Whelk.

The eyes narrowed and the muscles on the damaged side pulled in strange ways. 'I will be your Catechist,' he said. 'Do you know that word, *catechist*?'

Whelk shook his head. Pipi did not move at all.

'If you please, sir.' The Surveyor thought to distract this man somehow from his focus but again, the man only glanced at him, a flicker of contempt, and returned to Pipi and Whelk.

'From the Greek, children. I will be teaching you about God, when we reach the place where we will settle.' He looked slightly to either side of himself. 'All children are filled with God's divine light, you see. But you can only come to know Him by knowing *me*.'

The sun finally fell below the hill behind the trees and the air cooled. The shadows under the man's hat became part of all the shadows and he stood now, knees cracking again on the way up, unfolding until he towered into the dusk.

'Don't you wander too far,' he said in his musical voice.

Then he turned his back and was gone.

PART TWO

~

Hobart Town
April 1833–5

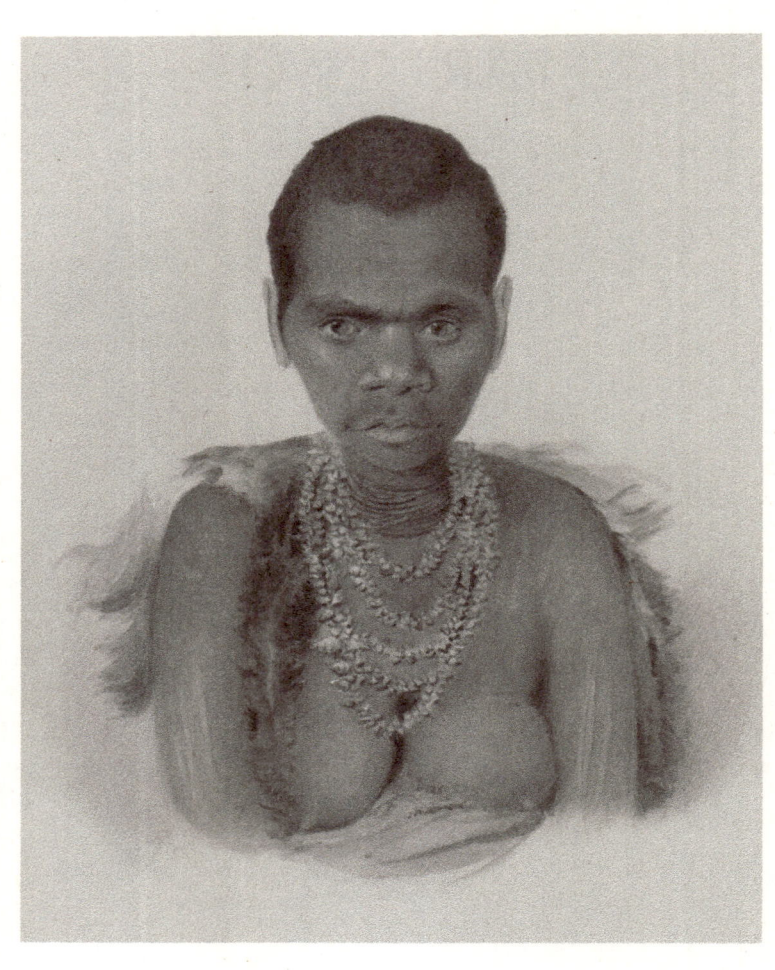

Truganini

Ah good, now. Yes. There…no, there. Bring it over here. Right. Thank you, you may go.

Now you would be Truganini. I am Mr Thomas Bock. How do you do. Such an honour…let me look at you.

~

Birmingham. I won the society's silver medal for an engraving, you know. I suppose one may succumb to later infamy but such a thing is long remembered. Is why, is why they pardoned me. Skill. How I ended up in this studio.

~

Fourteen years, but they commuted it. Mrs Underhill and I, we both stood the Assizes. She was—she *is*, I suppose—somewhat notorious. A maker of blights, a shedder of linings. Someone that you go to in a *situation*, you understand.

You don't understand. No, of course, quite reasonably.

Can I explain it this way: the allegation was that we *Administered Concoctions of Certain Herbs to Ann Yates, with the Intent to Cause a Miscarriage*. A young woman, my mistress. I needed her to, ah, to not be pregnant. I had a wife and five children.

~

Can you tell me about the shells? They seem to glow.

Mair—*maireener*. Thank you. Do I emphasise them? I rather think they will compete with your eyes, and your eyes are everything here.

~

I've not had a living sitter in months. I have been drawing—you may find this distasteful—post-mortem portraits of deceased infants. The face of a small child does not lose its form in death as that of an adult does. Impossibly delicate.

…to feel something. To retrieve love from death; for that existence to have meant something. And peace for the mother in her grief. *This was my child*—d'you see?

My children? No. Adults now. Come to me in my dreams, but do not answer my letters. You have similar dreams, do you not? You have felt loss, I can see it.

Generous of you, but my losses are of my own making. Yours, I feel, were thrust upon you.

I am trying at this moment to capture your loss.

~

We are almost finished here. You have been very patient. Some exalted souls have occupied that chair and my, don't they fuss.

Your eyes. I believe I have painted you only as eyes, Truganini.

Woorady

You haven't moved. Forty minutes now and you haven't moved.

You have me in mind of stored energy. If I threw a powder flask in the coals—that sense that nothing changes until it combusts.

I don't expect you will understand me here but I am trying to, er, to depict that. Motion in stillness. *Ha!* This is what I tell the students.

~

I was telling your wife about the infants. Most often I paint the dead, you see, which is why I am unperturbed by your silence. They bring me criminals fresh off the gallows—body this way, head that way. I drew Pearce the cannibal for the Colonial Surgeon. Did the murderer Charles Routley as a head and a skull and I told them, I said there is nothing to this phrenology business, you know. Nothing at all. A skull is a skull. A lump tells you nothing you wouldn't learn from a callused hand.

~

I study bodies all my days. In yours I see the physical power, oh yes. But I see time coming for you, too. The force is there in your shoulders, but the lightning has gone. Only recently: you may not even know it is deserting you.

I had a son this autumn just gone. *Step*-son; complex business. Young Alfred: his baptismal certificate says a sailor named Alexander Cameron is his father and the convict Mary Anne Cameron is his mother. But Mary Anne is my housekeeper, and her husband, well, he is often away at sea. So I have a boy. Which is nice.

At some point Alexander Cameron will go missing, I suppose. It's what mariners do.

Mannalargenna

They told me when they brought you in that you did not want to come. That you believe you have been lied to, which is what I see this very instant in your eyes. A sense of outrage. A man who looks—and I can tell you this is rare—looks past the artist, beyond the matter at hand and into the future. It will be hard to render.

I see the work that has gone into the ochre. Your hair, your beard. I will not ask to touch. I imagine that would be unwelcome.

~

My aim here, in case you are wondering, is to depict your body settled and at peace. An ageing body that yet remains lithe. Eternally a sapling.

~

I thought they told you. No?

I see. Mr Robinson has commissioned me to create these images. Posterity. They will go in the book that he will publish out of those diaries you have watched him creating all these years.

~

Is it possible that we can—how shall I put this?—dispense with the smouldering stick? I have captured it now, and the smoke is filling the room.

Yes, I said to be yourself, but—

Very well.

~

You know they are going to make him commandant of the settlement? Of course you do. An island, he says. Well, you must come again and sit for me when you return from your island.

But how can you know? *Ye know neither the day nor the hour,* hmm?

Perhaps you are right, old chief. Perhaps he has heard of my singular gift. Perhaps the commission is to retrieve…something. Something from, oh…death.

PART THREE

~

Pea Jacket Point
October 1835

The Stop on Green Island

The wind whipped fiercely over the low island while the western sky turned dark.

The Commandant had seen seasons in Van Diemen's Land that arrived late, or inverted, or did not arrive at all. Dry winds in autumn, snow in summer. Should a wet gale in spring have been any surprise? He hurried to get the last of the provisions into the boat, glancing at the towering granite of Flinders Island, wrapped in cloud.

The government brig could go no closer to Flinders: the approaches to the settlement, miles to the north, were too exposed. The procedure was to lay up at Green Island to the south, transfer everything and everyone into the whaleboat and row it there. Five hours now and they had only completed two deliveries. The convicts were struggling with a ram that had briefly tasted freedom on the little island and now refused to be lifted over the gunwale into the longboat. It kicked and bucked, and a young lag swore as he caught a hoof near his throat. He punched the ram in its face and the others laughed and bleated.

The Commandant smelled the wet animal and the tobacco from the men and hung his head. There were grass seeds on his trousers. They tested his faith, this lot. The idle ones entertained themselves standing on penguins as they waited. The pitiful creatures cried under the boots, too slow to escape. One man had his foot on a bird even now, imitating a squawk as he turned his heel and the penguin's entrails burst from its beak. The Commandant was well outnumbered, as always. He gritted his teeth: God's work was among people, but it was people that made it so difficult.

A holler from the rise: the last of the convicts coming down the boulders, framed against the sickly sky.

'Sir, he won't come.'

'Well…' The Commandant wanted to explode. 'Tell him to!'

The lag's response flew around in the gusts. 'Dare not, sir, if ye pardon.'

He breathed deeply, tamped down the fury and made his way up into the tussocks, where the convict was indicating. As he passed him, the old lag added, 'Careful sir, he's got a shard o glass…'

'Well, who gave him that?' he roared back.

The convict was a broken man, half-shaved, dirty hair plastered down over his forehead and food or blood or something congealed in his neckerchief. 'Cannae rightly say, sir.' He looked at his feet.

Pointless. The Commandant picked his way over the boulders until he found Mannalargenna at the centre of the island's modest rise. From here the grey sea was visible all around, rocks and minor islets dotted everywhere.

The chief was cross-legged on a small patch of earth and grasses that had collected between the boulders. He looked small there in the protective hollow while the sky curdled around him. The purpose of the glass was immediately clear: Mannalargenna was cutting into the matted hair over his forehead. As he took a clump of it away from his head, he regarded it mournfully and placed it on the ground in front of his feet.

He cut again, this time over his ear, grimacing slightly as he pulled the thick lock tight. Great chunks of the heavy, ochred hair were gone, leaving a fuzz of short tufts over his scalp. Either he had not noticed the Commandant's approach or he did not care.

'What are you doing, my friend?' The Commandant took care to project authority in his voice. Confidence. But when he lowered his gaze to look into the chief's face he could see that the great man had been crying. This rocked his certainty. Never in all of their travels on country had Mannalargenna shown himself vulnerable.

Only once had the Commandant seen him display emotion at all. When the brig passed by his homeland on the northeast coast of Van Diemen's Land, only days before, his whole demeanour had changed and a great urgency had overcome him. He had snatched the eyeglass from the bosun and stared desperately at the low hills behind Swan Island. When the boat moved on and he could see them no longer he had paced the deck, muttering painfully to himself. It was raining at the time, the hills wreathed in mist, and all of the passengers below decks. Only he, the Commandant, had seen the chief's distress. It was over swiftly and he returned to his steely indifference. Aside from those moments, the suffering he had endured—and there must have been some; the man had lost four daughters and two wives—remained a bitter secret.

When Mannalargenna finally looked up his face was so fierce that for a moment the Commandant was unsure whether he was safe, so far from the boat.

'This all done now, all gone.'

The Commandant weighed the words carefully. 'It is perhaps inadvisable to cut off one's hair in such a…climate.'

'*It is perhaps inadvisable,*' echoed the chief. 'Nothin else now.' He coughed and flicked the green flake of glass away. 'Your hair'—he waved a tired finger in the direction of the Commandant's head—'just your hair. *This…*' But the fingers danced away, leaving the conversation. 'Too hard…'

He picked up the glass and started with it again, this time over the other ear.

The Commandant looked down at him, willing himself to understand. On the voyage from Yarmouth to here, through foul weather, through changes of course and of schedule, Mannalargenna had been stoic. But he had laid down his aura of authority, withdrawn inside himself. His eyes no longer explored the world but appeared to gaze at an abyss that swallowed everything. Mannalargenna, he now realised, believed himself to be on a journey from which he would not return. He had said goodbye to his homeland, to the handful of his people who were left there. Whether he saw himself as their betrayer, the Commandant could not tell. It was sad but unavoidable. His will to go on living was his own concern. For the Commandant, the power over life and death was a matter for the Almighty, to be exercised in His own time and His own way. He could not abide the notion that a person might refuse to go on living, might even presume to call upon themselves the right to make such a decision. These simple people were nonetheless capable of surprising complexity.

The chief hacked again at his hair and laid a new tuft with the others. He sang softly to himself as he worked, a tuneless roll of vowels that was unfamiliar to the Commandant. The wind swirled in the hollow and the severed locks at his feet shifted a little. Overhead the seabirds circled.

There being nothing else he could do, the Commandant took a seat on a nearby rock. A convict approached, saw the two of them sitting there and returned to the boat with a shrug. Once the chief had sawed off the matted ropes of hair he began to run his left hand over his scalp, feeling and searching, the glass in his right hand following to take off the stray lengths. He did it delicately, as though introducing his fingertips to his scalp for the first time. Then he set to work on his beard, and the Commandant saw the sharp line of his jaw, shaped to fit his inexorable nature.

Finally he laid the glass down, bowed his head towards his lap and with both hands rubbed his scalp vigorously. The stray hairs flew free and he stood: the Commandant did likewise. They faced each other and Mannalargenna seized him by the arms, not embracing him but regarding him coldly. The Commandant saw that face as something profoundly sad: a man of advanced years who was a boy inside—and a boy who had lost everything.

The Arrival of the Dog

The wind moaned over empty plains and found the settlement. It moved the grasses, pushed at the walls and fences, the structures of Pea Jacket Point, made in haste. It flowed through the tough fronds of the she-oaks, and each frond made a tiny thrum over its fluted surface as it whipped the air and all of them, collectively, built the moaning.

The fronds and the pale grasses gave form to the wind so that each blast and retreat could be seen racing over the saddle of land and out across the water. The Commandant would write *boisterous* in his journal: his word for the breeze, not the mood of the people.

~

The Storekeeper had been sent to the sawpit that morning, and had returned to find his wife hurrying back to the house from across the settlement. He did not enquire; he had taught himself not to enquire. Instead, he invited her to walk the beach with him, and to his surprise she agreed: these days she seemed alternately too busy or too listless for such diversions.

He had mapped out the things he wanted to say. That he knew this life had proved disappointing, that it felt like exile and not advancement. That he could return to surveying and they could go back to Sydney, or try their luck again in Hobart. There had to be a way of reshaping their future. There were no children to consider, and even if at some point there were… he would have to reconcile the thing they never discussed: the likelihood a child would not be his, but the Commandant's.

He knew. She knew he knew. And somehow the thing was beyond bluster, beyond rage, and was only a source of sadness to him. That he could not fill up her life and that she needed the love of another man to be complete. It was galling that in such a small settlement the man who was his rival and his superior occupied a house not fifty yards from theirs, that they were obliged to bid good morning to each other every day; that the man enjoyed the authority to deploy him as he pleased in order to have impunity with his wife. *Split me a cart of wood: the heavy stuff from over the hill. Go with the bullock driver to see whether the Pats River is running. Take the natives to Stony Castle so they can hunt.*

At least, walking now, he knew what his wife was doing because she walked beside him. But she was in no mood to talk. When he pointed out the birds in the late afternoon sky, or the moss by the track, or the studded, glittering boulders, she sighed and said yes. Lovely.

He wanted a drink. He was beginning to despair that there was anything he could use to begin a conversation when he saw the two children, Pipi and Whelk. He knew they liked to escape to the beach just north of the settlement, separated from it by a hundred yards of scrub. Their furtive ways, among the wallaby tracks.

Friends for most of their brief lives, Pipi and Whelk were now allies against the sorrow of the place. Pipi was still too small to be allocated chores or even very much schooling. Whelk had been placed with the Coxswain, never on the sea but sweeping and practising knots and rigging at the little boatshed, learning he seemed to enjoy.

The children must have slipped away during the time allocated for afternoon prayer, and now they were huddled out of the wind in the cleft under a suspended boulder they called the Fat Badger Rock. They often told the old people in the settlement about this place of theirs: *probelattenner*, the old people would reply. *Don't you go callin it a badger.*

No one else went there. No one else knew where it was, not even the other children. So the Storekeeper was surprised and secretly pleased to have seen it, to recognise how closely it did indeed resemble a badger. The rock had a bulging belly, a snout and a black imperfection that could have passed as an eye. The space beneath would be tricky to crawl into, available only to them. He felt a wave of pleasure for them, in there without officers, or church services, or sick people or punishments.

He turned to his wife to see if she had noticed them. She had not. She was looking back over her shoulder as though she was vaguely interested in returning to the settlement, from where it was impossible to see the sea at all. The movement of her body under the dress called forth regret for everything: not blame but a dogged wish that things had been otherwise. She had taken a risk with her future in coming to him, here.

The risk appeared to be curdling into failure. But how could he condemn her for having tried?

The very highest tides pushed some seawater into the bottom of the crevice under the Fat Badger. There would be limpets under there: he'd seen the natives knocking them off the sheer sides of granite boulders with the heels of their hands and taking them to the old people to cook. He tried one once: his tongue on the grippy surface of the limpet's foot a distant memory of a kiss that had shocked him with its urgency before the sharp fishy taste swept sentiment aside.

It was October, spring, and the wind was supposed to be blustery. But this gale carried winter endlessly from somewhere to somewhere else. He walked across the end of the beach and onto the first of the rocks that fringed the bay. He was uncertain about approaching the children: worried they would be scared by his presence and would abandon their hideaway like frightened shorebirds fleeing a nest. His wife trailed behind, reluctant. By the time they emerged onto the tops of the boulders and could see the ocean, he realised that the two children had left the Fat Badger Rock anyway.

Pipi was now a tiny figure in the distance, hurrying away from the settlement. Whelk stood beside the rock, whistling to her. He had a good whistle on him: it cut the air. He had not noticed the Storekeeper or his wife yet, although they were closing within speaking distance. The seals lazing at the back of the beach looked up at the whistle, but Pipi did not, and Whelk's body betrayed frustration.

Now he saw the Storekeeper. The boy was startled, but good at deference. 'Afternoon, sir,' he breathed under lowered eyes.

'Young Whelk. Out walking?'

'*Ah.*' It was more a release of annoyance than a response. 'She won't come back. Says she seen something.'

'Something where?' The Storekeeper tried looking beyond where the girl was standing. There was nothing on the sea but the heaving of the grey-green waves, and explosions of white when they collapsed.

But now she was skipping on the spot. The Storekeeper's wife had caught up with him and the two of them stood watching. Pipi looked at the sea, looked back at the three of them. Something was tugging at her attention. She looked cold: the heavy serge of her frock flapped and rippled against her ribs, and her hair swirled so that she had to hold it flat with her fingers to see clearly. The boy had stopped at the near end of the beach and started picking through the dried kelp.

The Storekeeper bent down and studied the wrack alongside him. Thinking of the flagon on his desk, still a quarter full, as the reflex flared again: the salt, the thirst, the longing…

'What are we looking for?'

Whelk shrugged. 'Mebbe take something to the Connerdant.'

The Man had only taken to calling himself the Commandant since they had been here. He wore the same suit and hat, he spoke the same way, but he insisted they use the word, even though it invited mispronunciation. *Combalant. Commerdat.* He patiently corrected the stumbles, lavishly praising those, like Pipi, who could say it perfectly. It mattered a great deal to him.

The Commandant was a collector, always pleased by shells and stones and other pretty objects. But it was the dead things, strangely, that pleased him most: a dried-out porcupine fish, a sea dragon or a paper nautilus. The children had once taken him the claw of an enormous crab, a heavy, cruel-looking thing that the Commandant had received eagerly, as though it were a treasure. It stank sweetly from a far corner of his desk.

Pipi was calling back to Whelk now, apparently indifferent to the presence of the adults, tiny and somehow defiant on top of a tall boulder. The Storekeeper still couldn't see anything in the direction she was looking: he was down too low. He took his wife's hand and they stepped together awkwardly until they had come up to Pipi's level. Whelk had reached her first.

'What is it?' the boy asked.

She did not look around, but continued to stare at the sea.

'Something there,' she said eventually. The Storekeeper looked where she was indicating but could see nothing. There were cold flecks of salty water in the air and he licked them off his lips.

'Wait,' she said. 'Wait.' The swells rose and fell, hiding and revealing patches of sea. Foam, strands of kelp, voyaging birds.

'*There.*'

And it appeared. Out at sea, beyond swimming, something rode the restless surface. Its edges were straight lines, and in its centre was a small peak that was rounder, softer. It lacked the symmetry of a vessel, sitting low to the surface and moving sluggishly, as if half-sunk. It disappeared in the troughs, rose on the waves.

The Storekeeper watched the floating thing in silence. His hand reached for his wife's, though she did not return its light pressure. A whale, perhaps? No. The edges were too sharp. A house, that had somehow unmoored itself and sailed away? He glanced at the side of Pipi's face: there was no fear in her.

It baffled him, this abstract shape. The children's eyes would be sharper, not so maddeningly slow to focus. He asked his wife what she thought it was, and she shrugged.

'A boat?'

The arrival of a boat would bring the settlement to life: the Commandant would want the place cleaned and tidied.

Everyone knew he was hoping the Governor would visit. He had drilled them in a plan to take effect if the Governor's sail was seen: singing, marching, reciting scripture. This floating puzzle clearly didn't carry the Governor: such a grand man would hardly arrive on this shapeless sinking thing, waves washing through his breeches. But still, it might be important. The store was low on many items. There was so much mail to send, and presumably just as much to receive.

Pipi hopped on the spot, like the excitement was passing through her and heating the rock. He worried that if she moved forward any further she'd reach the periwinkled downslope where a wave might snatch her. The boulders were smooth, pale granite, glittering with minerals. When they were wet, the steep curves of the big domes were slippery. He took her hand and led her back.

'Come,' he said to her. 'You can go to see the Commandant, and tell him yourself.'

Her hand was warm in his, just briefly; impossibly warm in this wind. Then she was gone, running with Whelk up the path to the settlement. His wife looked at him expectantly and he smiled and began to walk after them.

~

The Commandant and the Surgeon were in the store, sprawled on timber chairs behind the counter, smoking. The Surgeon was a young man in old habits. Jowly already, but still dark-haired; creases in his nankeen trousers, but also stains of a bodily kind. A short housecoat over a shirt, no waistcoat. About his ruddy face there was no sign of the years of study, nor of devotion to anything much, save perhaps ease. He looked as he was: a single man in a lonely outpost who had learnt to stave off the boredom with drink.

That morning the Commandant had sent the Storekeeper away to examine the new sawpit to the south, so he could spend a vigorous hour with the man's wife. The Storekeeper's long, sad face had betrayed no emotion in response to the request. He must have known it was a pretext: so be it. Awkward truces were the Commandant's specialty, and she was worth the bother.

He and the Surgeon had no great regard for each other, but both considered the other the only intellect in the settlement worth exchanging insults with. Their disagreeable, smoky silence was broken now by a tentative knocking at the door. The two men glanced at each other, and as the Surgeon showed no sign of moving, the Commandant heaved himself to his feet with a sigh.

When he saw it was Whelk at the door, with Pipi a few steps behind him on the grass, he arched an eyebrow. The lad was meant to be working at the boatshed. The twigs and sand on their clothing, the windblown state of their hair, should not pass without comment. But the boy was already speaking.

'We found something,' he said breathlessly. 'Pipi found it. It's floating.'

'Floatin,' Pipi repeated from behind him.

The Commandant managed a dry chuckle. 'You have disturbed me from my conversation with the Surgeon to tell me something's *floating*?'

He hated to be interrupted when he was writing, thinking or conversing. He preferred that people brought their business to him when he was engaged in practical tasks: not settled into a contemplative state, but available at the superficial level. Many people in the settlement—those who hadn't seen him during his sojourns in the bush—thought writing was all he ever did. That, and helping the Surgeon with the dead people.

'Well, come in, then. I'm not having that infernal wind in here.'

He swung the door closed behind the two small bodies and the Surgeon eyed them both. The Commandant did not return to his armchair but chose a chair behind the table so as to appear more formal. He pointed his long nose at them.

'Now: tell me.' He was quite fond of these two. He noticed the boy held the girl's hand. The girl had inhaled and forgotten to breathe out: her chest was inflated and her mouth half open, holding the breath in terror.

Whelk explained about the floating thing. The Commandant picked up a feather from the table as he listened.

'It will go past,' the boy was pleading. 'It will go up to Stony Castle. Might break up there, sir. We think it might be a boat.'

'*Break up?* Coxswain's got you picking up the lingo, boy.' His mouth projected forward when he spoke firmly. He ran his pinched fingers along the vane of the feather. Firmness was needed here: children were apt to get carried away. 'It is a boat or it isn't. A boat is not something one confuses with another thing.'

'Then it is not a boat,' parried the boy.

'So what is it?'

'W-we don't know.' Pipi nodded beside him.

The Commandant sighed deeply. He remembered that he was nearly done with his list of names, taking the long and complex ones that the natives used, and replacing them with kings and queens and counts and dukes. It conferred dignity and simplified conversation, something his predecessors had been unable to achieve. He needed to come up with something more serious for these two than *Pipi* and *Whelk*.

'Well.' He opened a decorative box next to the pen stand and dropped the feather inside. 'Since I have not yet had my walk...' He rose and herded them towards the door with a brisk nod of farewell to the Surgeon. The smell of paper and dust swirled around him. 'You, boy, bring that eyeglass with you. And for heaven's sake do not drop it.'

~

The Commandant and the children reached the shore as the last of the light flickered and fired on the edges of the waves.

Whelk and Pipi led the way, the fat grey geese scattering before them. The boy gripped the glass tightly, his other hand on Pipi. Out on the high boulders, they saw that the thing had gone past, carried by the wind and swell, and was now well to the east of them. There was a brief impasse: the girl wanted to continue east to where the thing would eventually fetch up on the shore, and would only communicate this by muttering to Whelk.

The Commandant had matters to attend to, but seeing their excitement he agreed to be led there. They pushed on in the half-light, and he felt the stirring of a memory: the walking, the endless walking in search of the Big River people, Mannalargenna guiding them through the heavy scrub. It was a tiny satisfaction to him that the great chief no longer went walking; had even lost interest in hunting. Only he, the Commandant, could reprise those efforts at will.

The track meandered under low overhangs and through tight openings that forced him to duck. His enormous cloth cap made him artificially taller: he would otherwise have slipped through unimpeded. When they emerged into the open again, east of the settlement, the coast was a series of smoothly ramped beaches. At the third beach, backed by walls of granite, the children ran ahead again, feet plunging in the damp sand, to where the object had washed up and was rocking in the foam. The swell faced squarely onto the beach here, rather than sweeping past as it did in front of the settlement.

The Commandant took his time stepping through the mounds of dried seagrass at the top of the beach. By the time he arrived he was out of breath, but there was no need for him to speak: the children were speechless also, staring at the thing the sea had delivered.

It was a timber triangle, many yards across and rising at its centre to a point, which was unmistakably the broken-off corner of a vessel. It rocked and shuddered in the foam, wet planks gleaming in the dying light. And at the apex of the raised corner there stood a dog: black as soot, finely built and tall; soaked enough to peak its fur, but perfectly balanced, even as its strange raft bucked and swayed.

It watched them calmly, nose slightly raised to take in the scent of a new shore. It did not bark; did not yelp in anxiety to be delivered from the sea. Its tail did not move. It eyed the breaking waves and, when the moment allowed, it stepped off onto the sand and was among them.

To the Dormitory

The Commandant left the Storekeeper's house in a mild hurry, out through the scullery and into the garden, along the narrow brick path the man had laid for his wife (laid it with the hands that had been on her) and between the young orchard trees where the bees droned in clouds of scent. He pressed down on his cloth cap so that it did not snag as he passed under.

The monkey on the pedestal screeched as he passed, baring its fangs, and he hissed at it. The yellow eyes of the thing were human enough to disconcert him. Had it possessed the power of speech, it could tell the Storekeeper some tales. He ran a hand over the buttons of his trousers. All was well: only a tired half-pressure persisted.

He eyed the monkey eyeing him, and he saw it as a lurid parody of femaleness with its long, pointed nipples and the cleft mound of its vulva. Then he stopped, stared more intently. Its belly had swollen. There could be no doubt now. He had seen it two days before and thought it was his imagination—he was acutely wary of fertility just now, as a man borrowing another's wife. But no, there it was. A distinct curvature. *Christ*, he muttered to himself, *how long do the damned things gestate?* It may yet be a tumour.

He rushed on, looped around the front of the house as though he had come from elsewhere, and saw the Storekeeper hard at work on his stupid Sisyphean wall. Monotonous and unceasing: the perfect task for an inferior intellect.

~

That night, the Storekeeper prepared the evening meal: a hen that had stopped laying, slaughtered for him by the Coxswain, and some vegetables from the store's little field.

He closed the store early and abandoned his work on the wall so he could prepare the fire ahead of time. He laid a table—cut flowers and a bottle of claret he had taken from the victualling room—carefully placing his coins in the drawer. He admired the glow of the bottle: was it too early to pull the cork? He had no plan in mind. This was no grand seduction: merely, he hoped, a starting point.

But missteps accrued from the beginning. His wife, unoccupied, sat at the table looking restless while he chopped food and prodded the fire. When she had said nothing for a long time, he turned around from the hearth to find she was studying the backs of her hands.

She spoke without raising her eyes. 'Do you think we will ever have children?'

The Storekeeper felt panic rise. Was this the reason for

everything? 'How can I tell? I know you want to. I suppose it is up to—'

'But you. You want to also, don't you?'

He had his wish now: they were talking. About something that terrified him. 'Yes, I—'

'I see you with those native children. Pipi and Whelk. You're very fond of them, aren't you.'

It was no trap. She had raised her eyes now, was looking at him in earnest.

'I suppose I am.'

'The girl is so small and quiet. I think she is comfortable with you because the boy trusts you. But I see her around the Catechist…' She shuddered. 'The poor child shrinks from him.'

'I must say, I can find no warmth for that man.' He pulled up a chair opposite his wife.

She was adamant now. 'And he knows she's terrified. It must appeal to him somehow, because he smiles all the more, and he, those…*hands* of his! He strokes her cheek, or he touches her hair.' She made a small sound of revulsion. 'Any liberty he can get. I watched him on Sunday at the chapel and I swear he was *purring* at her.'

'She's withdrawn from the old people,' he replied. 'They were good to her. It makes no sense.'

'Who is she?' He thought he saw redness in her eyes now.

'I don't think anyone knows,' he answered. He could smell the ashes again, could see the dead woman and her splayed hair, her delicately outstretched hand and the pups spilling free. But it would not help to explain those scenes. *Her mother knew what was coming. She hid the girl before they murdered her.* Letting that spiral take its course was too much to bear. In the end he simply said 'An orphan. The boy is an orphan too. We thought she was

Big River at first, but those people haven't claimed her as theirs. We have gone to little trouble to find the families.'

He served their food in silence, suddenly disconsolate, and they ate without speaking.

The Catechist had once remarked of Whelk's parents, over dinner at the Commandant's house, that perhaps they had decided to wander off. *It happens sometimes with the nomads.* The Storekeeper didn't believe it for a minute. The Catechist, and others like him, had a vested interest in such children having been abandoned: lost souls to gather under their black robes. He wasn't sure if that was the greater horror, or the idea that there were people out there who loved their children and had lost them.

He knew that Pipi and Whelk slept in different parts of the settlement, but he had seen them in the early mornings, meeting on the damp grass and poking at the fire until the blue smoke popped a flame. During the days, Whelk would go to the Coxswain, to scrub and caulk and fix nets, and Pipi would be absent from his attention for hours at a time: he had much to take care of. And she was small and quiet, talking to herself in a muddy combined language. There were other secret places the two of them had learned to inhabit; not just the Fat Badger Rock, but overhangs, the clefts of boulders, the tunnels under bushes.

Their secrecy, he felt, was a way of dealing with despair. They were children watching old people dying. Some of them bed-bound, drowning in seas of filth and horror. Others deciding simply to sit down, refusing to be patients. Within hours or days there would be a cry as they were found stiff and windblown under the trees, currawongs cawing above them.

He found himself urging the cork out of the claret and

splashing it into the glass in front of him. His wife declined with a hand over the rim.

The graveyard paddock at the foot of the hill grew fuller week upon week. Unfinished knitting, rows of pegs and stakes that reached the fenceline and started again in the other direction. *How will it end?* his wife had asked him when she first arrived. *Will the paddock fill and the people empty? Will there be another paddock after this one, if there are more people coming?*

The Storekeeper was sure there were no more people coming, that this was all there was of the natives. He had walked all over Van Diemen's Land with the Commandant, and if there were more out there, they would have known. The Surgeon maintained that there were plenty more in Port Phillip and in New South Wales, and someone would eventually try the same approach and bring them to the island. That the thought of it crept upon him when he was idle was a reason always to be occupied.

His wife had pushed the remainder of her food aside and she was speaking now. He forced himself to attend.

'...said you found Pipi with a dead woman,' she was saying. 'And there were pups.'

He nodded, tipped wine down his throat. The old dread returning.

'What happened to the pups?'

'Why does it matter?' he asked, and he could not conceal the prickle in his voice. 'There was a dead *woman*...'

'I'm only asking.'

He remembered them. When they'd reached Campbell Town the Man had said he would take care of them, and no-one saw them again. And now the Man's lie became his lie, because he did not want to further upset his wife.

'They grew up on a farm at Campbell Town. I'm told they're all fine big dogs now.'

She smiled slightly at this, a faint, wretched smile that was also a lie. The Commandant had clearly told her something different.

~

The little hopping mice had been getting into the grain sacks again, and though the Storekeeper thought them rather sweet creatures, the sharp tang of their urine was becoming noticeable in the store and he felt obliged to take action. The sacks were piled on the floor under the tall shelves that housed everything else: tins and jars and boxes and bottles. He began dragging them all out and sweeping away the mouse droppings and spilt grain. He arranged for a prisoner to bring him a cart of bricks so he could raise the sacks off the floor. The mice would have to earn their food like everyone else.

He left the door open as he worked, stopping occasionally to issue rum to the Coxswain or flour to the Catechist's wife. Later in the morning one of the old native men appeared, shuffling silently. He was after tobacco. There was effort in his exhalation as he mounted the three steps into the store. His muscles had gone slack with the years, with the slow decline in movement. Above a white beard stained gold by the smoking, his eyes were inflamed and weeping, a curse all the old people seemed to share.

They did their business—he had coins from the Tuesday market—and the old man silently retreated. As he hauled another sack out from under the shelves, the Storekeeper saw he'd sat down outside the front door and was filling his pipe. The aroma of the tobacco was accompanied by voices: Whelk had come to sit with the old man. His interest in the old people was as strong as ever, the Storekeeper realised: he seemed to love nothing more than coaxing their stories from them.

The old man's story was broadly known to everyone in the settlement. He'd had three children but he had them no more. A place called Meander River. *They done that thing with a swivel gun charged with nails,* the old man had said once. *Paddy Heagon was the devil what done it. Doan you never forget that name.* By the time they brought him here the old man was all thrashed out; had become a child again.

'Spose you want tucker,' he was saying to the boy. The old people laughed about Whelk's ways, his habit of engaging them in conversations to see if he could wheedle food out of them. They delighted in his soft belly, the squish of his upper arms. There was something sad in it too, he thought, the unspoken longing for more children who pulsed with the same good health.

'S'all right. I can ask this one.' The Storekeeper smiled as he listened: the boy meant him.

'Mm. I was gonna tell you how I wound up in this place.' More smoke, drifting gently in the door. There was some throat-clearing, a cough. The Storekeeper imagined the man settling, choosing his moment.

'Well then. You know that the Commandant fella come through Big River, where I was. This was, this was after that business with the, ah, the shootin. So you know how that goes: my family here, family belong clan, clan belong tribe an I was senior man in the tribe, senior man. Same for Oyster Bay lot, all the same.

'So we all there. An he come through with that ol man, Mannalargenna. Big man.' There was a harsher note in his voice. 'They lookin for weapons we got: gun, blackfella weapon.

Had em all wrapped up, in shirts an that, tucked in a tree. An they found em—we saw it—found, ooh, lot of spears, waddies, gun, bullet.'

The Storekeeper had returned to the sacks, rebuking himself for the eavesdropping, but working in silence so he could listen. He ran a hand over the cool glass of the brandy bottles. He was intrigued by the disagreements between the old people, their running battles over truth. The things that made up the truth had now all happened: what remained was to settle the stories, because here there were no conflicts, no raids, no killings. Just life turning slowly with the sun and the moon.

'—plenty shootin,' the old man was saying. 'Throwin spears back at em, all right. Get em in the gullies, from up high when they come through a breakaway.' His voice fell at this point. 'But people got to sleep, they got to eat, have a fire. Sometime, you know? Can't do it forever. Every night, every night, whitefella creepin up, waitin, watchin. *Num lagger*, we say. White man coming. Sometime if they dogs barkin we get a warnin, take off.'

The words were quiet now. 'People get tired of runnin. So what you do then? Got babies cryin and people need to hunt an nobody can go out? What you gonna do with them old ones that can't run anymore?'

'But anyway, that fella, that Mannalargenna, he was with em.'

'With the whitefellas?' There was shock in Whelk's voice.

'Nother story. Anyway, whitefella, Commandant bloke there, he couldn't find us. He was in the right area, but every day we get around him again, gettin tired, gettin tired. So he say to Mannalargenna, hey, you find em! An Mannalargenna, ben talkin to a devil in a dead tree and that devil showed im where we was. This was…'

His voice stopped, then returned as a mumble that the

Storekeeper strained to hear. '…lemme see…what year we in now?'

'Eighteen hundred thirty-five,' Whelk recited brightly.

'So this be…thirty-one I think. Rainy season. What they call that?'

There was a discussion about spring and summer, something about honey. The boy contradicting him gently; talk of rainy seasons and snow. The Storekeeper remembered all this, and he felt like stepping out the door and correcting them. They were both right: it had been summer and it was snowing. He remembered the children clutching at their burning feet with their fingers, trying to warm them. Wrapping kangaroo hides around themselves. Events he'd seen, told from the other end. All three of them had been there, in the same storm, and four years later they remained bound to each other, either side of a doorway. Did Whelk really not remember the storm, or was this just a game of his, a way to keep the old man talking?

'Are they really friends?' Whelk asked the old man.

'Who's that?'

'Mannalargenna and the Commandant.'

'Probly just their business.' There was a pause. Perhaps the old man was watching the sea eagle making its slow circuits over the flagstaff hill. 'No, don't think so. Not friends.'

'Are you friends with Mannalargenna?'

The silence was longer this time. 'He killin some of our people, long time ago. One other year, Big River mob kill his boy, you know. Speared im. Same enemy's not like same friends.'

~

Around this time it was decided that Pipi must live in the Catechist's house.

The reasoning was unclear: the Commandant said it was the Catechist's decision. The Catechist said he'd been told to arrange it, but did not say by whom. All the children at the settlement were orphans: Pipi was not unique in that respect. She'd lived among the aunts and uncles for as long as anyone could remember. The old people had the coughing sickness among them and that may have presented a reason to relocate her, but the Surgeon knew nothing of it. There was talk among the officers that Pipi was alone a lot, although in truth she never was—she was always with Whelk. It was noticed that she was at the beach more, that she had lice, that she was *insolent*, which meant only that she could not summon politeness in response to the Catechist's oily charm, nor submission under his rage.

There had been reports of children bruised, children stunned into a strange remote silence, under the Catechist's care. The Storekeeper thought he must be the most hated man on the island, but when he considered it more deeply he wondered if this was something beyond hate: if he was just an embodiment of the place, the hands and face of an otherwise formless despair.

The Storekeeper heard the reports because he was a post for casual conversation, someone to gossip to. Turnips, ears of corn, *did you hear about the fight in the barracks?* And he saw the evidence, a child pushing a coin over the counter with a hand striped purple by cane or belt; another who could not be encouraged to say anything at all, who shook with fear at nothing more than an adult's smile.

There was no announcement and no great occasion to Pipi's move. She was held back as the children filed into morning classes, and told to take her blanket from Seven and put it in the dormitory room at the Catechist's house. This the Storekeeper learned from the Commandant's son, who despised the Catechist but was hopelessly loyal to his own father.

She crossed the grounds with her blanket that day, Whelk as ever by her side. He knew she had taken a mother mouse full of babies that she was keeping under a tea box, because the two of them came to the store to show him. She solemnly cradled the tiny animal, placing the box on the store's counter and her fingers on the bulging abdomen. He thought her eyes were impossibly huge when she looked up at him.

'You can feel the wingling,' she said.

'Wiggling,' he corrected her gently. 'What are you keeping her for?'

She merely pressed her lips together, a thing she did when she did not want to talk. Whelk was watching her closely, protectively. There was something going on with the mouse, and it was not the first mouse he had seen them with. 'Pipi?' he asked, as another thought occurred to him. 'Did you take the classroom kittens? They're all looking for them.'

She hesitated, just long enough that the Storekeeper started to be alarmed. 'No. Too big. I only get mice.'

He felt a wave of relief. They hid the box under the bundled blanket as they left.

Months earlier, when the Catechist had decided to establish a room in his house for the orphans, the Storekeeper had helped to place the beds in there. It was the one time he had been inside, and the memory of it lingered unpleasantly. The room was long and narrow and they arranged the iron beds in a row along one side. It had a door to the outside of the house that was kept locked, and another one to the inside. There was a lock on this one as well. The room was fiercely neat: the light that came in showed the dust, and the dust just hung there as if it dared not settle.

He tried to be positive about it; tried to imagine Pipi would be warmer there, that the Catechist's wife would bring her food. There would be other children to talk to, not just Whelk. But his misgivings persisted.

He stood on the front step of the store and gazed across the field to the Catechist's house. The two of them were taking their time: all they had to do was deposit the blanket—and perhaps the mouse in the tea box—and leave. The late morning reading and writing was taught by the older children, so their absence from the schoolroom might pass unnoticed, he thought.

But as he stood in the sun worrying for the two of them he caught a flash of movement. They had run from the Catechist's house, skirting into the near edge of the scrub and the tunnels that led to the northern shore of the peninsula. They would be headed for the Fat Badger Rock. He tried to think why that mattered, what it might signify. In this slow place events turned without fanfare, and signal moments could be missed. This mattered somehow.

A Fortunate Marriage

The Catechist's wife was in the scullery in the middle of the afternoon when she heard his footfalls in the hallway. She stood perfectly still to listen, and there it was: a second set of footsteps, much fainter. The front door closed and the door to the first room opened and then shut. The sounds were muffled: she knew to keep the door to the kitchen closed at all times—she had been firmly instructed on this—so as to prevent draughts.

Providence had granted her a fine kitchen to work in: an iron hob over the fireplace, a swinging arm for the water. Crockery and glassware that weren't made for a boat but could be served to guests without shame, should there have been any guests. Fine knives and a whetstone, a central table that crowded her a little towards the edges of the room, but gave her a working surface. She was content to eat at the table alone when her husband was working: she found conversation arduous at the best of times.

She rubbed at the table's surface with hot water and a rag.

To lose a husband to drowning at forty had been a misfortune, but not an outrageous one: to gain another at such an age was nothing short of a miracle. He did not fill her days with laughter or affection: that was not his way and besides, she had no taste for frivolity. But to be the wife of the Catechist, even in this bleak place, was no small thing.

He could be difficult, she conceded. He had a temper, a hot streak of cruelty, and unexpected surges of lust. He would take hold of her not only in the bed, in the dark, but sometimes during the day, in places that risked discovery by others. He'd bent her over this very table, ready or not, and rutted at her till the chairs tipped, laughing as she bit down on the pain. When that faded she recalled mainly his black robes swinging over her, as if she was being attacked by some great priapic raven.

Such thoughts. Not befitting a Christian wife.

He controlled the children absolutely. They had none of their own, and she'd had none with the drowner, but he owned the orphans in all ways other than affection. They did not run or shout or laugh in his presence, nor in hers. They did not make things or explore or heaven forbid *play* in this house. For all she knew they did not even dream. He had created a world in which all they could do was absorb the Word of the Lord, or risk his fury. Part of her abhorred it. Another part admired his effectiveness: if one could curb the native children, it might be possible to contain the wind itself.

She wrung the cloth and dunked it, began again to scrub. The sounds were coming now, weaving through the lining boards like smoke. Trouble. Probably to do with the missing kittens. Not her business. They were not her business.

She rammed the cloth into the table's surface and the weave

began to catch in the tiny splinters and pull away in threads.

Who was he, anyway? She'd known him intimately four years now. She knew his trousers, his shirts and underclothes from washing them, over and over. She knew the shape of him in a chair. She knew the feel of his nobbly prick inside her, though she'd never seen the thing. She knew the broken landscape of his face, the crescent nose, the lost eye, the great gouge of pink flesh through his brow. Quiet nights she had felt a longing to touch the devastation, to examine all the pits and furrows, to know the lives he had led.

Because none of his stories added up. No one in Launceston knew him. He had no friends, no professional acquaintances, as one might expect of a spiritual leader. A shepherd with no flock, he claimed to know Sydney, to have passing acquaintance with the new aristocrats of Port Phillip, Batman and Fawkner. He'd seen the Hunter Group and Western Port, he said, but was himself an unknowable land.

She pressed harder into the unforgiving timber and her nails turned white with the pressure.

The sounds were louder now, more emphatic. The first time she'd heard such sounds she thought she would never live with them. But people adjust to the most remarkable things. Now she could hear a child screaming in her own house and not feel the least distress.

Dissolution's Approach

West of the creaking timber chapel, a cluster of the adults milled around a doorway. They were family, come to see the woman in Fifteen who lay on a bower of blankets, straw beneath her to stop the cold seeping up from the bricked ground. Fifteen was no different to the other huts: walls of lined timber, papered for appearances but thin enough to shake in the wind, a thatched roof, a hearth and chimney of convict bricks and limestone rubble. The air inside was viscous: this was a place of waiting. It was all of the damp paucity of a prison cell, built with indifference as to escape: where would one go, having determined to leave? The liberty to walk out was the cruellest of hoaxes. The world outside was a saddle of grassy fields between two hills on an island in a strait that severed Van Diemen's Land like a fingertip from its vast northern neighbour. The Commandant had been given no role in the selection of the site, but he suspected it had been chosen especially because the people could not see their homelands from here. Even the sea was blocked from view unless they climbed the hill.

His predecessors thought it was from the old woman's tongue that they got the name of the place. *Wybalenna*: the Commandant could imagine the logic. It created the impression of an enthusiastic adoption by the natives themselves. But no one recognised it. It was just something they'd mistaken and not bothered to correct. The people called it *the settlement* and ignored the name.

And here at the settlement, in Fifteen, this woman lay suspended between life and death, a series of endings taking place within her. *Her dissolution approaches*, the Commandant wrote, seated on a plain wooden chair beside her. He tried to be observant, tried to hold fast to his place in posterity. Her body formed a shapeless mass beneath the blankets, one that moved only to cough and sigh. Her hands, knotted by kindness, were hidden: her feet just points under the bedding. They had been a girl's feet once, he mused. They had known grace and childhood pains and they had felt the land, as the land had felt them, walking unconquered ground. He did not write that.

Her days of illness had been undignified and full of cruelty. The Commandant had watched the Surgeon hauling at her clothes, baring her breasts and demanding to *auscultate*. Old tobacco and sour breath would waft from him as he prodded among her ribs, but that was not the worst of it.

Three times the Surgeon had bled her. Nobody knew what it achieved. He came now to do it again: unpacked the long box and assembled the brass and ceramic implements; made notes as he went, drawing back the sleeve, smoothing the skin on the underside of the forearm, slapping for veins. Who were the notes for? Did they go somewhere? With the mail, perhaps? He must find out: they should be Government property.

The blood spurted until it was channelled, and lay in brilliant red droplets on the white ceramic. It ran off the curves of the instruments, losing brilliance when it spread as a darker stain on the bedclothes. It was a messy business, imprecise.

She coughed, and the effort pulsed more blood so that the Surgeon reeled back from her, throwing his arm dramatically over the lower half of his face, eyes peering wildly over the top of his sleeve as though he had beheld some horror beyond imagining.

The Commandant made notes on the cough and the blood: the Surgeon was too busy flinching. Posterity would want to know this. That he had taken a quart. That *the lancet was had recourse to*, that he had taken four ounces, *diem*, that the patient showed no response. His frustrated declaration, each time, that the treatment needed time to take effect. He snapped shut the cases, wrapped her arm in gauze and drew the covers over. *How can I help those who would not help themselves?* he sputtered on the way back to the store afterwards. And *Try to keep them from bothering her*, and *She is listless and appears resigned*.

Her final hours were filled with other people, as her life had been. She talked and wept with them, and the Commandant withdrew to stand outside, still writing in the journal. He confined himself to trying to regulate who came and went. If the thing was infectious, it wouldn't do for the dying to pass it to the living.

The women came first, addressing the urgent things. They would care for the little ones, tend the garden. Take no nonsense from the men. The men came quietly, their bellies buttoned into coats, abashed and cloaked in gruffness. They came in staunch, ignoring his presence, and left in tears. The

Commandant lacked words for what he was seeing and hearing: it was beyond the range of his reporting. The woman admonished the men gently, just audible to him outside the door. Behind the beards they were shaken: she had made them heartbroken boys. She had words for each of them that were theirs alone, and even now in the sapping of her last hours she was easing their sorrow, working whispers from inside her soul and her exhausted body.

Once they were all done the children came to her, their voices quieter than the creaking timbers. They understood what was required of them in this room—the Commandant felt sure they had absorbed these habits from their schooling. Pipi and Whelk were among them, he saw, the boy leading the tiny girl forward. There had only been a handful of other deaths in the weeks since he had taken over management of the settlement, but the children would have seen the burial yard with its rows of humped earth. And these were only the dead among those who had been *saved*. Back in the bush near Lake Echo, the woman with the spilling hair would be merging into the soil now, with no one to give her stories to. He wondered if they remembered her the way he did, if she visited them in their sleep, too.

He was conscious of his intrusion. Pipi and Whelk had climbed onto the bed. Their searching hands found her blanketed form and held on to her. She kissed their foreheads, stroked their fingers with a gnarled thumb. She had words for the boy, words that sounded like instruction.

Through the endless walking in the bush, and later in Hobart, the old woman had been a constant for those children, he realised. She had been their summers, squinting at the light and beaded in sweat as she waited for them swimming; their winters, when they'd enveloped themselves in the itchy rumples of her clothes.

She was food and comfort, embraces and smells, sanctuary from the unrelenting strangeness of this place and the cold austerity of their keepers. He did not write any of this either.

And she would leave them, imminently. They must have understood. They cried and couldn't conceal it, from each other or from the gathered adults. Yes, he was intruding. He took his journal out into the evening, with a gruff nod to the people holding vigil.

~

As night fell, the Storekeeper knew the old lady's time was near. The catarrh would be drowning her now. He had brandy, and he watched from the steps of the store with the bottle between his feet as the convicts appeared with the old circular rug that was used for burials. They hauled the heavy roll of it from the guardhouse where it was stored, and thumped it down outside Fifteen.

The weeping had been constant and widespread through the day: now it increased in pitch and intensity. Talk of the devil, the *Raegeowrapper*. Darkness approached, deeper than the sea. Tonight, it came for the old lady, but it could circle back for any of them. Time spun randomly here and only the strongest would live to grow old. The Storekeeper went alone to offer his company, though there was nothing he could do. The Surgeon and the Commandant were dining together. He had ensured that the people had plenty of tea, and they had maintained a steaming pannikin of it on the fire outside. All he could do was stand there.

Shortly after nightfall a great peace came over her and she sighed in its arms. She hadn't eaten in days and now she wanted no water either. Too weak to decline it, she merely averted her eyes when the cup was brought to her lips. She was far away.

At the yawn of a tired infant near her feet the woman smiled, ever so faintly, and was gone.

The Storekeeper went outside and looked first at the early stars, then down to the grass. The fine black dog that had come in from the sea sat facing out at the night, its back to the doorway, head down and snout pointed at the earth, listening. The families sat nearby, each around a small fire. Only a handful of people had been allowed inside, among them Mannalargenna, who spoke to no one and seemed taken by a great foreboding, and the small figure of Tanganaturra and her fat baby daughter, Fanny.

When word of the death passed through the vigil they wept anew and held on to each other. Whelk had fallen asleep on Trugernana's lap: the cries woke him. Under his arm curled the sleeping form of Pipi, twitching in restless dreams. The convicts returned and dragged the rug into Fifteen. There were grunts and curses from within as they loaded the body, still warm, onto the rug and then curled it over her. They shouldered the rug with her inside and staggered out of the room and across the grass to the hospital room, where the Surgeon had instructed the body was to be left ahead of the funeral.

The Storekeeper saw Whelk's eyes follow the geometric patterns as the rug passed, abstract designs in black on the fawn weave that appeared like screaming heads in rows. He hated the rug and all it stood for.

No words were spoken now. There were none to say. All that could be done was to endure the slow tide of the sorrow, and wait and hope for sleep.

The Parable of the Monkey and the Kittens

Afternoon, the long shadows and the currawongs taking over from the wrens, and it was about now that the craving started to bite.

The Storekeeper knew how to meet it: he broke up the fire in the store's hearth and screened it. He locked the drawer that had the coins, locked the door and the windows, and walked the short distance to the wall to keep working on it. Every stone he could place upon it was another sip he could avoid, or at least delay. Push it back into the night, push it back where it belonged.

The tools in the bucket, the rock piles. The task so slow and endless that it could stave off desire for as long as he could keep at it. He breathed out, hands on hips as he surveyed the gaps in the wall and the rocks pleading their cases for filling them.

He had laid two, a wide flat plate and an internal locking stone, when one of the women came to him. She had come from the hillside directly behind his house, hand in hand with

Pipi. He briefly wondered why she hadn't turned the other way and gone to bother the Commandant, but it was not his way to make a point of such things, and instead he smiled at her.

'Sir,' mumbled the woman. 'Sir, please.'

Pipi's cheeks were washed with tears. The unwelcome vision came again: the dead woman in the highlands, the litter of pups. The girl's chest jerked with sobs.

'What is it?' He dusted his hands on the sides of his trousers.

'Sir, the lady-monkey.'

'Ah, the lady-monkey.' The animal repulsed him, though he could see that it had no control over its fate. The Commandant had shipped it here to entertain the children: no one had considered that it might be pregnant, as indeed it was, or that pregnancy would turn it hostile. Squatting miserably on a yard-square platform at the top of a pole, it surveyed the world in empty despair. A collar and leash confined it to a circle around the base of the pole only eight feet or so in diameter. In any case it rarely climbed down. It would do so only to defecate or to drink, and once a day a convict would come by with a rake to sweep the turds out of its circular domain, taking care to stand out of reach and probe inwards with the rake lest the animal attempt to gouge his eyes out.

'Sir, we need you come see her.' The woman's eyes shifted sideways. 'It bad, sir.'

'Is this not something the Overseer could deal with?' He was almost pleading now.

'Already there, sir.' The woman was not budging. 'Please come.'

He sighed, then stood, plonking his hat on his head. Tonight he would have to stay away from the grog. Tomorrow, when the Commandant tried to send him to collect the new timber from over the back of Flagstaff Hill to gain some time alone with his wife, he would refuse. He was too passive in these matters. He could become a more difficult man.

But first, the monkey. As he followed the woman and the small girl through the orchard he could see that a modest crowd had gathered around the monkey's perch. Natives, three convicts, a couple of children. The Overseer, swearing loudly.

The Storekeeper moved in, took the blasphemer by the collar and pulled him back from the perch. But as the man turned to face him, he stopped dead: the Overseer's face had been laid open in two clean lines, and blood coursed down his jaw and into his shirt. His eyes burned with rage.

The monkey stood tall and defiant atop the perch, the leash trailing from her neck. Her hands met at her chest, and each was clutched around a kitten. The mad eyes were fixed and desperate: the kittens' heads were pressed against her nipples. As the small crowd looked on in horror, the monkey changed her grip so that one arm pinned both tiny captives while she used her free hand to stroke their heads.

She looked up from the kittens and she snarled at the sun, then stared down every one of the humans who had come to look at her. And her face transformed into a mask of pure hatred.

~

The Commandant was hunched over his correspondence. He'd been told about the business with the monkey, and it had unsettled him. It wasn't so much the injury to the Overseer, who had no doubt provoked the animal, but the depravity of the attempt to suckle the kittens. Women were emotional creatures, lacking the cool rationality of males, but he had been shocked to see the deficit exhibited in a monkey.

The only human sound that reached him here was the continued wailing from the mourners, which rose and fell abstractly like the wind. He tried to concentrate once more; dipped the pen and brushed irritably at a fly.

Another knock: formal, measured.

'Yes. What is it *now*?'

The ageing sergeant stepped in and gave a gruff nod where a salute might have been. He carried a sharpened knife, and he placed it formally on the front edge of the desk, then stood patiently back while the Commandant dealt with the fly. The man had stood at desks for a lifetime. The wind rattled the casement of the window and the Commandant glanced at it.

'Will it never end?'

The sergeant remained silent. The Commandant stood and surveyed him, maintaining a gaze that was steady and intimate. A uniform that was beginning to mock itself, dusty and frayed by this abrasive place. Thoughts made shadows as they crossed the Commandant's face, but he uttered none of them. His gaze returned to the front of the desk, where the knife lay. He picked it up and examined the edge. 'Good.'

'Sir.'

'You will confine them all to quarters for the night.'

'Sir.'

Outside, the wailing faded into the early dark, lost in the wind. The Commandant placed the blade across the soldier's outstretched hands and looked up into his eyes. He named his request precisely, shrouding with his authority the obscene thing that he wanted.

'The head and the hands.'

The Placing of the Mice

It was Monday, the day before the markets. The Storekeeper had unlocked just after dawn and was preparing a ledger when there was a shadow at the door and he saw that it was his wife. His heart leapt; he tried to conceal his delight in case it somehow dissuaded her.

'You will be busy,' she said quietly. 'I thought I might help.'

'Yes,' he replied, too eagerly. 'Yes, of course.'

Together they brought stock down from the high shelves, and up from the hatchway beneath the floor. They spoke little but worked closely, preparing small amounts of the staples like sugar and tobacco, flour and tea. Three dressed carcasses on ceiling hooks, a tin dish on the scales. He left her to her work and went across to the small paddock where the dairy cow was kept, wanting to ensure that she had been milked and that butter was being churned. He could see the natives gathered outside the huts, wreathed in smoke. They sounded lively, some even garrulous, and the relief from the mourning made him happy. They would be bartering among themselves already, planning small indulgences, gifts for the old people. They saw him and he could hear his name in their conversation. This was a day for optimism.

He stood shoulder to shoulder with his wife throughout the morning, brushing against her occasionally, wondering if she felt the fleeting contact as loudly as he did. He saw her blow her fringe away from her eyes as she handled the muttonfish in the small cask the Coxswain had brought in. Her wrists were pink from the cold seawater the cask contained and her hands were strong and capable. She was vivid, physical, and he knew he still loved her.

The work eased off towards noon, and it was only when he stopped to make tea that he noticed Whelk there, and knew something was wrong.

He spoke his wife's name and she looked up at him. His eyes shifted to the boy, and she followed them: saw the distress on Whelk's face, and the question on her husband's. She nodded. He came around the counter, put a hand on Whelk's shoulder and guided him outside. He sat the boy on the steps, wide of the doorway. There were dried tears on his face, and his lip quivered a little.

'Thought you'd be down the boatshed.'

Whelk did not reply.

'What is it, lad?'

There was nothing but a little gasp and then his mouth formed the word *Pipi*.

The Storekeeper felt the first stirrings of dread. He looked forward and not directly at the boy, in the hope that he would not feel daunted.

'Tell me what it is, Whelk.' Inside he could hear his wife beginning to sweep.

'Don't know where she is,' whispered the boy.

~

The Storekeeper worked patiently to open up the story. The boy wanted to tell him: only his horror at what had happened made him hesitant.

She had fallen asleep in class. It happened often, the Storekeeper knew; he had seen Pipi and other children sent to the Catechist's house for punishment before. Spelling and arithmetic were taught by the older children, and they'd simply wake her up with a rough shake, but Whelk had warned her not to let it happen in front of the Catechist.

As he listened, the Storekeeper recalled the little differences he'd noticed in her: the increase in her frantic twisting of her fingers. Her shoulders pulled heavily over her neck as she had done all that time ago when it was a shield against the sleet. Her refusal to talk.

The Catechist demanded of the children that they remain bolt upright at all times. Failure to sit thus would result in the cane. Allowing the stool to scrape on the floorboards would result in the cane. Silently mouthing the words of the prayers or the names of the apostles or the English monarchs, rather than speaking them clearly, would result in the cane. Such a dizzying array of sins did the Catechist proscribe—and he blithely listed them in conversation among the officers—that the sting of the cane was inevitable.

The Storekeeper had seen him through the windows of the old timber schoolroom as he passed during the mornings:

always at the front table, towering like a carrion-eating bird. He wore a black robe over his long frame when he taught and it swished around him as he flung his arms for emphasis. The middle of his forehead and his shelled prawn of a nose would blotch when his mood ran high.

He had been telling them about the devil coming to Jesus in the desert, Whelk said. Pipi had been watching, eyelids drooping. Whelk had tried kicking her from under his table, but couldn't reach. There was a moment when the Catechist smacked his hymnal down on the front table and the bang was so loud that Pipi jerked forward and snorted. Her eyes flared and locked on the crow in the cloak. Whelk had watched it all. Now he felt responsible for what had happened next.

The boy was speaking in a flat monotone now, droning, as if to himself.

He had seen that both her hands were nested in her lap under the little table, and at first he had no idea what she was doing. So he'd whispered to her, with his arm curled around his lowered face and had not only failed to alert her to the danger of falling asleep—he'd alerted the Catechist: *Something to share, boy?*

Whelk had said that no, sir, he had nothing to share. When the preacher replied *Good*—and Whelk unconsciously imitated the Catechist's half-open mouth as he repeated the word—he had turned away. For a moment Whelk thought disaster had been averted.

Pipi still had her head down. Her hands were still balled in her lap, and in the end it was simple: the Catechist had reached the end of his walk to the front of the room, *making Bible verses*. Then, said Whelk, he turned around fast. The Storekeeper imagined him pivoting on one heel to face the children.

'You,' he'd said…*an he was talkin to Pip.*

He hit her with the cane, *thwack* across her neck and her cheek. Whelk mimed the impact on his own face; he made the sound with his mouth. The Storekeeper imagined the great black bird lowering the cane, the welt already rising.

Whelk's voice was climbing in pitch and tempo now as he retold it. The Catechist reached out a hand, he said, jammed a thumb into the side of her little mouth and pulled her by the cheek, off her stool and onto her feet. Whelk said that Pipi didn't move her arms at all, that they were still clutched together in front of her, *because she had the, had the…baby mice.*

Whelk's face suggested he had revealed a treasured secret, but the Storekeeper didn't notice it. He was imagining the Catechist there, mouth open and the strange, bright teeth visible. His grip would have been powerful far beyond anything needed to restrain a small child.

The preacher had noticed her hands were still together and he forced them open. He knew what was in there, Whelk said, because she did it all the time. Mice.

This is why, he had roared. *This is WHY you do not deserve to hear the word of the LORD.*

The Storekeeper wondered if he could hear more than just distress in the boy's words: was there a hint of something harder, some quiet fury? The Catechist had turned to him: *What do we do with those who disobey?*

And what a terrible betrayal it must have felt when he gave the correct answer. *They are to be punished. Sir.* He had had no choice, but he would blame himself—although the Storekeeper was quite sure Pipi would not have fixed him with that blame.

Whelk had been told to take Pipi to the front step of the Catechist's house, and to ensure she remained there until the class was dismissed.

'He pointed in my eyes,' Whelk said miserably, 'like this,' and he pointed his own index finger within an inch of his nose.

Then the Catechist had thrown Pipi towards the door, slung her from the mouth-grip, and according to Whelk she fell onto the boards. She didn't put her hands out, he said, and when she landed the boards made a bang. He picked her up, and—he looked up at the Storekeeper now and his eyes were large with wonder—her hands were still cupped with the mice nestled inside.

'I took her out the door and down the steps,' he said. 'We stopped on the grass, and the cane...cane made a big stripe down there'—he pointed along the side of his neck—'an I said *why you got them little uns in there?* cos I was that wild with her, but she jus sniffed.'

He fell silent.

'So why *was* she hanging on to the mice, Whelk?' asked the Storekeeper. Her desperation to keep the mice sounded deliberate.

'Lucky he din kill em all,' the boy responded. 'Lucky he din kill *her*.' He seemed puzzled now, frustrated. 'Maybe her head's not right.'

Whelk had walked her across the grassy field in the mid-morning sun, towards the Catechist's house on the far side of the soldiers' barracks.

The Storekeeper thought back: he had been serving the customers and secretly admiring his wife. If he had looked out he would have seen them passing. The smoking, polishing soldiers at the barracks would have seen them passing, too, and would have made the usual disturbing noises to frighten them, being no better than animals.

The Catechist's house rose square and grey beside the quarry that had yielded its foundations. The Storekeeper could see it now, in the distance, as the boy talked. His wife was pinning washing to a wire between two poles; the Catechist's drawers, source of the convicts' forbidden rhyme, *The Catechist, he shat and missed*. The wife had no name, only Ma'am. Pink, as if he'd boiled her, always busy. Busy pretending her husband was a fine upstanding fellow.

'Thought Pipi'd wait at the door,' Whelk continued. 'But she just went right past the house, and I said, *where you going?* All we had to do was walk to the house!' He nodded towards the orchard beside the Catechist's house. 'But she wanted to look at them kittens.'

Whelk looked around desperately, and the Storekeeper could see that his story was coming to its point. 'So there was no one around and Ma'am couldn't see us there. But I thought someone might come, and she was already in trouble, so I tried to, to grab her an I said *please don't*.'

He was distressed again: the frustration gone and terror in its place. 'An she said *it's gonna get bad*, that was what she said. An she pointed at the, the cane mark, an it'd gone all purple an she said *this, it's nothin* an I think she was right now, I think she was right.'

But she had pressed on into the orchard, and as they came through the branches, Whelk said, they could see it was all over. The kittens hung in the monkey's fists. One was dead. 'Other one was makin a noise but he din move, an the monkey was lookin at us, an Pipi said *the milk's poison for kittens*.'

They had fled the orchard and returned to the Catechist's house, and still Pipi didn't wait on the step as she'd been ordered to do. She had gone down the stairs. 'Down there in the garden,' Whelk said.

The Storekeeper felt he had missed something. 'What was

she doing in the garden? You mean round by the chimney, beside the front stairs?'

'Yessir, that one. Well, she gone in there an she pulled out a stone from the, the bottom bit of the house…'

'The foundations?'

Whelk shrugged and continued. 'An there's a…' He concentrated. 'A little door there. Down the bottom.' He looked at the Storekeeper to see if he was making sense.

'Yes, I know where you mean. It's a firewood hatch—it goes into the front room, next to the fireplace so you can put wood inside.'

'Well, she got the stone outta the foun, foun…she pulled it out, right next to the hatch there an she put the mice in the hole.' He looked up at the Storekeeper, surprised at his own story. 'There was some o that stuff. White, um, dust on the ground there like she done it before, but I never seen her. Then she jus put the stone back in.'

The Storekeeper had no idea what to make of this tale. He resolved to go and look at the spot that Whelk was describing.

'She put the mice in the *wall*?'

'Mm-hmm. Yeah, an then she come and sat with me on the steps, an we were talkin about, about…'

'Whelk? About what?'

'Sposed to be secret.'

'Will it help you telling me the story if I know the secret part?'

Whelk remained silent.

'Whelk, where's Pipi?'

The boy seemed to shudder faintly, and his eyes searched wildly across the scrub. 'She wanted me to promise.'

'Promise to do what?'

'Escape. I know we couldn't,' he added quickly. 'But I jus used to say yes cos it made her happy.' Tears came to his eyes now. 'I promised her we'd go when it was time, but I was just *sayin* it.'

'Where were you going to go?'

The boy sighed like he was much older than he was. 'Cos I work for the Cox'n. She thinks I can sail a boat. So we gonna get a boat an…sail it to Sydney.' His eyes, upturned to meet the Storekeeper's, were vulnerable. 'I never been off the beach. Cox'n never lets me.'

The Storekeeper understood. 'Yes, Sydney. All right. But she's tiny, Whelk. She couldn't have gone alone.'

'Nope.' The boy scratched at his head. Lice again. 'I tole her *Pipi, lookit the sun. Middle o the day. They'd find us quick smart. Got no food, no water. No boat yet. No good doin it now.*'

'Ah. Good lad.'

A ripple of agitation passed through the boy's body. The Sydney thing wasn't the nub of it, clearly. 'She said he was gonna hurt her.'

'Who, the chaplain?'

'Mm.'

'I'm sure…' A surge of panic. What he was sure of was that this was highly likely. 'I'm sure he wouldn't do that. He teaches the Bible, after all.'

The boy's agitation turned suddenly to anger. His face darkened to a furious scowl. 'Yes, he *would*. Summin's wrong in im.'

The Storekeeper thought about those words for a moment, and considered that perhaps the boy had intended to say that something was wrong *with* the Catechist. But he knew the phrase was spun intentionally: something was wrong deep inside the man, something foundationally wicked, and Whelk's instinct was true. 'It's a…sometimes a hiding is the right course, Whelk. As sad as that is. Had she done something that…'

'*No!*' he responded fiercely. 'It weren't just a whackin. He come along an picked er up and drug her in the house an he banged the door an I went and I listened at the hat—the hatch, where the mice went an she was *screamin* in there.' His body rocked now and he plunged his head into his hands.

'He picked er up an I saw her eyes an she went *whaah, whoosh…*'

He swept his arms out to his sides and the Storekeeper saw the poor girl vividly: enveloped in the dark arms and taken aloft as her little mouth registered the shock.

~

He walked the boy back to the old people so they would care for him. His words were coming apart and remaking themselves in unsettling new sequences. That wall, the foundation wall. It made no sense: perhaps Whelk himself had misunderstood what was going on.

He crossed the grounds to the Catechist's house. Seeing no activity around the place, he stepped down and retraced the path he imagined Pipi had taken into the garden. Here and there her feet had left impressions in the crushed green, the cool bright leaves so foreign to this barren island. The greenery ended against the foundations of the Catechist's house. When he stopped there and looked around, he realised he could not be seen from out in the field and, deep in the lee of the house, he was also hidden from above.

He stood and waited, not knowing why. He would be unable to explain this if he was found. The stones were cool under his hands, rounded because the builders had scavenged them from the beach. There was the stone that Pipi had removed, easily identifiable by the scraped-out mortar. The insects came and went around his head, and further out the currawongs swooped past.

He nudged the loose stone and it shifted a little. His curiosity grew. He thought he could wriggle the stone out again without being overheard. And—*yes*—it came free easily, heavy in his hands as he placed it on the ground at his feet. Cool air flowed from under the house, smelling of damp soil and rot. He pressed his face to the opening, no wider than his eyes. There was darkness while his vision adjusted, then the beginnings of light. He could hear movements on the floorboards: heavy adult feet. The light was coming from in front of him, and he had to squint to understand it. There was no sign of the mice, beyond a scattering of dark pellets on the floorboards just below his eyes. He could see now that he was looking into the foot of the inside wall, and that the timber box of the firewood hatch formed a barrier immediately to the left of his eyes. A large gap in the skirting board, opening into the Catechist's office, was admitting the light.

He was looking at the feet of the furniture, the curled corner of a rug. Dust, shreds of dried grass. His vision adjusted to the light: the darkness around the edges deepened. Then he could hear a human sound.

The Catechist, speaking softly. The wooden squeak of furniture.

The Storekeeper was transfixed, and then rapidly ashamed of himself. He should not be here. And as these thoughts came and went, in the darkness to the right of his eyes, something large shifted inside the wall itself, and he recoiled in haste and fright.

He scrambled away from the spyhole, replaced the stone and hurried from the garden.

The Hours That Had Already Passed

In the hours that followed, Pipi did not reappear.

Whelk wandered alone, came and went from the boatshed without any apparent interest in the children around him. The Storekeeper kept a watch over him. He knew the boy was avoiding the officers, and above all the Catechist.

He was worried himself, now, too. In the afternoon he asked his wife what she thought, but she said only that it was remarkable more of them didn't take off. He spoke to the Coxswain, who told him the boy was coming along well, that he could rig lines now, and he knew his sails, but that his spirit seemed wanting; he seemed to have despaired of things. There were no boats missing. Pipi? No, he hadn't seen her for days.

He went to the Fat Badger Rock several times. He tried the long beach where the piece of ship had washed up. He studied the black dog, and when it wandered he tried following it. But the black dog was engaged in business of its own, and it only led him in circles around the settlement. He checked on the monkey, wondering if Pipi might be there at the foot of the pedestal, studying her. But the animal sat disconsolate on her platform, head bowed over her swollen belly. The kittens were matted into the ground below, dead and speckled with ants.

This was an island. A big one, yes—he had not himself walked the whole circumference—but it was finite. The girl had not fulfilled her fantasy and sailed away. She was on the island, most likely close among them even now.

~

The market went ahead on the Tuesday. There was no agitation about the girl's absence, and that infuriated the Storekeeper even more. Women sat on their rugs in the half-cleared forest behind the Commandant's house, selling their work. Things that none of the officers needed, but they would arrive with their best clothes on, big false smiles on their pink heads, and they would buy everything. Sugar plums, fishing lines, pipes and kangaroo skins. It had been the Commandant's idea. *You will all learn the ways of trade and the value of property.* Most of the women had no idea about the money.

The Storekeeper knew the officers were not just pretending eagerness in order to encourage the women. There was a purpose, fed by greed. Once the Commandant had confiscated every amulet and necklace and brooch and hairpin and replaced them with hymnals, there would be no more trinkets of the lost natives to sell to the collectors. Diminishing supply, increasing rarity. This was a little industry, disguised as a lesson in civilisation. *This 'un sir is a Rare Example and was Made by a Woman known to be among the Last of the Tommeginne.*

Attendance was compulsory. Whelk was there and so were all the other children, and he watched the boy approaching the old people, the urgency in him. It was clear that he was asking them about Pipi, and that it was futile. The place was so tight, the flow of gossip so efficient, that Whelk would know by now if there was anything to tell. They'd all know.

When the Storekeeper had tried to accost the Commandant about the girl he'd blustered and harrumphed and claimed to be busy. He wasn't. The Storekeeper had even gently interrogated the other children from the Catechist's dormitory, though he suspected Whelk must already have tried this. But they were too scared to help, and the Storekeeper couldn't enter the Catechist's house without his consent.

The Catechist was out there in the crowd, doing his rounds of the sellers, his wife shadowing his every move. Despite his age, he loomed over them, a ghastly black banner in a parade. The sun beat down on the robes, stark against every other muted colour. Each time he doffed his hat the light would catch the white hair and the pink scars and the dead eye, and a chill would pass through the Storekeeper. His fat wife crushed her vast umbrella of petticoats against him so that she could keep hold of his arm, and the pink health of her cheeks made her look like a giant swaddled baby.

One of the senior men wandered over. The Storekeeper registered by the missing arm that it was Tongerlongeter, the chief. He had authority among the natives but did not keep counsel with white people, and though the Storekeeper knew who he was, they had never spoken.

He glanced at the Storekeeper as he approached, then sat down and crossed his legs. The shade caressed him; stark white whiskers searched out from the canyons of his face. The stump of his amputated arm was pinned inside a sleeve. With his remaining hand he pulled at a strand of grass near his knee and picked it apart.

'You lookin for that little girl.'

'Yes, I am.' The Storekeeper found that his whole body thrummed with sudden tension.

'Well...' He breathed out a long sigh. 'She up the hospital.'

'At the hospital? The little girl Pipi?'

'Yep.' The tone of a man who was not to be questioned. 'That one the boy's allus gettin round with.'

'I hadn't heard she was sick.'

The old warrior shrugged. 'Din say she was. But she been in there. I know cos I took some meat an bread in there for her. That lag, helps the Surgeon fella, said doan tell anyone she there, but she there.'

'When was this?' He felt a growing alarm.

'Yesserdee.'

'But why? She's not sick.'

'You said that before. I dunno. Got her all wrapped up under big blanket. I jus put the food down an left. But the ladies said the boy ben lookin for her, an looks like you ben lookin for her. So there you go.' He squinted off, far into the trees. 'No good, eh.'

Time was slowing now. The man sitting there, the sunlight and the shade. Something had happened to her in that house. Her wriggling mice, the floor. Under the floor.

The Catechist was out there in the market, braying and handling people. The big china dish of teeth under that smashed-up nose. He *knew*, that man. He could hide it even while he led his fat wife around and made himself big with everybody.

Tongerlongeter was watching him watching the Catechist.

'Wouldn go tekkin that one on, mister.' His voice was dark. 'Nasty one, that.'

The old chief was right, of course. The Storekeeper was a large man, but not skilled in violence. The Catechist blocked the sun, and even at his advanced age there was a physical threat in his honeyed speech, and in the squared blocks of his great hands. The religious talk was the thinnest of veneers—he invited brutality and would welcome it.

~

He had to wait until the market was finished. He was expected to tally the promissory notes and collect the coins because, as much as he was a dispensary and a victualler, he was also a banker. He collected a few good coins for his project, pocketed them and wrote a note to cover them. The women packed up their rugs in the golden glow of afternoon, the light that always made him think of cane spirits, and when the last few were gone he hurried to the little hospital. The search would be quick: there was only one room with a bed, and the kitchen.

He knocked on the hospital door before he had thought what he would say. But there was no answer. He knocked again, louder. The sound died within.

She might be tired, in need of rest. But surely there was an adult in there who would have heard his knocks. He looked left and right to check if he was being observed—did anything happen here *un*observed?—and slipped around the far side of the hospital to the back door that led into the kitchen. It was locked. The side window was firmly curtained; no smoke in the chimney. He returned to the front door and tried it. The knob turned in his hand but the door held fast. They had locked it too.

There was no escaping it now, the thought that something was drastically wrong.

Or it wasn't, and was instead a mere apparition in his fevered mind.

~

He paced the short verandah of their hut while inside his wife tried to sew in the dim light. The silences tormented him. His wife's silence, the Commandant's; the whole settlement's silence. He was filling the silences with his own thoughts, trapped in an endless argument with himself. The night was still again, and cool. The voices of the natives carried from the outskirts of the cleared ground where the wallabies thumped.

He thought she would need a blanket: she was so slight that the cold would pass straight through her. Did the person who had taken her consider this? He took a blanket from inside the hut, from the chest where it was kept in case of a frost.

He tucked it under his arm and continued pacing, and as he paced a boobook piped a soft note, and the sound of the officers' drunken laughter drifted across the field. And the wallabies thumped, and the she-oaks moaned softly, and the strange music of it all accompanied him through the anxious hours.

In the Garden Shed

The Commandant raised his fist to knock at the door of the garden shed, but a shuffling within told him the Surgeon had already heard his approach. As the door swung open he glanced briefly about. Satisfied he was unobserved, he stepped in, bringing with him a swirl of cold night air. His coat and hat were jewelled with water, and he thumped both as he removed them. There were wet grass seeds clinging to the hems of his trousers.

The Surgeon said nothing in greeting. He returned to slump in the deep chair he had put there specifically for these moments. When the Commandant fished the watch from his pocket and squinted at it, he saw that eleven o'clock had come and gone. He didn't like the lack of space in here, the smell or the chill that came up through the floor. He didn't like the company in here.

'Apologies,' he grunted, shrugging the coat. 'Much to do.'

'Lock it from the inside, please.'

The Commandant turned the key and looked carefully at the younger man. 'Can we turn the lamp up?'

The Surgeon obliged, then pointed at the window, and the Commandant pulled the curtains across so that no slice of the night was visible.

On the bench before them lay the small body of a girl, her skin both dark and pale as the flickers of the fire lent deceptive warmth to her face. It was a child's body and had not begun to change. A sheet had been draped over her hips, and her hands were crossed over her chest. The hands were all knuckles and bones; her ribs poked high under the hands and even the balls of bone in her wrists and elbows stood proud of her flesh.

Something stirred in the Commandant and he suppressed it. 'Poorly nourished,' he murmured.

'So I have noted.'

The Surgeon had set his writing materials on the bench at the girl's feet, and his surgical implements at the other end, behind her head. The implements were the only indication that anything medical was happening in the crowded space: it was otherwise filled with shovels, hoes, picks, the poles of other long-handled tools. The pegs either side of the Commandant's hat were all occupied with scythes and saws.

The Commandant looked at the bench and the girl with careful detachment. Regret; of course one felt regret. But it was a small thing in the greater march of history.

'Do you require anything?' The Surgeon looked to him, a blade in his hand.

It took the Commandant a moment to understand. 'Er…no. Just, just a cause.' Considering his choice of words, he added, 'I mean, just confirm it was the catarrh.' He cursed inwardly at the shake in his voice. 'They infect one another, and…*ad seriatim.*' He stepped aside and placed his own writing materials on the bench.

'Obvious marks about the face...' began the Surgeon.

The Commandant was writing by now and did not look up. 'Childish misadventure.'

The Surgeon shrugged. These were not his battles. The Commandant wrote steadily as the Surgeon worked, looking up only occasionally when the other man uttered a medical word that appealed to his sense of order. *Mediastinum. Pleura.* After a long period of silent concentration, he took a bucket of water from near his feet, sloshed some under the body and wiped it away with a cloth.

Placing a hand behind the head, and another on the calves among the mosquito welts, he rolled the body over. As it settled on its front, the two men gasped.

It was the Commandant who recovered first, and found the calmness of voice that the moment required.

'You are to write nothing of this.'

Resistance Falters

What was a locked door? Nothing beyond his physical power. Why had he not broken the lock and entered the hospital and seen for himself what was there, or was not there?

It was the usual problem. That you knew and could not bear to know. That, whatever you knew, the power to affect it was unimaginable.

This was when the danger of being in charge of provisions became clearest. All the poisons and the antidotes, there in the shelves with their whispered offers of sanctuary.

It was a storehouse, and he had tried to run it well. He had tried to dole out the supplies as equitably as he could and to stay clear of whatever went on between the Commandant and the Surgeon and the Catechist.

The flagon and the cup, there on the table in front of him.

Having control of the store made him the postmaster: a token title, perhaps—the bags of mail could as easily be placed on the beach when the supply ship came in and people could be left to ransack them until they found something with their name on it. But the office represented some greater order.

The natives who were learning to write letters to each other, and making their complaints in letters to the Commandant. The steady stream of invective that passed between the Surgeon and the Catechist which required the Commandant's intercession.

He traced a finger over the paper label on the flagon.

And the letters that came in from the museums and the colleges in London; the rhythm that evolved between those letters, with their fancy seals, and the boxes—long boxes, square boxes—that would go back to those addresses after a week or perhaps a month. After someone had died.

There was plenty to do as postmaster, aside from running the store. The shame of it was that he could not interest his wife. She had always been a worker: he could not fault her effort. So often he admired her secretly as they laboured: her gift for words and numbers, making displays or calculating measures.

But something had gripped her here, and he thought he would never understand it. The silences, the wind seemed to have smothered something behind her eyes. The spiral curls of hair behind her ears still promised loveliness, but not to him. He saw the place work its leaden influence on others, too—there could be no doubt the natives were uncommonly listless. Were the officers such miserable schemers when they were back home in Sydney, or Hobart Town, or Fife?

She no longer curled into him in the night, no longer favoured him with tiny smiles or laughter or the silken curves of her skin. He had probed for a cause—some careless utterance of his?—but no, there was nothing wrong, and that only made it worse. She cooked for him, she washed and cleaned, but she would not raise her eyes to him, nor her voice. He mourned it daily; gazed at her face and her lean, graceful body and wondered if whatever season she was passing through would end.

To be fair, something gripped him here too. Right there, gleaming softly on the table in front of him. Every day he pushed it grimly back into the sunset by working at his wall. His back ached with the effort of staving it off, lifting rocks, putting them down. Every day the warm liquid sang to him from among the rocks. *Enough. Come and rest.*

He tipped the cup on its side and let it roll in a circle, his hand on the neck of the flagon.

He'd locked the door at three, worked on his wall. The insects stung, the sun was angry; his neck and the backs of his hands were lobster-red. When he'd finished and locked himself in again, she had not come to ask why.

He took the cork from the flagon at a quarter after the hour, poured a measure and stared at it. Then he swallowed it in one languorous draught. The burn. The glow.

He refilled the cup.

Counting, always counting. Six dozen pairs of boots for the military, three dozen pair for the natives, although their feet outnumbered the military by a factor of six. It was not his role to do the thinking about that, but perhaps the idea was that they would not wear them out so fast. Only five of the Scotch caps—*reorder!*—a box of slates and a smaller one of stylii. A burst of clumsiness in the classroom and they would be out of those, too. A great many trousers, no problem there, and enough yarn and fabric for the native women to make more shirts and jackets.

It took foresight to predict the shortages and write the requests, to know months out that candles would deplete, then to ration them and wait for the supply ship which could arrive at any time and might have too many or too few. He had no idea whether he was a person who craved order—he supposed he did—but he felt obliged to paint a scene of reassurance with his store. As if a row of jars might be a bulwark against random death.

The boy was a counter, too. He'd watched him, alone since the girl disappeared, and he knew the tendencies: the irregular gait that fitted the right number of steps into a certain distance. Three steps across the schoolroom verandah; one step on each of the pavers in the vegetable garden. The boy had always had his tics: he could remember noticing them all the way back on the frozen scree of the Western Tiers, but they were more pronounced since the girl had gone. He hoped the footfalls or the muttered numbers or the touching of surfaces comforted him. If the Coxswain could teach him to navigate he'd be a natural fit: he could memorise all the numbers he needed. He was a good boy.

The second rum. He sipped it as if he might find character in it—as likely as discovering fine tailoring in the bloomers and the neckerchiefs. There was none and there was none: all was rough approximation. He ground the base of the cup on its edge. His back hurt. There were cuts on his fingers. He picked at a deep scratch beside a fingernail until it bled anew and he had to dab the blood away. Poured again, drank again.

He could endure the winter that had descended over his marriage. Love was provisioned, love could outlast. He could use it to wait for the thaw. Love was a measurable thing like pounds of flour and packets of buckshot. It would take some thinking, and there was time for thinking. They had time in abundance. One day they would understand each other.

He would write her a letter: that was it. If he caught it all, if he set it down, there would be none of the awkward fumbling when they tried, and failed, to talk. The Colonial Office could spare him a sheet of writing paper from the reams that no one wanted.

Another pour, another fiery swallow. He stared at the page. *Just start in the middle,* he thought. And so he did.

> *Can I move you? Can I lift your eyes from where they are downcast? Can I help you to find the capacity to love again, or is it that you have found the love lies elsewhere? It should not be this way, it should be a spreading warmth. Not a thing that flows only one way*
>
> *I am lonely, I am lonely, and even more so because I know that you are not.*
>
> *If we try*
>
> *but how can 'trying' ever be the answer? Love exists, or it does not.*
>
> *Yet if you tell me, I will abide Tell me, if only for mercy and no other reason, tell me what I must do*

He could not think how to bring it to a close or sign it off, so he simply stood and walked to the door. A mid-afternoon torpor often settled over the place, and this afternoon it was deep in slumber as heavy clouds rode by. One cloud had settled over them and was drizzling lightly. In such moments it was just a saddle of land again, a lost peninsula on a lost island, and it could be imagined all over again without the petty grievances and the suffering. The rain didn't know where it fell.

Across the grass where the bullock ruts disappeared into the scrub, he could see a dark shadow that he mistook at first for a stump. It shifted ever so slightly and he saw it was the black dog. He sensed the dog had noticed him—a tiny inclination of its head. Leaning on the frame of the door, he imagined it knew his sorrow. Foolish.

He turned to step back inside, but as he held the edge of the door to swing it, the dog stood up and walked nearer, only a few places, then resumed its seated position. The rain was increasing, blurring the animal's finer details into black silhouette with the gleam of water on its haunches.

He closed the door and turned up the lamp so it lit the fluid in his glass. He knew the real problem. It wasn't her; it wasn't them and the failure of their love. It was *him*. All their blind eyes, all their pretending there was nothing going on. In the midst of their wretched piety, the Catechist was a dark malignancy that all could see but none would discuss. And the horror was made worse by his wife, the bloody great blanched crab, smiling and fanning herself and affecting city manners while these things went on. She *knew*.

More of this stuff. Fiery as hell and the better for it.

How the boy had looked at him: as if he might be trusted. Now he seemed to be coming apart, unthreading before his eyes. And the girl Pipi, with the deep silent eyes of a prey animal, always poised for flight. Whelk was warm with people, persuasive; had done the talking for both. The severing of them had hit him hard. A distress that tore at the Storekeeper's heart.

He felt surer now that he knew what had happened. The girl had been moved into the Catechist's care, a move that was at best unnecessary, given that she was well looked after by the old people, at worst a catastrophe. Something dreadful had happened in the Catechist's house. And he didn't ever want to see a child look at him again the way that Whelk had then: a look that held him culpable.

He poured again. Wretched *bastard* man.

Why was he the only Englishman on the settlement who was worried? Where were the Overseer, the Coxswain? Where was the bloody Surgeon? And where on earth was the Commandant? He was there, that was the answer. Right there all along, refusing to see. If it wasn't this child, it was another one. Wouldn't do his aspirations no good to be involved. Mustn't make its way into his precious journals.

He got up and began to pace, uneven lurching steps. The poor girl, the poor girl.

A hand on the wall while he steadied himself. The room keeled left. He went outside again into smothering darkness, stepped down from the doorway and fumbled in his trousers, aimed his piss at the wall. Damn them all.

He stumbled forward, then stopped: something he'd remembered. His head spun free like a compass needle after his body stopped moving and there it was: the black dog, watching him. It had come forward out of the scrub now, halfway between the tree line and the storeroom. He let the drizzle settle on his hair and his shoulders, and watched the dog's eyes. There was no glimpse of the whites to lend depth, yet he felt the eyes were kindly. They saw his shortcomings and forgave them. He thought so.

'Sorry bout the…bout pissin.'

The corners of the dog's ears contracted slightly: it was listening. He excused himself formally and stumbled over the grass by the edge of the woodland where they held the markets. The water soaked up through his boots which, despite his access to the stores, he had not replaced since he had been there.

The Commandant's house. There. And beside it, with only a garden between, the Catechist's. Warm dry place for a cockroach. He forged ahead in the downpour, a champion storming the infernal keep, where an observer would have seen a man veering all over the place. At the front of the house he took hold of the banister and hauled himself up the stairs.

Cockroach.

His eyes landed on the chimney rising from the side of the house, the stonework of the foundations, the loose stone. Something he needed to resolve. Something. He frowned, mounted the last step and stood for a moment, unsure of himself. Then he pounded on the door, over and over, so that a gap opened with each blow where the hinges were screwed into the frame. He roared the Catechist's name over the drumming of the rain on the roof, forcing his face in close to the jamb of the door. He rattled the doorhandle and hammered again at the door with the side of his fist.

There was no reply.

He waited. It might be a long walk to the front door, he thought as the part of him that made allowances momentarily overpowered the booze. Then he began again, hammering and shouting. The violence of it warmed him against the cold night. His swung his sodden boot at the foot of the door and the impact hurt his toes, but he kicked it again and again.

Now the curtains of the front room were moving, just slightly, spilling warm light from within. It might only have been the effect of his kicking, shaking the wall and thus the curtain, but he felt sure that someone had heard him.

He slapped the door with his open palm, wondering if that would make more noise. It stung, clear and bright through the fog of the rum.

'Come out, filthy cowardfilthycoward.'

He kicked again, this time with the whole of his weight, as though the foot would meet no resistance at all but would swing through, high in front of him. It did not, of course: it crashed hard into the timbers and he felt it crumple with a crack inside his boot and a bright flash in his vision. The pain felled him and for a moment he lay on the doorstep, whimpering.

From that strange sideways perspective he looked across the short distance to the Commandant's house. The side door was open and the Commandant stood there in a housecoat, hatless, staring at him. A small portico above the door protected him from the downpour and the lamplight behind him framed his thick black hair.

'Sir,' the Storekeeper called feebly from where he lay. The figure did not move. 'Sir. Muss confront him. We both know…'

He grimaced, but could not raise his voice without adding to the pressure inside his boot. He released his breath in a long sorrowful sigh. A tear joined the rain trickling through the complex delta of his whiskers.

The Commandant turned and went back inside his house, closing the door behind him.

Funeral Notice

There were moments that filled the Commandant with pride, and reminded him of the importance of his mission. These took precedence in the journal because he would need them to forge a satisfying narrative for the publishers. Bock's portraits, his words. Posterity.

But there were other moments. Moments of tedium, of demeaning triviality, and of sadness. This, undoubtedly, was one of the latter kind.

The morning had started out bitingly cold, and he had waited and written while the clock inched towards nine, when the classes would begin. Normally the children would be teaching each other, but today the Catechist would be doing scripture with them. So he would have to address that corrupted face, would have to swallow his repugnance. It was clear what had happened to the girl. Equally clear that, in the eyes of Hobart and London, it must not have happened at all.

Such…problems did not arise under the eye of an effective administrator.

He licked the pen, transcribed the rainfall figures from the ledger into the journal. *Damn him.* When he was done with the day's business, the clock had passed its zenith. He gathered his hat and pursed his mouth into the indomitable line he believed was his signature.

Outside, the ridiculous geese waddled at him on the short grass. He hated them for some reason. Not long ago he had alarmed the whole settlement by running out of his office and charging straight at them with the dried pelican held high above his head, wings outstretched as though it wanted to snatch him aloft. He had ordered the tanners to dry it and then strung it—*why?*—so that its wings spread across his office wall like some terrible Valkyrie. The great mass of feathers, the bones and the dried bands of muscle were gruesome enough: but the head, hanging limp with the great beak swinging, was the hellish part of the vision. A bird that was entirely inoffensive in life, rendered terrifying by amateur taxidermy. When the geese saw him they lifted their heads from their stolid grazing and ran—hauled themselves into the air in comical alarm. He'd lowered the carcass and laughed breathlessly. He remembered stooping there, hands on knees, and looking around, hoping others would laugh along. But all he'd seen were averted eyes.

These are moments in which authority erodes. This time he merely swung a kick at the geese and watched them scatter.

The children were in class in the new chapel; a treat for them to celebrate its opening. He stood in the sunshine one last moment, then went in. It was quieter inside, the air heavier. The grassy hills were framed in the squares of the windows, but the outside sounds were muted. The floor was made of dry, even planks: the rafters of the roof were exposed and above them the light made patterns among the timber shingles. He took it all in quickly and reached up to his hat, but decided to leave it in place.

The Catechist roosted in the far corner of the room, talking. Half a sentence, and the Commandant knew he was making no sense. *My thoughts are not your thoughts, and my ways are not your ways.* Terrible man, he was unchanged by whatever he had done: biting his words with the awful dentures, good eye roving to compensate for its blinded companion. And the children, good God. A kind of stunned haze lay over the lot of them.

All of these things he took in, wanting to toss the grenade and leave. The Catechist's eye shifted his way but he carked on regardless. There in the middle of the room was the boy Whelk, head down and hauling his eyes open against sleep. A table next to the boy had been removed and the absence pulsed like a missing tooth.

The obscene confidence in that droning voice. The children fighting the narcotic spell of the sunlight. The missing table. The burden of the words. The Commandant felt the world beginning to collapse just a little. It was cracking and groaning and a bloody roar was coming. He pushed further into the room, unable to look away from the man who had caused all this, still droning on and on as though this was any other day.

'Stop.'

He had surprised himself, as much as the room. The Catechist did stop.

'My dear children.' He cleared his throat. 'I bring sad tidings. The orphan child known as Pipi died last night in the hospital.'

He exhaled now. It was out: the remainder was details. 'As you will be aware, she was suffering from the catarrh. She was in a state of good grace with the Lord, and may rightly rest in expectation of heavenly reward.'

The Commandant's gaze swung from the Catechist to Whelk, the boy who had found her those years ago. The ashes, the woman and the pups, the flowing hair on the powdered ground.

His words had struck the boy like fists or rocks raining down.

'She was not sick.'

'I beg your pardon, boy.' This level of impertinence would ordinarily merit punishment.

The Catechist watched them both from some secret place behind his smashed features.

'She was not sick. *Sir.*' His face was not a child's face. It was a wall. The room spun and the sun darkened and the wind knocked at the shingles above them and every grain of sand in the cosmos had poured itself down their throats. He should censure the boy. He should rein in this confrontation. He should leave.

'*She was not sick.*'

'Quiet, boy.'

'*She was not sick!*'

'Be silent!'

Whelk bit his lip but did not move. The Catechist came forward suddenly and raised an arm and looked down it and over the heavy silver ring on his fist at the boy's face, at where the blow would land, but the Commandant moved between them, into the line of it. The boy was not himself; clemency was the proper course. A tiny smile curled the corner of the Catechist's mouth as he lowered the arm.

'The funeral will be at three o'clock this afternoon,' the

Commandant finished. 'Coats on, shoes on, clean hands.' His eyes scanned the stunned rows of the children, avoiding the boy. 'That is all.'

Without another word, and without any acknowledgement of the Catechist, he placed the hat on his head and swept out of the room.

PART FOUR

~

Pea Jacket Point
December 1835

Each Tending to Small Tasks

The easterlies arrived, and the December days were warmer. The bulbs in the gardens collapsed into pale brown shreds and the roses burst into strange parodies of the dun-coloured world.

The east wind came over the spine of the island—from a different sea, the Coxswain was apt to say—and on ordinary days it was dry. But when it was wet it could drown the place. The vegetable gardens and the nursery beds had been planted out in expectation of such soaking rains, which this year had not materialised. The settlement was deep into a dry run, and grasshoppers sprang in the golden fields.

The Storekeeper rummaged through the pile of rocks at his feet. Limestone fragments, bigger and smaller, abrading to white dust on the dry grass. His hands had adapted to the rigours now. The most significant marks on them were the dark red crescents, the colour of old blood, that had appeared in his thumbnails the week that Pipi died.

He had thought at first that they indicated some disease in him, and his wife had made him go to the Surgeon. The Surgeon only shrugged and said that he had never heard of such a symptom. Late at night, awake and probing at the sadness there in the dark, he had formed his own diagnosis: the grief was leaching out of him like a ring in the timber of a wounded tree. Every time he saw the strange marks, he thought of Pipi and his heart cried out.

His hands hunted among the rocks like brown animals. He saw a flat triangle and hefted it at his waist. There. Along the rickety teeth of the half-made wall there was a perfect place for the rock. He kept his eyes on the place to ensure he wouldn't lose it as he carried the rock over. Still limping: eight weeks since he'd kicked the bastard's door, and the foot had healed all wrong. He placed the stone and it balanced; he pressed a little at both ends to ensure it wouldn't wobble, and it sat true. The grating sound of the rock against the other ones was a tiny pleasure.

The wall had begun as a way to remove rock from the arable ground, to give the settlement's beasts a little more to eat. A thirty-foot line of flat stone, then a right angle to a long fifty-six and the storehouse would be enclosed. He had been at it since the autumn and he felt at times that it might outlast his mortal days. But someone would finish it. And then there could be a garden out of reach of the Commandant's rabbits and the Commandant's goat. A stone wall would not disbar the Lord's wrens, nor the devil's serpents, nor whoever had dominion over the skinks. They would have to sort it out among themselves.

He made his way back to the rock pile and surveyed the abstract shapes in search of something satisfying. Out of the corner of his eye he saw Whelk, watching the men at their cricket. Every time he saw the boy he felt the claws of desperation. It was impossible, frightening and impossible, to imagine how the boy himself felt. He had never been the same. So awfully lost; he came and went like vapour, concentrating fiercely on whatever was in his hands, or whatever was under his feet. He had stopped going to the boatshed to learn from the Coxswain. When he was spoken to—and the Storekeeper always tried to engage him—he seemed shocked, as if he had been shaken out of sleep.

The Storekeeper had a heel of bread in the bins where the scraps were kept for the deer; new bread, too good to give to an animal. He dusted his hands and went to find it.

When he came back the boy had not moved, though a heavy black wasp droned around his hair.

'Young man.' The boy jumped, registering the wasp and the Storekeeper's presence simultaneously. 'I thought you might like this.' The boy swatted at the insect and took the bread.

'Thankyousir.' It was a performance: the boy had been trained to meet friendship with chanted words. He expected him to tear hungrily into it, but to his surprise he tipped one hand with care into the other and then cupped that hand against his chest. He wiped the free hand on his shirt and broke an end off the bread with his thumb. Then, with great precision, he crumbed the bread into his cupped hand.

'What have you got in there?' he asked gently. The boy's eyes shifted. 'It's all right, I don't mind,' he went on. 'Just wondering.'

The boy relaxed slightly. 'Mice, sir.'

It sparked a distant memory. 'What will you do with those? Sell them to the others?'

'No, sir. Feed em.'

He considered this. 'And then? Do you breed them?'

'No, I give em t—' The boy caught himself hurriedly. 'Jus let em go an start again, sir.'

'They like the bread.' They both looked down for a moment at the writhing velvet shapes in his hands, the fat of their haunches, guided over and under each other by their noses and followed by their tails.

'Sometimes I get frogs, or little lizards,' the boy volunteered.

'Ah, the skinks, you mean?' Receiving no reply, he got up from where he had crouched next to the boy. 'Sometimes they sit on the stones and watch me. If I see any I shall let you know.'

The boy nodded gravely at this, and lowered his head again over the cupped hands. The Storekeeper returned to his rock pile and tried to remember where he was up to. He toed at a couple of round stones, assessing them. There was a shout from Walter and the Commandant's lad over at the cricket: the lad claiming a wicket. From the rock pile, the Storekeeper could see not only their game against the hospital wall, but the window in the same small building at which sat the Surgeon. The blind was up: it was often pulled down during sensitive work. Every time one of the players hit the ball, every time they called out or laughed, the Surgeon would look up from his work and grimace. He lowered his pen now, rubbing his eyes in annoyance, spectacles riding his fingers as he did so.

The Storekeeper took another stone, this one rounder, and weighed it in a hand. A monkey-skull, a rough sphere, smaller than a human head. Sometimes they had divots in them, unnervingly like eye sockets. The flat stones were peacemakers, because they could be placed to resolve the wobbling of ill-matched ones below them. The small stones he used for fill were knuckles and peas, and the triangular ones were cake slices, and there were chips and flakes and mothers and orphans. He had named them all: a secret nonsense language he shared with the earth.

Across the field and behind the stone wall, the Commandant's monkey was chained to the platform on the pole, screeching at the sky. Every time he saw it, he was reminded of the dead baby it had delivered in the spring: the unmoving mass inside the pearl-coloured caul. When the monkey unwrapped her sad gift, she'd licked at the fur, streaked with clots of dark blood, and made small sounds of grieving. The Catechist had come by the pathetic scene and stepped towards the mourning animal with a thin laugh. For a moment he thought the preacher was going to strike the monkey, but he reared back when she saw him and bared her teeth.

The Storekeeper had privately hoped the ordeal of the stillbirth would be the end for the wretched creature. Nobody felt affection for it anymore, not since it attacked the Overseer. It hissed and slashed at anyone who came near. It was not a pet, not a beast of productive use, just a malign presence on a stick.

The skull-rock made a grating sound as he lay it. The dust chalked his hands. The triangles formed the outer surfaces of the wall, cambered in slightly as they rose, and the skulls and stones and knuckle-pebbles filled the inside. And the wall would slowly advance. The natives watched him sometimes, perplexed at a man so concerned by the relationships between stones. They smiled at his clumsy efforts to retouch the pieces, taking a harder stone to shape a softer one. You would smile, he reflected, if you could flake razor shards from a mother stone with ease.

The wall, indeed all of the settlement's fences, were lines that followed no contour in nature: in fact, they fought the contours, dividing one man's ground from another's, and some creatures from others. The old people, who'd lived in the other world, must have been baffled. Offended, even, since drawing lines on the land was where it all started. Perhaps the younger ones understood a world where fences set the arithmetic of giving and taking. It was there in the catechism: this is mine, that is yours. *Thou Shalt Not Steal*. Until a thing was owned, it could not be stolen.

Each stone he picked up, he wondered what would be underneath. The convicts had dumped this pile here weeks ago, and the drinking had been winning: he hadn't laid them promptly enough. They had rested so long that creatures were beginning to take residence under them: stinging ants, a scorpion, millipedes and skinks. His rummaging fingers weren't hunters at all: they were soft things, pink and vulnerable.

~

Out to the east of the Storekeeper and his wall, the bullocks returned with their burden: a great lead tank on a cart, sloshing with water. Their route from the lagoons near the beach to the cistern behind the Commandant's house had become a deep wound in the earth. Day after day, load after load, the weary beasts trod the same soft ground and their hooves pounded it into sludge in the wet, and compressed the sludge to a trench in the dry. The great tonnage of water would lurch with their efforts, then settle, forcing the animals to break inertia once again to move onward. The beasts were slick with sweat, muscled and slack, muscled and slack as they struggled through the swampy ground near the lagoons and the mud made its gluing and ungluing sounds. The flies assailed them relentlessly, but the bullocks were beyond irritation.

The convict bullock driver trudged beside them, made falsely tall by his position on the outside of the trench. This task was his alone, because he was consigned to hard labour. He walked with a stoop, hot and exhausted but ordered never to remove his blue coat. His lesser bulk had cut its own track beside theirs. When he and the animals ended their ordeal at the cistern and the water was decanted into it, the hundred and fifty humans on the settlement began emptying it with their buckets, and the animals turned around to repeat the journey under the half-hearted whipping of their driver, a man who was master of nothing and no one but them.

They plodded down the path, momentarily unburdened, only to repeat the torment over and over.

The Matter of the Deer

That same afternoon, the Commandant gazed down at the carcass of the chital deer, still roped by the neck.

An unfortunate thing, an avoidable thing. The children were instructed to take it from its yard and tether it to a stake while a pen was built to house it. They loved the deer: a yearling they had named Bess. For reasons he would never fathom, they had staked Bess in the bottom of the empty waterhole, and in the torrential rains of the early afternoon the basin had half-filled: enough that the poor animal had panicked and drowned. The children discovered it as they ran through the newly washed world after the rainstorm to see their pet, only to be confronted by their terrible misjudgment.

Now the collected water had drained away, leaving a muddy bowl and somewhere, the cronking frogs. The deer was a pale slick on the peat. He picked his way down until he was knee-deep and had the corpse by its tail. He heaved until it came free and slid over the mud towards him, then he buried his forearms under its flank and lifted it. The animal's shoulder, pressed against his face, smelled of both the clean fur the children adored, and the eggy gas of the mud. The damp pelt touched his forehead and anointed him with a dark smear. He sighed at the waste of God's nature; the spangled auburn coat, the velvet snout. There were deep lacerations around the animal's neck where it had fought the rope and the rising water. These were a particular shame. A chital was a sought-after pelt. He would have the hide cut short of the wounds, which would make a clean edge but spoil the traditional tannery shape he had hoped for. As for the meat, he could see it would upset the children; he would have it served to the officers.

He sent the prisoners down to attend to the carcass and walked back, skirting the Catechist's house. The journal awaited: there was history to record, and no time for fake piety. The man unnerved him.

He passed the natives' huts and saw them huddled around a fire. Three young men over by the hospital wall with their infernal cricket. Old women squawking their arguments in the wind. And the dogs, always the dogs, ribs and slobber and mange. All of them but the black one that sat apart and watched. It watched him now, as if it was about to take out a notebook and jot something down.

The hollering continued unabated and now a woman was pointing, beckoning. Her effort was directed not to him, but to a man in the distance. The man came running, and the Commandant felt a prickle of alarm. He knew the patterns of their somnolence. This was urgency. They spoke fast, over each other. Their hands grabbed at the air. The Commandant was concentrating on them, so it took him some time to notice the

Surgeon, who had leaned himself against a tree by the store. He was smoking a pipe, but also attending to the exchange between the two natives. The Commandant approached him and they watched together.

'You heard?' asked the Surgeon out of the corner of his mouth.

'Heard what?'

'Mannalargenna, the chief.'

'What about him?'

'Sickening. Be gone soon.' The Surgeon puffed at the pipe he was straining to keep lit. 'Usual culprits: catarrh, pulmonary distress. At a certain point they just'—he sucked at the pipe again and flicked at it with a fingertip—'they just *give up*, don't they?'

'They do, or you do?' The Commandant could not conceal his irritation. 'I suppose you've bled him?'

'Thrice. There's no end to the blood in the man.'

'I would think there is a definitive end to the blood in all of us, wouldn't you?'

The Surgeon ignored him. 'I mean it. They tuck their legs up under themselves. This, this gesture of absolute capitulation. Medical explanations, of course. Imbalance of humours, so on, so forth. But once that point has been reached, it's all futile. You've seen it yourself.'

The Commandant sighed. For a long time he did not respond. 'I have seen most things now,' he said eventually. 'They are a benighted race, and before we can study all the fascinating traits wrought by their isolation, they will be gone. It is inevitable.' He grimaced. 'But so fast…'

The Surgeon smirked. 'You think this is a collective suicide?'

'No. It is a letting go, an acquiescence. Which of course is terribly sad. At least when they rose up against us…'

'Yes. Well, it certainly legitimised the killing.'

The Commandant looked sharply at him. 'It was at any rate some measure of defiance against all that's been imposed upon them. Futile, of course. But…would you not fight back?'

'Not if my lungs were riddled with pustules.' The Surgeon seemed even more amused. 'It's your first year here. You're still prone to messianic thinking.'

'What?'

'Like a spring-loaded Jesus. Mostly your kind wander in from the desert rather than the trees.'

'I'll thank you not to blaspheme in my presence.'

'Well, where is the blasphemy? Perhaps in confusing oneself with our Lord and Saviour?'

'I refuse to listen to this,' said the Commandant, though he made no effort to leave.

'I think,' the Surgeon continued, 'you must have been very brave in Van Diemen's Land. They say you risked your life. Drove yourself twice as hard as your companions.'

'I did what was necessary.'

'Mm. You won't last, if I may be so bold. I won't last either. I've long since tired of it.'

The Commandant could no longer conceal his affront. 'If that's the way you feel, perhaps you should tender your resignation.'

'Perhaps I should. And then you'd wait—how long? Six months?—for my replacement. And how many of these people would die untreated in that period, do you think?'

'No worse a thing than dying treated.'

'Is that a comment on my work?'

'An observation that, given a choice, I would avoid your interminable blood-letting and go quietly. That's what they're trying to do, by and large.'

'And there, sir, you have come full circle. You don't understand why they won't fight back, and yet you say in their position you'd allow yourself to die. You moved them out of the path of the bullets in Van Diemen's Land, and they're no better off; so the next line of justification must be that they seek their own death.'

The Commandant sighed. 'Your task is only to diagnose and treat the failing body. Mine is to explore deeper causes and find lasting remedies.'

'No no no.' The Surgeon seemed nettled. 'You barely know *what* you want for them. You cannot see past what you want for yourself. It's the same for all of us. What do *I* want? I want surgical experience so I can lecture at Bart's when I return home. The Catechist—he's too old to want much in the way of a career, but for now he wants a steady stream of children through his house'—he arched a ribald eyebrow—'and the convicts want their leave. You probably want to make history. That's why you keep diaries like no administrator I've ever known.'

The Commandant had been staring at him as he spoke, light and shadow dappling him as the breeze swayed the she-oak above. His expression was ice-cold.

It had no effect on the Surgeon. 'All these deaths,' he continued, 'all those pegs in the ground: what are they for? If you are trying to burnish your reputation—and I feel certain you are—then you should know that every passing month tarnishes you. If you do not leave and strike out in a new direction, the world will pass you by. As it has'—he gestured at the couple in their desperate conversation—'as it has for this lot.'

He eyed the Commandant with vehemence now and jabbed a finger towards the earth at their feet. 'This place eats human lives.'

'Encountering precious little opposition from you, doctor,'

the Commandant sniped absently. He had been looking up the rise, away from the couple, and his eye was drawn to a movement in the Catechist's garden. A native boy had emerged from among the foliage, bright against it in a pale shirt that stood out sharply on his skin. It was Whelk: the Commandant knew him by shape and movement. With the sight of him came the ashes, the smoke. The woman and her hair. The girl's post-mortem.

The boy was crossing the open grass now, looking left and right in a way that the Commandant thought suggestive of guilt. He'd been crying and his nose was running—three tracks of moisture on his dark face. He was headed for the natives' houses. The Commandant made a mental note to find out more.

The Surgeon was still talking, placing a conspiratorial hand on the Commandant's shoulder. 'And while we're on fame and fortune, any response to our…*packages?*'

'It is not a matter for your amusement, doctor. It is no small thing…'

'…to dismember a corpse? Couldn't agree more. It's me that has to do it.'

'It is *no small thing*,' the Commandant continued, exasperated, 'to be party to the advancement of science. You may content yourself with being a practitioner of it, a mere functionary, but there are higher roles.'

'And do they pay well, sir?'

'I've never accepted a penny, as you well know. I do it because I believe we ought to extract some knowledge from these tragedies.'

The Surgeon smiled mockingly at this. 'You should visit your old friend. He won't last long.'

'I shall do as I see fit, doctor.'

'Quite. Shall I have the corporal sharpen a blade?'

Grievance

In a room like the other rooms, along the bleak row of the natives' houses, Mannalargenna lay dying. The Storekeeper had made it his duty to bring meals into the room, something he found difficult, yet indefinably soothing.

The smell in the room was unpleasant: this was a dying man, after all. The mood was grim; the Storekeeper's role unclear. He was not made to feel unwelcome, and indeed there was gratitude for the food, but he had no place in the storytelling, in the arguments, the instructions, not even in the laughter. He remembered Van Diemen's Land; the reverence for this man and his unquestioned authority. If he himself was an irrelevance in the room as a great man lay fading, then he understood.

Mannalargenna cared little for displays of suffering. He continued to use the grease on his skin and the ochre in the short tufts of his hair, in defiance of the Commandant's wishes. He persisted in adorning himself in other ways, and in speaking language. Far from rendering him an alien in their midst, it made aliens of his captors. Like a holed and smoking ship of war, he would slide beneath the waves imperious.

The Storekeeper had heard him say it many times, back then in Van Diemen's Land and even here: he had not come willingly. The Commandant had deceived him, back when he was just the Man, a man making deals, and not a *Commandant*. Yes, the chief had delivered up his people, but that had never meant the Man's civilising project was a thing he aspired to, for himself or for them. He did it because otherwise only slaughter remained.

These were the arguments the Storekeeper had absorbed over the four years he had watched the chief. He heard the grievances, and he chafed at his inability to think of a response. And meanwhile, Mannalargenna lay there. Outside the finches and the wrens swooped the grass stalks and made off with their tiny burdens. The sun went round, revisiting his slow decline. Mannalargenna's eyes were wide in the gloom as visions came and went. A swarm of ants dismantled a heel of bread, took nourishment and left a husk. Small spiders wrapped their prey.

And he lay there. Late in the afternoon the wind got up in the southwest, and it thrashed and moaned under the incoming rain, and still he lay there. The black dog was now a fixture at the door of his room. The rest of the dogs outside rehearsed their rituals of lust and aggression, but the black dog was always apart from them. In the mornings when the eastern sun warmed the ground, it would lay itself at the foot of the wall, absorbing heat, eyes pinched closed. The rest of the time it sat upright and alert, watching the comings and goings—the *Pairrebeenne*, the Surgeon, the Commandant, the Storekeeper bringing and taking dishes. The dog would incline its handsome head towards the feet that went past. In the pools of its dark eyes some register was kept.

~

The Commandant was tired. The words were not coming easily.

He had managed no more than the words *Third of December*, and a note about the rainfall. He rested the pen in its holder and took up the amulet he'd got from the dying woman in the autumn. The thing had been secured around her neck with a length of twine so that it hung somewhere among the ribs of her back. It was touching, he reflected, her belief in its power. She did not want to part with it, believing it would ward off the ills that besieged her. She was wrong, of course: the post-mortem had shown that the lung adhesions, the purulence, were worst right under the point where she had fixed the thing.

He had tried buying it, tried wrongfooting her with talk of the Lord being affronted by it. And he meant all of it. It was impossible to explain to a native woman, but the fact was that the use of such trinkets made progress from their pagan nonsense to any state of grace impossible. He had no doubt the beliefs were sincere, but sincerity wasn't the point. Medicine and religion stood together on one side, superstition on the other.

She had received the best medical care the settlement could offer. That was what he wrote to London. *Venesection, clysters, compresses, warmth and cleanliness*...it would have cruelled the pitch to mention that these remedies had been administered under the questionable hand of the Surgeon.

The amulet was kangaroo skin, stuffed with what he believed to be the cremated remains of an infant—Hers? He had never asked—drawn together at the top with a fine leather cord. He had described it in his letter to the broker as *a braided cord of animal skin*. The broker had had that letter six months now. There would be a reply on the next vessel, he felt sure.

But letters yet to come were flights of fancy: distractions from writing the letters that were yet to go. There was the Colonial Office to upbraid:

> *I do not believe my request to be unreasonable. I have not forgotten, though perhaps you have, that it was I who freed your settled districts from the oppression of constant battle, of raids and thieving, rapine and murder. It was I, should the matter be now beyond your memory, who cleared—single-handedly!—the natives from the entirety of Van Diemen's Land, without violence, without financial impost. It was a feat most likely unequalled in the history of the British Empire. And in doing so, I vastly increased the wealth of many of the great families: with their tenure unchallenged, and their assets in stock and crop now safe from banditry, I have handed them, and their sons, a future of limitless wealth.*

How she had wept when he took the amulet from her.

He wondered now if it caused some deep wound to the soul of a person to be separated from the totem they believe will heal them. It was remarkable how fast she'd slid once it was gone. The Surgeon had reassured him on this point: with her ribs sprung open between them he'd pointed out the chronic *phthisis pulmonalis*. 'These are not matters of the mind,' he slurred. 'Nor 'f the spirit.' He spread his bloody fingers for emphasis, a butcher in broadcloth. 'Degradations of the body only.'

The Commandant hefted the small thing in his hand. A draught of damp air, fluttering the candle just a little. It wasn't like he'd prised a prayer book from the hands of a Christian. All the same, he wished to be rid of it.

The letter, the letter.

And what do I have in return? A paltry amount, such as might be paid to one who had cleared the tree stumps, not the original inhabitants. And I find myself in a form of exile, here in these windswept isles. You will say but no, you chose this fate! And aye, so I did, but I chose it in the clear understanding that I would be justly recompensed for the enormous benefit I have conferred upon others.

I led them out. I rid the fields and the towns and the beaches of the last great obstacle to progress. And when I came to the aldermen and the merchants and asked for my sack of coins I had only scorn for my trouble.

In fable, a man scorned for his trouble was an agent of terrible vengeance. That was not his way. But scorned he had been, and it didn't hurt to make the point.

Visitors

At dawn on the third day of Mannalargenna's illness, the dog began to bark. Nobody had heard it bark before: barking seemed beneath it. But even in this it was true to character. It did not yelp as a pet might, nor was the sound pained or urgent. It was of a low register, powerful spikes of canine voice, bracketed by long silences.

It was so early that the light was a soft pink. The wind had not got up yet. No one came to tell the dog to stop. No one complained to anyone else about the sound but every human ear on the settlement registered it and, at first, each person reacted in their differing ways. Within hours it became a part of the landscape, stitches on the fabric of the wind that hissed in the she-oaks, and soon no one noticed it anymore.

~

The Commandant went outside, pulling his collar tight around his neck.

Eight short weeks and it felt like he'd been here a year. The ordinary idleness of the place would be the hardest fault to eradicate. Illiteracy, godlessness—these were things that could be worked upon, but the sheer indolence ran deep in them. It had been established early on that nobody could be forced to do anything. That decision looked like hopeless naiveté now, now that they had all chosen to do nothing.

The smokers playing marbles, the cricketers, the women gossiping, they all turned to register his presence as he emerged, because after all he was their Commandant. But then they returned to whatever it was that filled their day.

He strode to the bald patch on the ground outside Mannalargenna's hut, and in front of a dozen of the early risers he kicked the dog as hard as he could. It yelped, then whimpered loudly, and it pleased him to have got a different noise from it. No one was prepared to incur his wrath by intervening on its behalf but, as he looked around at the natives staring at him, he felt a sudden shame. Then he spied the Coxswain standing sentry halfway up the rise of the hill. He beckoned to him, trying to conceive of a way to do it that looked official. There must be a semaphore, he thought, that designates *come here, you simpleton*.

The Coxswain sauntered down, in no apparent hurry, fiddling with a clay pipe.

'Sir,' he offered, still nonchalant.

'Stand to attention,' the Commandant demanded.

The Coxswain made an approximation of the right posture, clearly feeling under no authority from this pompous civilian. The Commandant pointed at the dog. 'Have that thing shot,' he said.

'But sir—'

The Commandant came in close to the Coxswain, who was considerably taller than him, and looked up into his eyes. 'Do I need to speak to the sergeant about you?'

'Sir, it's just—' The Coxswain was more earnest now. 'The natives regard the dog well, sir. There'd be trouble.' There had indeed been trouble—he'd read the letters—when the previous administration had tried to cull the camp dogs.

'Return to your post,' he sighed.

The Coxswain gave him a puzzled look and complied. The Commandant turned his back on the dog and went to the tool store, where he found the corporal who'd taken care of blades and other implements for him in the past. He explained what he wanted, received a curt nod of assent, and left.

By the time he returned to the huts, the dog had moved and was now positioned outside Mannalargenna's room. The bare ground had been taken up by a group of the women, their skirts spread around them. The dog watched him pass, and the dignity of the animal caused the Commandant a slick of guilt. He'd forgotten why he returned. But a task announced itself: the Coxswain was returning down the hill from his lookout, more purposefully this time than before. He was out of breath.

'Sail approaching, sir,' he puffed. 'From the south.'

'From Green Island?'

'No sir, not one of our boats. Most likely straitsmen. Maybe Preservation or Gun Carriage. Dozen or so on board.'

'The bloody wives, then, I suppose.' The Commandant sighed. 'Very well, talk to the Storekeeper. Tell him to think about food. Tell the women they'll need to make room.'

He retired to his office once more, this time to think about his plans. There was interest in London, he felt sure of it. If he was to advance his case to be made Protector of Aborigines, if he was to expand his field of influence into Port Phillip, then impressions must be made. The Colonial Office wouldn't be handing higher roles to a man who merely languished in competent obscurity.

The journal would be his proof. It would tell the ages what he had achieved on this windswept saddle of misery. But the journal could not carry the load alone. He needed samples, evidence. Proof. The numbers could not be denied: these poor innocents were headed for extinction, and when they were gone, future generations would ask: who strove to collect evidence of these lost tribes? They would look for a name to attach to compendia, to halls of learning. A name to etch in marble. His name.

The incoming sail presented a problem.

Whoever they were, they would want to be involved in the chief's final hours. He could not anticipate what their funerary demands would be. If he went back through the journals he'd kept on the northeast walk he could work it out. Some wanted rituals; some would need a cairn of rocks, or a pyre. A bundling or a burial he could undo, provided he was quick. But if they demanded a cremation; that would be a problem. Why couldn't they standardise these things?

~

The Commandant strolled down to the southern beach alone, through the small forest with its secretive air, the path winding in pleasing fashion around the granite boulders. He stood on the highest of the small dunes above the beach, wanting the arrivals to behold him profiled against the sky. His coat and his hat, the rule of law.

The boat that came in was a lighter, a single mast with a simple boom and a tiller, beamy and low-swept for working between the islands. He recognised it as one of Munro's. The morning was cloudless but the air still cold and the passengers had huddled themselves deep between the thwarts. It was overloaded. He would write to Munro and warn him: if there was a disaster such carelessness would come down on his head, and Munro's.

The breeze was so slight that the boat struck the sand without momentum. But the tide was up, and the bow sliced over the oyster beds and through the dried clumps of the seagrasses, almost into the saltbush that lined the beach. The Commandant didn't move. He watched as the passengers began to disembark. They were carrying bundles and he knew that to be a bad sign: they were settling in. Where would he put them all? He could add a bed-roll to each of the rooms, except for the rooms where sickness had struck. They would want to be close to the dying chief. Crowds and noise and smoke, and nobody would get any rest.

All of the skin he could see was dark. No straitsmen aboard, then. He was beginning to make out faces, smeared with white ochre. They wore heavy cloaks of kangaroo and possum, maireener necklaces and amulets of one kind and another, and he was reminded of the many ways the straitsmen had frustrated his plans. These women should be living on the settlement: the pagan trinkets should be gone. They were here to make vigil for their countryman, and their presence was going to be a thorn in his side.

He watched them helping the older ones out of the vessel: mostly women, one or two with child, or nursing them, some infants around their feet. A grown man, Jack Williams. The short woman would be his New Holland wife, Ninjit. Kardingorroke, she was Morgan's but there was no sign of him. Bet Smith and Dumpy and Maria Portoyer from Guncarriage. Abyssinia Jack from Woody Isle with Emue and her children.

As he watched them gathering on the beach he could see that they centred themselves around one woman. He watched her, watched the authority in her movements, and before long he could hear her voice ringing through the sharp, new air. The lists rolled by in his mind: the Friendly Mission. Oh, early, early. 1828? Maybe earlier. One of the first. Some significance to her…something.

Then he recalled it.

~

The Commandant did not want to waste time doling out civilities on the beach. He turned on his heel and walked briskly back to the settlement and into the store, where he found the Storekeeper already stoking a small fire.

His wife was nowhere to be seen, a small mercy given the embarrassment that always caused. He had no idea what the Storekeeper knew: his long face was as hard as the granite but craggier. Its only variation was a faint twitch in one corner of the mouth, with which he would signal anything from a smirk to a tremendous outburst of goodwill. It registered in hundredths of an inch.

The Storekeeper nodded slightly and uttered a grunt that might have been 'Sir'. He reached under the counter at which he was working. 'They dropped this in. From the workshop.'

He handed the Commandant a wide leather collar with a row of holes at one end and a brass buckle at the other. The

Commandant opened its length between his hands.

'Good.'

The Storekeeper did not ask what it was for, nor did the dark eyes appear to guess. He gave the disconcerting impression of having lived through everything before. The Commandant had to remind himself why he had come: the vessel in the bay. He set out the numbers and his plans for accommodating the new arrivals. He ordered more bread and a hunting party to fetch meat, and he warned about the likely demands for tobacco, tea and sugar—none of which were held in abundance. The Storekeeper nodded and his face registered nothing at all. The Commandant felt an irrational urge to confess, like the urge to jump from a height: *We should talk about your wife.* He restrained himself.

He walked west along the short road they'd cleared, the rising sun throwing his shadow on the ground ahead of him. Where the grass was hacked off there was a grit of hardened quartz sand, and the road was silver-white with it. It sparkled faintly in the new light, revealing the tracks of things that had crossed in the night.

The dog was there in the first patch of sun outside the terraces, a sphinx in black. When the Commandant approached and his shadow fell across it, it looked up calmly: took in the collar, and its eyes narrowed slightly. Damn the creature, inscrutable as the Storekeeper. He squatted down and braced himself—there was no telling whether it was going to erupt in response to this indignity—and he reached under and over the warm fur. The collar slipped around its neck; the dog did not move. When the Commandant had secured the buckle, he removed his hands slowly and withdrew until he stood above the animal once more. *There*, he breathed. If the dog wanted to be a part of the community then it would comply with certain minimum standards.

It flicked its eyes down, pawed at the collar briefly then ignored it.

Satisfied, the Commandant walked north and found the rutted track that led to the waterhole behind the beach. The furrows were cutting ever-deeper into the ground, and had rippled into large potholes. The ground was so porous that none of them held any water, but they were clearly a problem. Here and there, shovelfuls of gravel had been poured into them to try to level them out. He stood by the track and listened carefully.

At first all he heard was the birds: the resounding chatter of the scrub and its countless wrens. Then there came a deep thumping to the south of him, nearer the settlement, slow and rhythmic. The squeaking of timber followed, and finally the bullocks' tormented breathing as they rounded a bend next to a tree stump and came into view. The driver walked behind the near-side flank, flicking at the closest animal with a long stick. He saw the Commandant but did not greet him, only stared in dumb exhaustion.

'Morris, isn't it?'

'Murrell, suh.' He doffed his hat, no further than his nose. The endless return journeys, day after day, occupied the corner of everyone's vision. Not something you watched but something you saw, like the hours of a clock. The Commandant had never stopped to study the man's face: the despair in it was immense, emptiness collected like grime in the long creases. The man stared at him now, awaiting whatever it was that the Commandant had to say.

'The ah, the animals. How are the animals?' He reached out awkwardly to stroke the near one's long muzzle, and the bullock shied warily from his hand. Over the brass ring through its septum, the Commandant saw the whites of its eyes.

'Best you don't handle 'im, suh.'

'Ah.'

'Tell the Overseer a number o times now, they's weary, I say. Hard goin, see, up and down the path. Ye can, if ye look back yon, path's split in all sorts o differn directions cause it's too rough.' He lowered his eyes, looked at the Commandant's feet. 'More work'n we can do suh.'

'Ah! Sounds like my job!' The Commandant's laugh fell dead at his feet. 'Merrett, I need you to step up the pace. I need more water.' The bullock driver's face did not move, so the Commandant continued. 'There has been a party arrive, unexpectedly, and I am sure they will want to wash.'

The convict was appalled. 'But this un's near dead on 'is feet,' he pleaded. 'Look at 'im. There's no more can be got.' The bullock hung its head as if to illustrate the convict's words. Mucus frothed in the wide nostrils and the tongue licked obsessively at the corners of its mouth.

The Commandant considered this appeal for a moment. Water would be in short supply within a day or two unless they got rain. Because none of the roofs had been shingled—a matter he had repeatedly written home about—there could be no prospect of collecting water off them. The Surgeon had advised that cleaning and washing would slow the ravages of the catarrh, which was well and good, but necessitated water.

He clapped the convict on his back, because he could, because he was the Commandant. 'You will have to find a way, I'm afraid. We must all make sacrifices…Just find me two more runs per day, hmm?'

The convict was horrified. 'Takes me over an hour to do

a run! I cannae—would ye have me start before the dawn, suh?' The morning sun caught a long string of drool from the bullock's snout.

'When we reflect on our lives, Mullett, we always find instances in which we can improve. I will relay our agreement to the Overseer so that he can monitor your efforts.' He smiled brightly at the unfortunate man and left him there.

One further errand: the Catechist. He found him at breakfast. The Commandant felt his temper rising: must every worry be left to him? The Catechist watched him from his single eye, unawed. He forked eggs under that grotesque nose, until an arch of his good eyebrow invited the Commandant to state his business.

'We must ensure we have a eulogy ready.'

'For whom?'

'The chief, Mannalargenna. The residents appear to have given up hope of his recovery.' The Commandant eased himself into a seat at the table: the Catechist had made no move to offer one. The man's wife hovered nearby, evincing even less interest in good manners. He couldn't look at her without wondering how she put up with the man. The rumours about her husband reached every corner of the settlement. How could she not know? Any woman would be aware of what went on in her own house.

'A mourning party has arrived,' he continued. 'Somehow it has been communicated to the southern islands that his dissolution approaches. We must accommodate them. In any event, once he has expired I will want the funeral conducted swiftly and these people gone. So be ready.'

The Catechist took this in without reaction. He chewed open-mouthed, took a sip of tea. Where had he got that china? Then that voice of his.

'Why the hurry?'

The Commandant breathed deeply. 'My haste is not your concern. Just see to it that you compose something that is intelligible. Any repeat of the drivel you have been indulging yourself in will result in poor reports leaving the island with that boat. So keep it sharp. Do I make myself clear?'

'Who are they?' asked the Catechist, ignoring the rebuke. The eyes scanned and shifted.

'Southern islanders. Straitsmen's wives.'

'Oh, yes.' Something in the broken face had changed at the mention of the southern islands. Another sip. 'Who's in charge?'

The rigidity left the Commandant's body, and he felt the entire weight of the settlement. 'Maria,' he said softly. His mouth remembered the rhythm of the word. 'Toogernuppertootenner.'

The Catechist looked at him blankly.

'Mannalargenna's sister. So finish that tea and come immediately. I want this eulogy done.'

~

The Commandant had hurried back to his office and sat behind his desk. He looked around the surface of it, opened three heavy ledgers and scattered some papers in front of him. He lit an extra lamp and turned some books, all three volumes of *The Russian Dynasties*, so their spines faced the door.

Then he waited. His eye caught the draughts of the letter he had been writing to the Colonial Office, seeking a post in the Port Phillip district. He flipped the top page so that the script was obscured, and placed his pen on the pile. Smoothed his waistcoat, ran a finger over the dust on the inkstand. When the knock came he cleared his throat and bellowed *enter*.

It was not, as he expected, the delegation of natives, but the

Catechist. His dry bulk filled the doorway, and he placed an over-familiar hand on the jamb.

'Those natives are on the way,' he said. 'Perhaps the meeting about the eulogy ought to wait?'

The Commandant hefted his watch on its chain. '*Lord*. Yes, very well.'

The Catechist drummed his fingers on the doorway, just a little. 'Where are they...?' The fingers stopped. 'Oh, never mind.' He rolled the bad eye in the Commandant's direction and smiled his crooked smile. 'An hour or two, perhaps?'

As he spoke the floorboards rumbled and a crowd filled the hall and began to spill into his office. *Tyereelore*, dressed in skins. Their hair was nested; they wore pins and beads, and carried bundles they evidently had refused to leave at the door. The passageway was immediately crammed with them. Their full forms and obvious health were reminders of what had fallen short here.

A woman pushed her way to the front. Short, still heavily bundled against the chill of the voyage, she wore a look of impatience. She was about to emerge fully into the room, but as she did so she brushed past the Catechist, who had stalled in the doorway. She looked up at him combatively, did not excuse herself but stared into his eyes. All movement stopped as she focused on him. He broke the impasse by excusing himself hurriedly; he edged his way through the group and was gone.

Toogernuppertootenner occupied the centre of the room, facing the Commandant, and her companions arranged themselves around her.

'You remember me,' she began.

The Commandant did not hear it as a question, and in any event, he did remember her. 'Northeast?'

'Cape Portland. These people, some of these people my people, some from other places. We comin to see that sick fella.' Her voice was high and animated. None of the others made a sound. It was clear to the Commandant that she spoke for them all.

'Yes, well, of course,' the Commandant began. 'But you…'

'Where is he?' she demanded. 'Where you keepin him?'

'…as I was *saying*, you must understand that there are procedures here. I have the man separated from the others so that any disease might be contained.'

'The man? Thought my brother was your *friend*, mister. Now he's "the man"?'

'Mannalargenna was and remains my friend. All of the people here are my friends and we are all one in Jesus Christ. I neither hold grudges nor play favourites.'

'So let's go, then. Let's see that fella. Your Jesus friend.'

'Can I…' The Commandant's face twisted in suppressed anxiety. 'Can I ask that perhaps we visit him in smaller groups, so as to lessen the strain upon him? I must look to his health and the health of the other residents.'

'You worryin bout his health now? Maybe shoulda thought about that earlier.' She turned and said something indecipherable to her companions, and they began to file out of the crowded room. The smell in the office had changed from an abstract note of dust to something richly human. The Commandant looked at their backs, feeling the loss of control over this encounter.

'Maria?'

She stopped, turned. *'Tooger. Nupper. Tootenner.* Try bit harder.'

'Yes.' He smiled thinly. 'I imagine you and your party intend to lament him.'

'Lament?'

'You will want to sing and so forth when he, hmm.'

There was a tiny change in her face. 'Yeah. Sing him proper way, bury him. You had your go.'

The Commandant stood up now, his whole body tensed with pleading. 'I ask of you, do not create a confrontation over this. That is not what your brother would want.'

The woman's eyes widened. She stepped back into the office and immediately it was hers again. 'Must've heard my ears wrong, mister. Did you just try tellin me what my brother wants?'

He held her gaze for as long as he could. Then he dropped his eyes to the desk and made another gesture at sweeping dust from it.

'You stay clear of us while we do our business and there be no trouble.' She turned to go, but hesitated. 'That preacher fella,' she said. 'Where'd you get im?'

The Commandant laughed without amusement. 'I hardly think that is any concern of yours, Maria. He has been appointed to the settlement and he is doing a fine job.'

She narrowed her eyes. 'Don't see too many white fella with all them scars an only one eye.'

'That would be his business and not yours, don't you think? Now if you will excuse me…'

She wasn't done. 'Might have a think about that fella. Talk to these others. Might be you got a crook one there, mister.'

She swept out of the room and the group left with her. When the last of the footfalls had ceased and the voices of the visitors had faded across the yard, the house fell into silence. He turned and opened the window and the dry air of the day flowed in.

He slumped in the armchair under the bookshelf and considered his position. There must not be a scene. It could do tremendous discredit to the settlement, and ultimately to him, if it emerged that he had been compelled to use force on the women. Equally, they could not be allowed to interfere with the post-mortem or the burial. He had decided that at the very least he must have the head. The greatest of the Tasmanian chiefs, emblematic of a dying race: it had fallen to him alone to preserve this vital piece of evidence in anatomy's long journey to understanding. The Hunterian would consider it a prize beyond all measure. Such an artefact must not be lost, must not be left to decay under a peg in the infernal wind. It was a matter of respect: imagine what a travesty it would be if some badger tunnelled the thing out.

Yes: it was unarguably the right way to proceed. The trick would be managing the visitors. Give them something they could imagine as a victory. Access to the chief, yes; singing for him. Let them mingle with the residents and spread their hateful assessment of the settlement and their self-serving lies about life as straitsmen's wives—fine. The singing, the gathering, unavoidable. They would want a hand in the funeral arrangements. They were unlikely to stay for long after that: they had work to attend to back on their islands. He folded his hands on the desk, examined his knuckles. If he could have the chief anatomised during the post-mortem and then ensure the coffin was nailed shut, they could be given free rein over the subsequent funeral and burial.

He hurried from the office and found the group already gathered at Mannalargenna's room, mingling with the residents. Old tribal loyalties had been resumed. The crowd parted as he approached and he found Toogernuppertootenner crouching by the bedside, holding her brother's hand. Mannalargenna showed no sign of comprehending her presence; his eyes were peacefully closed, though his breathing was shallow and irregular.

The exhalations were punctuated by the barking of the black dog. The animal had taken up vigil by the doorway, so that all who came and went had to pick their way around it. It did not push its snout at the passing legs and sniff them for friendship as another dog might. Its head remained as still as the mopokes', and its eyes gave no succour. Every minute or so its narrow chest would expand and it would give voice again.

The Commandant had come to tell them he had relented, that they could share in the man's last hours; eulogise and bury him if that was what they wanted to do. He had a plan for the contingencies. But they were already singing, long notes, low and quiet. The sound enclosed him, as if the song was taking the air from the room. He looked to the figure in the bed, but found no solace there.

Mannalargenna's head, there on the pillow they had fashioned him, he intended to boil down to bone and send to London in a box. Yet now, as he looked, it was the visible part of a struggling human body that clenched and wheezed in the gloom.

The Corrosive Effect of Doubt

In the middle of the morning the Commandant took his tea. It was scalding, and the china glowed warm in his hands.

Footfalls and a discreet knocking announced the presence of his clerk. He rumbled assent and the clerk ushered the Catechist into the room, shrinking himself in the doorframe as the man's bulk came through. The Commandant continued to write in the journal. The clock crunched out the moments; the pen dragged dry over the pages and the furniture squeaked faintly under him. Outside in the trees, the rooks carked their hunger from the thin canopy.

The Catechist cocked an eyebrow at the window. 'Old crow gets us in the end…'

The writing stopped. The Commandant looked up. 'What?'

'I said the old crow gets us all in the end.'

'That's patently ridiculous. They don't live anywhere near our age.' He resumed writing.

'Ah, yes,' the Catechist continued, enjoying himself. 'But this crow, that crow—can you tell them apart? No, you cannot. So for all practical purposes, generations of them, they are one crow. And in the end it's your bones they're picking.'

The Commandant scoffed quietly under his breath and did not respond, so the Catechist stood in sly tolerance. Halfway through the second minute he looked about himself in mock distress, then pulled out a chair and sat on it, smiling.

'Any word from the Governor?'

The pen slowed just slightly. 'He has been in touch, yes.'

'Oh! How *exciting*. When can we expect his arrival?'

'He assures me that the visit will be early this summer. And the letter was several weeks old, so I would say'—he flipped a page, did not look up—'an arrival is imminent.'

'I trust all the necessary measures are in place.'

Had the Commandant looked up at this point he would have seen the unconcealed mischief on the Catechist's face. But he kept writing, his voice a low murmur. 'I can say that everything of an administrative nature is in order. Can you say the same of your young charges?'

'Of *course*, sir. Their singing would please His Excellency no end. To say nothing of the good lady wife. But perhaps'—he poked out his lower lip doubtfully—'you ought to arrange some more drills for us all. To ensure readiness at a moment's notice.'

The pen stopped, and the Commandant flipped his notebook closed, took another, smaller one and began to write there. 'Yes. Very good. Drills.'

'A vital moment in your…*trajectory*, sir.'

The Commandant paused in the act of closing the small notebook and returning to his journal. He did not look up, but a tiny frown betrayed his detection that he was being ridiculed.

Above him hung the pelican, dried to a mineral brown, eye shrivelled and the great beak open to cry. His head, his pink and earnest head, bobbed in the chair beneath it, like a morsel the mineral bird might snatch.

The pen finally slowed and he jabbed it with a *pock* at the full stop. 'How long have you been here now?'

The humour still floated in the Catechist's eyes as he examined his watch. 'Four minutes.'

'Here. *Here.*'

'Oh. Hm. Hard to tell, isn't it? This is a place outside time. It was November, maybe? Thirteen months, I shall say.'

The Commandant wrote something. He wished to have the Catechist wonder if it was related to his answer. 'And what can you say you've achieved, over that period?'

'Achieved?' He cocked his head. 'Why, it is not my achievements that matter, sir. I am humbled that you might seek to draw attention to them, but it is the saving of souls with which we are concerned.'

The Commandant waited, tapped a finger. The golden voice continued.

'Eight of the children can recite the Beatitudes. Most of them can now identify the Commandments by number. Some of the brighter ones are familiar with the One Hundred and Twenty-First Psalm...'

'I lift mine eyes unto the damn hill every day, pastor.'

'Ha!' The Catechist clapped loudly and pointed. 'I tell them, I tell them all the time, *he's got personality, our Commandant! Not nearly so dry as you think!*' The teeth were preternaturally bright, and the Commandant wondered, not for the first time, whether they'd once resided in someone else's skull. The Catechist was still chuckling. 'I see evidence,' he went on, 'of a growing sanctitude in all that they do now. I see them clean and attentive at the Sunday services. There is a decline in their more…*licentious* ways.'

The Commandant wrote again, dipped his pen and blotted it. Then: 'And you? What of your ways?'

The Catechist's good eye searched the Commandant's face, looking for shades of meaning in the question. The smile uncurled itself. 'My ways are the ways of the Lord…'

'You have how many—eight?—children living in your house now?'

'A refuge from the storm, shadow from the heat, hmm?'

'*Refuge*…' The pen scratched onwards. 'And your wife? She assists with the…refuge?'

The Catechist appeared to think hard for a moment. 'It pays no man to heed rumours, sir.'

The Commandant looked up, looked away from the bad eye and into the sighted one. 'Pays less to ignore them.' A long silence ensued, and it was the Commandant who spoke first to break it, unwilling or unable to probe at the darkness. 'How have you found the new chapel?'

The Catechist's demeanour lifted instantly. 'Well, it is excellent. We now have the capacity to bring together the whole settlement in worship. Raises the voices, makes the absences more conspicuous. And naturally I prefer my homilies are delivered to a fulsome congregation.'

The Commandant was unmoved. His eyes wandered over the chaplain's face, climbed in and out of the gouges. 'Tell me where you came from, pastor. I have never asked.'

'You want to know about the injury.' He waved a hand near it: the dent in the line of his brow, shell-pink in there like a fingertip had gouged the soft wax of a candle. The turned eye, milky-white and curdled; some fragment of the iris fixed inward, in permanent stare at the crescent nose, smashed from right to left and never corrected. 'Sometimes I think bringing people to a benevolent god is made harder when you have the devil's face. How lucky that a voice is a harder thing to shoot away.' He laughed. 'A native did it, you know. Musket ball. Very lucky, I was, or unlucky. Of course, we know from scripture to lean not on our own understanding, but to—'

'Your *working* history, pastor.'

'Yes, of course. Londoner, originally, sir. So many Scots hereabouts but not I. St Judes, refectory, school of divinity. Life, sir, *life*! I came out on the *Elphinstone*, charged with the souls of one hundred and forty-nine prisoners and though we lost a number to scurvy and flux I will aver we did not lose a single soul to the devil.' He sighed. 'In the colonies I...oh, troubles here, troubles there. I came to Hobart and found myself ministering to the sealers in the western straits these past five years. Not all bad men either, but hungry for the succour of faith like any other. Much as these natives are, sir.'

Caught in the misaligned stare, the swirl of meaningless words, the Commandant felt deep unease, a trickling of poison. Meeting the good eye was akin to opening one's mouth and allowing him to breathe some foul miasma into it. It was not the Commandant's way to pay heed to ideas of evil, or of anything but the long struggle towards piety, but this *man*...

He composed himself. 'How was it that you came to have a letter of recommendation from the Colonial Secretary, might I ask?'

'Naught but good fortune. The hand of the Lord, perhaps. I was at George Town resupplying and I was invited to dinner at the Governor's house. One meets many people along the course; he had accrued, I suppose, a certain obligation and was keen to acquit. I explained my mission to the islands, the price I had paid'—he indicated the eye again, and a sly smile escaped—'and such was his sympathy that an offer was made then and there to recommend me for the post.'

The Commandant had the letter in his hands. He gazed at it while the Catechist spoke, scepticism etched on his face. None of it added up. Even the gibberish seemed to lack commitment.

'I am not happy with the number of children you have around that house.'

The good eyebrow rose.

'How are they being fed?'

'My wife attends to everything, sir. It is no trouble.'

'But *why*? Why are they there?'

The Catechist looked shocked. 'They are the Lord's children, sir. I cannot turn my back on them. You know the ones—Nelson and Finley, Min. And the boy Whelk. All lost their parents to the Englishman's ball or these terrible afflictions, to the catarrh. All of them sadly orphaned, none separated from living parents. If I do not extend the hand of charity then I beg of you, what is left for them?'

'No one is arguing with charity. The issue here is that people are suspicious of you, and therefore of the credibility of our entire mission. If it were to be *suggested*, pastor, merely suggested, that there was some kind of rot at the core of our religious instruction here…'

The Catechist's face soured; the mockery was replaced by a sneer. 'Have it out. Tell me what it is that you say I have done. Tell me how I can be a better Christian than to take in the world's orphans.'

'The Surgeon performed a post-mortem the other day. You know that I attend them all.'

The Catechist pounced. 'A rich source of...*souvenirs*, are they not?'

'What on earth is that supposed to mean?'

'Oh, medical curiosities, hmm? Hard to satisfy a serious collector with'—he glanced over the Commandant's shoulder—'pelicans.'

The dog still barked outside, steady as a convict hammer.

'If I read your insinuation correctly, pastor, I am given various specimens in the course of my work, and often by the natives themselves as tokens of gratitude. There are few Englishmen alive who have achieved the level of intimacy that I have with these people.' He drew himself up to a height, colour rising in his throat. 'My contribution to clearing these people off the settled lands has never been properly recognised. History will record it so.'

'Are you sure?'

'What?'

'Are you sure you want that to be history's verdict—Pied Piper to a race of human beings? He doesn't emerge from the story as the hero, exactly.'

The infernal barking. Why had no one forced the creature to shut up?

I have seen things in those autopsies, you animal. The Commandant stood now and the chair squealed back and a vein sprang with angry blood under his jaw. 'It isn't me that's come for the children, pastor. Now get out.'

~

He sat there long after the dark bulk of the man had cleared the doorway and the room had filled with light again. The Catechist had evaded the questions by raising a false equivalence, but his time would come. It tore at him—it caused him to pull at his hair and drag his fingertips down his face in angst: the devil had him perfectly cornered. If he raised the alarm about this man and his evil ways, he would destroy the careful impression he had built of an orderly, pious settlement. He would scuttle any chance of the Port Phillip assignment.

He took up the pen and instead let fly with his anger.

Philanthropy is nothing. The security of life and property is nothing. The immense revenue arising from the sale of lands consequent upon the increased value by the removal of the aborigines is nothing. The increase to individual property is nothing…thus it is when men are unprincipled, unjust and dishonest. All is nothing.

It seems passing strange that the Home Government should sanction the vast expenditure incurred on occasion of the military operation which achieved nothing and completely failed, and refuse compensation to me who effected without loss of life what they could not accomplish and at comparatively no expense at all.

A Reckoning

Around midday, the Commandant settled himself in the chair next to Mannalargenna's bed. He rested his elbows on the chair's arms, drew out his journal and took a pen from his coat pocket. He dabbed the nib on his tongue, then pinched at it with his fingertips. *Fourth of December.* The burden of correspondence had meant he'd made no entry for two days. Not since *Several natives sick: MANNALARGENNA expected by doctor to die.*

The fire struggled in the grate, a sickly yellow flame that fell to embers. It had sooted the fireplace, and the ash had spilt out onto the bare bricks of the hearth.

Mannalargenna, lying prone and straight, the covers at his collarbones, watched the pen-fiddling sidelong.

'What's this?' he said, after a while.

'I thought we might talk,' the Commandant replied evenly.

'Bout what?'

The Commandant looked kindly upon him. 'About our

friendship. About all we've done together these past years…'

A wry squint. 'Surgeon man's given up, eh?'

'There is always hope, my friend, but it is best that things are not left unsaid.'

He snorted weakly down his nose. 'Best they not written down. You put the book away, mister, an we can have a talk.'

An unexpected tone. The Commandant's eyes darted from the pen to the book. This was not what he had had in mind. However…

'You're right,' he said equably, and set the book down.

'So?'

'My friend, I don't feel the warmth between us that once prevailed. Have I done you wrong?'

'You must know the answer, bein you asked the question.' He drew breath: slow, painful.

This was going to be a test of his patience, but so be it. There were always roads around a difficult point. 'Can we assume I do not know the answer, and I wish to hear it from you?'

Mannalargenna let his eyes roll over the Commandant while the words formed. 'You told me we would have our land, and I told the people that.'

'I did not.'

'*Some* land. You promised.'

'You have land. You have land under your feet.' The Commandant inclined his head to indicate his forbearance. 'A people with some land is better than a land with no people, surely.'

'This land makin us die. It's the wrong kind.'

The Commandant screwed his face in exasperation. 'The land is not killing your people. A basic lack of attention to hygiene and proper dress, on the other hand…'

The chief looked at him with disgust.

'My friend, take your own sorry circumstances. Had you not cut your hair off at Green Island as you did, you may not have caught the chill, and you would not be so afflicted as you are. I told you—'

A long hand appeared from beneath the blanket. The chief jabbed a finger into the bedding beside his hip. 'This land you put us on,' he repeated. 'Makin' people die.'

The Commandant could barely contain his frustration. 'Look around you,' he pleaded, though the chief could look nowhere beyond the edge of the bed. 'It is not killing the Englishmen here.'

Footsteps outside, low voices and a heavy thud. The convicts had dumped the burial rug by the door. All the tact of stray dogs.

'Mebbe your God doesn't love us so much?'

'I would never suggest such a thing. The love of God is spread evenly across all men.'

'My whole life I ben walkin around my own country. Come here, other fella said I ben here fifty days, an I'm dyin. If this int a dyin place then that's a, a—'

'—coincidence,' finished the Commandant. Mannalargenna had watched the word come out of his mouth with cold satisfaction. The Commandant cursed himself for being so easily outflanked. But he had other defences. 'It's a topic that often fascinates me,' he began, eyes half-closed in thought. 'This thing about the land. The great mystery of property rights is that no other man can own the space you occupy. It follows that no man can own nothing.' The journal lay on the floor beside him. He should be recording this. 'The inalienable space you occupy, my friend. Within yourselves you remain kings and queens, and your domain can never be seized from you.'

'Is that what *you* own? This, what—space inside? Thought you had a place in Hobart.'

'That is different and you know it. I have a mission...'

Mannalargenna's eyes pierced the gloom, fixed in opposition.

'Why did you come with me, if you believed it to be a bad bargain?'

'Because.' Every word brought pain. Mannalargenna was tiring, pummelled down by each exchange as if it were a flurry of blows. 'Cos we had to. English give us war: war with your lot, war with ourselves. You remember that time you come to Big River with me? An I went out, found the devil of a dead man in a tree an he showed me where them people was. I took you to em, showed you them people. Because I *trusted* you.'

The Commandant remembered it differently, remembered being led foolishly by the nose. The long hours of diversion, giving Mannalargenna's countrymen time to escape.

The chief was measuring his breaths, gathering them up to begin again. They both knew those breaths were finite.

'You told me we safe. We not safe.

'Told me we get land. Got no land.

'Now, I made a mistake listenin to you. Just for me, that's my problem. But the *people*, see? They come, say, Mannalargenna, what do we do? White fella, he shootin at us, kill the babies. Women cryin. Where we go, Mannalargenna?

'An I look around and I see *you*. And I think: can't stay here. Not gonna win. Not gonna have guns, fight back. See you makin big promises. You think I hear anything else when you make big promises, think maybe I hear *be careful this fella*?'

The Commandant rose from his seat and turned his back angrily to stare out the window. 'You are running very close to accusing me of lying, and I will not abide it! Not from you, nor anyone.'

The dying man on the bed behind him was reflected in the panes. All the doubt and regret he had felt assailed him as he turned and pointed an angry finger. 'I demand to be respected! By the officers, by the prisoners. By your people. By you, damn it. There is no other way.' He swept an exasperated hand through the thick air. 'Without it the enterprise fails.'

'*Demand*...ah.' Mannalargenna was apparently too lethargic for melodrama. 'People mebbe give you respect if they want. Ones who demand it, they don't get—'

A coughing fit. He recovered more slowly this time.

'Nearly finished, mister. Be gone. You be here, one problem outta the way. But every one what dies, that's one more promise you broken.'

The Commandant considered this for a long time. He needed to resist the implacable logic, the coming judgment. 'The mission must continue on its own terms, Mannalargenna. The children learning their arithmetic, their Psalms. The adults must find their way to God. There is no other path to salvation.'

'God!' spat the chief. He was gasping, a landed fish in a bed.

'Salvation is universal, dear friend. The Lord God does not distinguish between the native and the Englishman. He loves the lowest of men and the highest the same. I am so proud of what we achieved toge—'

'*Lowest of men*,' the chief repeated. 'We done what we done apart. Me for mine, you for yours.'

'It sorrows me deeply that you believe that to be the case, that our friendship must close on such a note.' He paused, reconsidered. Smiled. 'But of course you are ill.'

The man in the bed furrowed his brow and the rage rebuilt

in him. '*Now I am ill* I see you clear.' Mannalargenna's eyes, so weary, so dimmed just a moment before, flickered bright with anger. 'Doan you stand up there at my grave and tell em I went off happy…and we traded our lands for some place in the sky, *mister Commandant*. I say it one time for good: I belong in the ground. Doan you go tellin em your God kingdom is my country now. None o them lies.'

'I have always been honest with you, old friend. I will pay you worthy tribute.'

'I belong…' He gulped for air. He was drowning. 'Belong in the ground.'

'You should rest…'

'I know what you ben doin with my people. Wanna put my head in a pot, boil all the meat off, don't you. Ole *friend*.' The coughing broke him down and he curled his body away from the Commandant's spluttered denials.

Mannalargenna's face was gaunt now. He was not the man the Commandant had met in the bush. The vigour, the humour, the glow of satisfied authority had all left him. What remained was a terrifying fixity, all doubt having vanished and judgment made clear. And he was not done. He hauled in a series of strangled breaths, determined to continue.

'Nobody gonna dig me up, you hear? Cut me, take my *head*. Nobody carry me way! You hear?'

'I know nothing of this!' The Commandant's breath was ragged and his eyes ranged wildly into the gloom. 'I would never interfere with the dead, much less a dear friend. Your grave will be the site of my fondest remembrances, my—'

'An I don't need your Jesus, *Englishman*.' That word: a word he had never used to address the Commandant. The final dark epithet.

For just an instant before he shut it out, the Commandant glimpsed the possibility that he had mistaken his own role in history. That he was that most wretched of creatures, the Judas.

Mannalargenna was fading before his eyes now.

'Doan need your gospel. Singin,' he whispered. 'Jus put me in that yard and doan you come near me never.'

The Song of Lamentation

½ 3pm a female aborigine came to my quarters and told me that Mannalargenna was dead. Went with the Surgeon, who had dined with me, to see the corpse. Soon after leaving my house heard the song of lamentation. I still went on in the direction of the house where the corpse lay, but was too overpowered to go. I therefore avoided the house of mourning and went around the back of the native huts to the Surgeon's quarters. A short time after the Surgeon gave directions for the body to be removed to the new store, when it was wrapped in a blanket and the lamentation ceased. I then went and requested the men to go with me to select a place for the grave in the burying ground and then marked the spot, when the natives at my request began digging the grave; and it was truly gratifying to see with what willingness they performed the labour, and moreover the Big River tribe, who were hostile to the deceased when alive, took a most active part.

Outside the day had turned unseasonably cold, and a southerly gale ran straight over the saddle of land where the settlement lay.

It suited the Commandant that it was like this. He wanted to walk, to escape the incessant business of being himself in that place. He was more position than man, queueing to take time with himself.

The chief's words had upset him profoundly. He walked east, up the slope of Pea Jacket Hill, taking care to avoid the burial ground at its foot. The wind grew stronger as he gained elevation, and the smaller sounds like the speech of the natives and the squeaking of the water cart's wheels were swept away on the southerly. The air was especially cold over his cheeks; he realised he had been crying a little. It surprised him, but then he understood that he was utterly alone, and pretences no longer mattered up here. No one could see him—they would see only the ant-speck of his meandering form from down there—and no one could hear him. There was no one to whom he might justify himself or make an impression. The queue had ended and there was only him up here.

The hillside was dotted with small trees: she-oaks and little gums. The currawongs alighted on them and scrawed loudly as the wind bounced their perches. He watched his feet for snakes but saw only the big bronze ants now and then, rearing back and waving their mandibles up at him in false bellicosity. A skink or two, crackling twigs underfoot.

He was high enough now to see north and south over the two bays, and to view the entire settlement on its short isthmus. The water broke over the rocky islet up close in the west, and out further on the horizon, the great hills of Hummock Island turned to haze and sky. There were more islands to the north and south: long, low, mountainous and flat, near and far. He was *standing* on a damned island. They were hemming him in. Thwarting him.

He sat on a small area of softer grasses and the truth came to visit him: any grieving was an act of gravest hypocrisy. He knew for certain that the moment he could secure privacy with the chief's body he would desecrate it, and he would do so for earthly renown. His mouth went sour. The fierce sadness he'd felt in Mannalargenna's company was what any decent person should feel, for he was talking to the living person whose sacred vessel he would defile as soon as he had the opportunity. And in those moments when the chief had met his eye and had glared at him with glacial hatred, that truth had stood naked between them.

~

The Surgeon was waiting for him at his table when he returned. He had made a habit of appearing just before the Commandant's Friday lunch, transparently seeking a share of the beef and red wine he would otherwise have to requisition from the store. They retired to the office after their meal and the Surgeon lit a pipe, and when the native woman came they absorbed the news in silence and the Commandant sent her away.

'Come,' said the Surgeon, yawning expansively. 'There will be much carry-on, and not much chance to have a look at his insides.'

As they rose and left the house, the wailing could be heard rising into the trees and above them to meet the southerly and blow away to the north, taking the chief and his memory further and further from home. This was the first act of scattering. It was less than a hundred yards from the house to the native houses where the sorrowful voices rose, and the Surgeon strode confidently towards them. Somewhere in the middle of that open distance, however, the dog stood waiting. It did not sit regally this time, but stood with its head and tail low so that the level plane of its back made a dark bridge in the grass. It did not look at the Commandant. It did not need to.

The Commandant's resolve failed him and he stopped. He placed his hands on his knees and bent towards the grass.

The Surgeon had walked on; he must have noticed the absence of footfalls behind him because he stopped and looked around, saw the stricken Commandant and paused. 'Squeamish?'

'Of course not,' he snapped, but without standing upright. His face was so contorted that the Surgeon wondered if he should intervene. From where he was bent, the Commandant cocked an eyebrow in the direction of the pitiful sound. 'This *place*...'

'Why don't you go to my quarters?' the Surgeon offered, placing a hand on the Commandant's back. 'They won't come after you there, and we can take our time with the rest of it. Hmm?'

The Commandant finally straightened and looked gratefully at the younger man. 'Yes, yes. Might do that. Don't know what's come over me.' Standing upright, he looked about himself to check that his distress hadn't been seen. 'Do you think of me as...?' He shook his head. 'No matter.'

The Commandant started along the road to the Surgeon's quarters, as the Surgeon continued towards the house that was the focus of the sound. The sun was high in the north above them, making squat shadows of the two men as they parted. The wailing rang out from the terraces, and it scattered the birds.

Divided Observers

By mid-afternoon, the wind had backed off. The sun clawed its way into the tight spaces of the store, feeling the gaps by the curtains, climbing the dark walls. It was gloomy in the high corners of the room; gloomy like an unresolved memory. But the stark lines of the incoming light made the table bright enough to work without a lamp.

The Surgeon stood by the table in the centre of the floor. It was normally used to measure out quantities, to make sales and to spread the paperwork of ordering and inventory. He had rolled his sleeves above his elbows, where they were held by metal clips. He stood frowning through his spectacles, clean hands on his hips. He looked older than his years.

In the centre of the table lay the body of Mannalargenna, shrouded by a blanket. The shape it made was long and narrow. The Surgeon had two buckets at his feet—one for wetting and one for wringing—and a small basket piled with cloths. He laid his hands lightly on the body as any doctor might lie them on a living one, contemplating. He glanced at the Commandant, who had drawn a chair up to the far side of the table and sat with his chin in his hands.

'What we might do with you'—the Surgeon tossed his own notebook so it landed atop the Commandant's—'is have you scribe for us both, hmm?'

The Commandant flipped the Surgeon's book open. The Surgeon placed a canvas roll on the surface of the table and opened it to reveal his implements in their gleaming, obedient rows.

'I am anticipating a standard pulmonary,' he began. 'Windpipe, lungs, thoracic cavity inclusive of pleura. Then the heart while we're in there, though I would wager it will be unaffected, given the man was drowning and not suffering from a failed pump. Then, depending upon findings, a dissection of the viscera. And after that'—he indicated with his eyes the clump of short hair that protruded from the far end of the blanket—'the decisions are yours.'

He went back to preparing his tools, and the Commandant gazed vacantly at the notebooks in front of him.

The noise of the door was so unexpected, and so loud, that it startled both men. The light flooded in and Toogernuppertootenner stood silhouetted in it. Her eyes went straight to the shape under the blanket. When she came forward to stand at the table between the two men, her face was soft with sorrow but her body was tensed. She reached out and touched the pinnacle of the toes, ignoring them both, until the Commandant finally found his voice.

'Maria?'

She looked at him, as if for the first time, and her face

hardened. 'They took our ochre. Why you tell em to do that?'

The Commandant knew what she referred to. The soldiers had seen the *tyereelore* women, shortly after their arrival, mixing ochre with charcoal at the fire; they must have brought it with them for the mourning. The sergeant had reported this fact, and he had ordered it be confiscated and disposed of. But he would not be drawn into that argument.

He stood. 'There is no need for them to be wearing ochre.'

She looked him up and down. 'So why you need them fancy clothes?'

The argument was coming, only if he allowed it. 'This is no place for you. I would be grateful if you would leave us.' His chin was up, authority restored.

'I know what you do in here,' she replied, eyes about the room. 'Cuttin people up.'

The Surgeon smiled tightly. 'There is a process of medical examination,' he began. 'Necessary to—'

'Not him!' Her raised voice threatened chaos in the small space. 'Got plenty of our people out there. More 'n you got. You don't wanna be makin trouble with me.'

She was wrong, the Commandant thought. Wrong mathematically, and wrong practically. There was no energy left for an uprising, and even if there was it would be cut down in minutes. But with it would go all his prospects. The Surgeon eyed the roll of implements discreetly. There were blades in there, closer to her hands than his.

'Now, Maria,' murmured the Commandant. 'I have been weeping myself, these long hours. This man...this great man, a terrible, terrible loss to us all.' His eyes darted to the Surgeon, who was watching him sharply. 'He must be given every honour. We must farewell him as a chief.'

There was the faintest slackening of the woman's stance. He worked towards the weakness.

'It could be that there is a misunderstanding about what we are doing. I do not know what you have been told about this procedure, but you see…it is essential that we understand what sickened this man. We must look inside him for answers. That is all. We will do so with the utmost respect.'

'Not our way!' she insisted, but the Commandant's confidence was building as he sensed her anger subsiding.

'No, but these diseases are not your way either,' he said gently. 'Sadly, nothing is the way it was, and we must make do. Perhaps if I'—he glanced again at the Surgeon—'perhaps if I explain to you what it is we do with the body, you may feel more at ease?' His voice rose just slightly to make it a question.

Toogernuppertootenner looked at him: still seething, but attentive now.

'We must, ah, open him up, as I said'—his hands were extended in front of him, warding off counterargument—'and we will look in there and write down what we observe, and then we will close him again, dress him in his good clothes, and we will hand him over to you and to the people to bury him. The entire matter will occupy as little as half of one hour.' He raised his eyebrows imploringly, and all the exhilaration of negotiating on the open country of Van Diemen's Land came back to him. When he harnessed his intellect and his charm to God's will he was convinced that he could not be denied.

She regarded him for some time in shades of suspicion and anger. The Surgeon was watching him too, well aware that the Commandant had just bargained away his opportunity to obtain the head.

Without a word to either of them, Toogernuppertootenner

walked around the table until she came to the far end, and drew the blanket back from her brother's face. His teeth were set hard, his lips slightly withdrawn so it appeared he was still enduring his last pain. No one had taken the care to close his eyelids properly, and the Commandant was suddenly alarmed by the sense that the chief was still glaring in fury. But Toogernuppertootenner had noticed it, and she tenderly rolled her brother's eyelids down with her fingertips. She touched the short fuzz of hair above his forehead and a look of puzzlement came over her.

There was a long moment when the room did not move; when the people in it were absorbed in worlds of their own and they were painted there in sheets of afternoon shadow and light. And the painter would capture forever two Englishmen in their attitudes of revulsion and scheming, the corpse in its vacant carnality and the woman in her grief.

'You wash him,' she said after a long time. 'And you leave him with us when you done so we can put him right.' She levelled a hateful glare at the Surgeon, who glanced at the Commandant and saw no opposition there.

'Very well,' he replied.

'And I be here,' she continued. She scanned the room, took a chair and sat by the table as though it was set for a meal. 'I be here watchin you. See if you do what you say.'

The Surgeon blanched at this, looked with alarm at the Commandant. 'It is not a spectacle suited to the viewing of laypersons...'

'Yes, all right,' the Commandant smiled. He was so full of confidence now that nothing could stop him. 'If you feel it will not cause you distress, I have no objection.'

The Surgeon shrugged faintly. He studied the tools in their canvas roll and chose a blade. With his other hand he pulled the blanket down the chief's chest, stopping at the peaks of his pelvis. He considered the body beneath his hands, and placed a fingertip at the small declivity where the collarbones met. The Commandant always anticipated this moment, when a body opened, when the secret interior became known to the waking world and its causes and effects were no longer mere inferences but the evidence of human eyes.

The Surgeon glanced at the other two: the Commandant was alert now and the native woman showed no sign of keeling over.

He pressed, and pointed the blade sharply down into the pool of shadow beside his fingertip.

~

The Commandant waited long beneath the pelican for the words to come.

The sudden burst of confidence had left him once the ribs were open. The grey sadness had returned. A man could not fail to be sad seeing the sister of the dead chief resting a hand on his bare foot, stroking it as though this was merely a painful procedure that must be endured momentarily, rather than what it truly was, a defiling.

A man such as Mannalargenna did not die this way, he had reflected as the Surgeon burrowed. He died fighting, or old age came gently to collect him, or he took himself away into the night and was gone. He did not suffer the fate of rotting alive. Small wonder he had been furious at the end.

But for the Commandant, the rejection burned. Never in all his years had another so fiercely denounced him. The maggots of rumour might feed on reputations, the plight of every man of consequence, but to be confronted eye to eye with such a repudiation, and from a man who would take it, unwithdrawn, to the grave…

He meant to go and make tea. He meant to walk the grounds, take in the evening light and a break in the southerly. He meant to examine the barracks, check on the Catechist, inspect the flagstaff. But his limbs would not obey him and he felt that his weight in the chair was more than he could ever raise to standing. With an effort he took the wick trimmer from the drawer and tapped the cool brass in one palm.

He clipped the string. Took a flint and rolled it thoughtfully. Struck the spark and lit the taper, then the wick. This poor man didn't, couldn't, understand the great transaction that wrapped around them both: bigger than men, bigger than individual wants and needs. He had been the titular head of a handful of families, but nations were moved by different forces.

And if Mannalargenna's worries about country were no more than a personal preoccupation, then so too was his insistence about his mortal remains. To ask a man—though he hadn't asked, he acknowledged that—to contribute his tissue to the great forward march of anatomical knowledge…Well, it incurred no pain now, did it? Why commit to the earth that which could advance human understanding?

He didn't feel convinced of the theories, that was the only real flaw. Doctor Hunter and the London men hovering at his shoulders saw anatomy as the evidence of intelligence, of character and moral worth, and they believed, as fervently as the Commandant did in scripture, that such things as the inclination towards kindness, or the deliberate wish to violate a woman, could be measured in the diameter of a cranial arch. It was nonsense to him. He'd spent enough time in the bush, at close quarters with all manner of people, to know that men came in strange arrangements, and no line could be drawn from lumps in the bones to decency or wit.

But he would send a box to London. Yes, he would. Was he a worse man for doing it anyway, despite his scepticism as to the purpose? What shape was *his* head?

Think it through, he admonished himself. Patronage was the lifeblood of all these endeavours. If it wasn't him who was known in London for his access to such wonders of the natural world as a Vandemonian head, then...then it would be someone else. All very fine to say you're above the work of unclean hands when others were willing to do it.

He turned the lamp up, took a bottle and drew ink into the pen. That was it. An ugly race between ugly competitors, but one he could not avoid and still expect advancement. What would he say to his Maker on the final day? He would say the whole business was inimical to virtue, but worse if lesser men did it.

God, the brandy. Where? In a cabinet by the chiffonier, the very bottle he'd been scrupulously saving for the night when the Governor would arrive. They would sit together—here!—and raise a glass to the King, and His Excellency would toast his remarkable success and his irresistible future. He picked the wax from the neck with a thumbnail and rolled it into a glob between his fingers, then took a glass and splashed the brandy in. The fumes, the warmth. He pressed the wax onto a corner of the waiting page. History: *I will write history.*

A mopoke outside. Listening, no doubt. Was nothing truly private between a man and his God?

Once Spoken,
It Is Truth

The funeral was conducted as previously directed by torch-light, and had a grand and imposing effect. The night was sufficiently dark to render the torchlight lurid. The glare of between forty and fifty lights moving through the dark shades, the sable countenance of the aborigines, the occasion of the scene the interment of the body of a fellow mortal which was borne to the grave on the handcart drawn by the aborigines and followers…it had a solemn and novel effect altogether pleasing and was well calculated to call forth most gratifying reflections…It well deserved the pencil of Glover or some other artist of first rate to delineate.

The procession left from the store at sundown.

It was no great distance. So far from anything else in the world, each part of the settlement pressed close against every other part: the prisoners' barracks and the store, the houses and the garden, the garden and the Commandant's house.

The burial ground lay only yards to the south of the store, where the body had been lying. Locating the graves so near to the business of the living had been a mistake: at the time, those responsible had believed the sight of headstones would be a reminder of Matthew's warning: *ye know neither the day nor the hour.* But no one had anticipated such numbers, and the lumpen graves had become a public calculus of failure. The Commandant often considered what he would say when the Governor arrived, and he had to explain them all.

To give the procession some gravitas, he had them circle the hospital and the gaol. The natives loved pomp. They would be disappointed if the exequy took its truest course and was over within a minute.

The evening was heavy and dark. A west wind pushed over the low forest behind the prisoners' barracks and cast cold rain over them. He walked at the head of the procession beside Tongerlongeter, the Oyster Bay chief. The Commandant had conferred upon him a more magisterial name—King William—and he would now need to anoint him successor to the dead chief. The people who ignored his letters might think themselves powerful, he reflected, but it was he who chose kings.

The men walked beside the cart that carried the coffin, all of them dressed with care in shirts and jackets and shoes. The load on the cart was not heavy: he had been shocked at how emaciated the chief was, there on the table. Under the sister's watchful eye, the Surgeon had recited words like *serous fluid* and *purulent matter* and the Commandant had written them down.

Then they had closed him up again. Not a shred of flesh nor slice of organ had been kept for the collecting jars, and in one sense that was no great loss: the pathologies afflicting the poor man were depressingly obvious.

The faces of the mourners were sombre, as was expected. He had told them there were to be no outbursts of dancing at such a solemn time. The women gathered behind the men, children at their feet, a straggle of the older ones bringing up the rear.

The Commandant eyed the fall of evening on the hill, the summer grass going dark. Anyone who walks beside a coffin considers their own mortality, and when all of this was over he hoped to God he would die in London, among devastated admirers. Borne in a carriage, not dragged in a handcart, to his final rest in the soil of Home.

The lads at the front opened the gate in the picket fence that marked the cemetery. There was a brief rush to be first at this important task: he scolded them for their exuberance. Once inside the burial ground they knew to veer to the left, where the flat ground was humped but unmarked—to the right the ground was reserved for settlers. The grass had not yet grown over the most recent burials; piles of dirty sand, speckled with fragments of limestone.

A handful of the older boys had been instructed to carry burning torches tied to long poles. He had rehearsed this with them: they formed a circle around the grave that had been shovelled out by the Big River men. He waited, the Book of Common Prayer in his joined hands. The gathering settled. He stood atop a small rise in the ground, and now he was taller than his companions. The men laid the coffin on the ropes by the grave, then withdrew. The sounds of the smaller children subsided, the dogs slumped on their skinny flanks at the outside of the group. By and by, the only sound that remained was the hollow pocking of the rain on the coffin.

Bow your heads, my friends.

He was aware of the Catechist out to his right, scowling. The stare, he knew despite the broken gaze, was directed at him: he could feel it like heat. In the end he had forbidden the man to give the eulogy, in part because he had no great familiarity with the deceased, but also to prevent the inevitable lapse into florid nonsense. The stare was sulphurous.

Mannalargenna, principal chief, was a native of the country between St Patricks Head and the Schoutens. He was my constant, my unwavering friend. In all our wanderings through the Gardens of Eden that are your homelands, he was the soul of discretion and trustworthiness and tact.

Another stare, a different one, from directly in front of him. Toogernuppertootenner, wrapped in a cloak and shawl against the wind. In there, eyes like deep wells filled with contempt. He felt no malice for her, only pity that she could not comprehend the forces at work. Like her brother. Some things outranked sorrow.

He was, of course, an ardent convert to the ways of Jesus Christ our Lord and Saviour and on that path to salvation, a salvation he now eagerly awaits, he urged so many of you to join him. Look around you, my friends! Hark to your brothers and sisters, your children, your parents. Take up the example that our dear departed friend has left you: hear the word of our Lord, guiding you. Repent your sins, as our dear friend repented his to me in the very hour of his approaching demise!

What an extraordinary scene they made, he thought. All of them out here, the rain in the torchlight, the faces speckled with droplets and streaked with tears. One or two were afflicted by lusty coughing fits, which detracted from the solemnity, but on balance it was most pleasing. If only such scenes could be more widely witnessed.

> *He will see God, see him face to face, see him the same as I see you and then he will never be sick anymore, never hungry anymore, but he will be happy, happy forever…he will like it, yes, he will like it much. He would not like to go back to his own country. He will have no desire to go there. If you could say to him will you come back to your own country again, he would say No. He would be displeased with you, he would not like to hear you ask him, he would say No. No. I like this place. I like it better than my own country. I like it much. I am happy here. He would say when I was in my own country you fought with me, you talk'd no good… When I was in my own country I was sick, I was hungry, I was cold, I was frightened, I was miserable. But now I am very happy indeed this is a good place, a very good place.*

The Catechist's gaze had left him now, had shifted to watch balefully over the children, gathered to approximate a choir. The sound of his own voice gave him strength, and he heard the fortitude and solace to be got from his words.

> *We spoke at great length yesterday, as you know. I will cherish the memory of that conversation, because he had found peace. He was reflective, and wise. He spoke about all of you, and with such tenderness.*
>
> *I felt very proud in our last hours together, my friends,*

because he said to me, he said: tell them to listen to the Commandant. Read the Bible. Give up all those old places and the memories that don't help you, those ways that lead away from the Lord. The songs, the dancing. Paint your bodies no longer because those are old ways, and the Lord, your God, wishes you to wear the clothes of a civilised race.

A nod to the young ones by the grave. They took up the ropes, ready to lift the coffin into the ground.

And so now we commit him to the earth, with all the solemn respect we would grant an Englishman: the King of England, no less. We would bury him the same.

The coffin descended until it stopped. One man held a spade with a mouthful of earth upon it. Had someone screamed, then and there, had they poured their grief and horror into the night and let it echo off the hill, it would not have been out of place: the night waited for it. The man with the spade looked unsure, until the morning's rehearsal had its effect and he threw the earth onto the lid.

The sound of it landing was a reminder that something foreign was being introduced into the earth. Another spadeful, and another: sharper knocking sounds when the stones in the thin soil hit the timbers. Soon the boards of the coffin were disappearing and the earth was rising to meet the night.

God will tell the angels to carry the chief's soul to heaven.

And the next available ship will carry his head to London. It is not for us to apportion God's burdens.

The Second Kicking of the Dog

...it is an appalling sight to view the mounds of earth now before us where the people are buried, as they are single graves. Each one reminds us that the body of a native lies there. This is their repository of the dead—no white man lies there. These numerous graves contain only the bodies of aborigines. God's will be done.

When the funeral was done and he had written about it, the Commandant returned alone to the graveyard fence and leaned his forearms on the gate, the ends of the timbers picking at his sleeves. He tapped out his pipe and slowly refilled it. The night was darker for the absence of the people and their torches. The gale was abating, smaller sounds now rising to the surface. The trees shivered the rain off themselves in the last of the breeze.

Out there was the new grave, Mannalargenna's. The wages of trust.

He struck a flint, and in its spark he saw eyes reflected back at him from the edge of the tree line to the west. He waited for his vision to adjust: the eyes were low. He struck the flint again and was surprised to see not the wallaby he expected but the black dog, neatly arranged on its haunches.

He worked the pipe until it smouldered and they watched each other. He felt a growing impatience with its cool appraisal. He hissed through his teeth, but it did not move.

'Bugger you,' he said, and it thrilled him. He looked over both shoulders then back at the dog. 'Bugger and fuck you, bloody dog.' The dog only watched him in its unearthly way and the Commandant fell deeper into the eyes and saw all sorts of things in there and wondered if one of them was pity.

He stepped closer. The dog was unworried. Its snout came up slightly to adjust its gaze, that was all.

'You think'—he pointed an admonishing finger at it—'you think you have the right to judge. You think you know. You're above your station, you...' He looked under it. 'All right, you've a cock and balls. But you're no less a bitch...'

He kicked it as hard as he could. This was the second time he'd felt the impact on its body. It was dense enough to stop his leg, soft enough that he imagined the dog's warmth. The blow forced a little air out of it, a vulnerable gasp that flooded the Commandant with shame. But the dog did not fall; nor did it snarl back at him as another kicked dog might. And this time it did not yelp. It merely stepped a short distance away from him. His shame turned back to fury and he went after it, aiming another kick, but now it loped easily through a gap in the pickets of the cemetery fence. He felt no desire to pursue the dog, not out *there*.

'Flaming cunt of a thing,' he said into the night air.

It moved across the cemetery, a black shape on the grass, weaving between the mounds. *It could not be headed there*, he thought. But unerringly, it was moving towards Mannalargenna's grave.

The grave lay fresh on the field, a disturbance in the pale grass. The diggers had done a reasonable job: the box was five feet down, the earth tamped to a faint rise, the largest of the limestones taken away to be used in the Storekeeper's wall.

The dog reached the grave now and took up a position at the foot of it, with its back to the hillside, facing him. Now its head was up again, framed by the sweep of the hill. The tip of its nose gleamed wet in faint reflection of the light that spilled from the settlement.

'Damn your huffling arse, you filthy mutt.'

The rain had stopped and the faint traces of light that reached the cemetery were picked up in glitters on the fronds of the grass and the wet stones. He turned his back on the dog and the grave and headed for his house. Up beyond the natives' huts, a lamp still burned in the hospital window. Unusual for the Surgeon to show such application to his work, he thought.

Reason returned the further he removed himself from the malign presence of the dog. Reason that pushed back the darkness, banished the strange speculations. His boots were filling with water, wicking it out of the soaked grass. He followed the light from the hospital as his feet tried to read the complex hollows and mounds that the animals had made in the ground. As he came past the back of the row of natives' houses he heard their voices, still preoccupied with their sorrows. He should take the opportunity and lock them down for the night; his long day was not quite done.

There was a man seated by the fire amid a huddle of four

women. It was Heedeweek, a whip of bone and sinew, chanting with them. The Commandant remembered Heedeweek from Van Diemen's Land. He rose from the mist of that time with relative clarity: a warrior, a malevolent phantom of the woodlands with ochred hair and terrifying ritual scars over his chest; a man who'd once made a very earnest bid to kill him. Now he was a spent force, his hair neatly trimmed and a standard-issue shirt and jacket covering his inscribed skin. They looked up at his approach: the Commandant positioned himself among them and their voices fell. He saw that Toogernuppertootenner was there among the women. She eyed him levelly.

'I have been clear, my friends,' he said. 'You are to retire to your quarters.'

There was some murmured complaint in languages the Commandant could not understand. He knew they would want to talk long into the light, to sing, to take up their inappropriate dancing. Toogernuppertootenner had her elbows on her knees and her chin in her hands. She appeared to be deep in thought until the others had finished. 'Din come all this way to get locked up,' she said flatly. 'Come here to sing him and be with the people. Besides'—she arched an eyebrow caustically—'why I gotta listen to *you*?'

He knew this game, knew how to slip back into the old ways: the passivity and charm that won him the trust of these people. 'Of course you feel that way,' he began, sitting himself down on the sandy ground with an affected grunt that made him sound old.

It was damp under his backside: he saw now that the natives sat on folded blankets. There was a shifting of eyes that might have been mockery.

'He was an important man, and we spoke of important things

together, he and I. These are sad days for all of us. But this lot'—he swept a hand around the terrace, where they were still gathered in families and clans—'they look to you for leadership. I cannot have them out here in the cold or I will have more sickness, more death. There's no good in lamenting him if it leads to more lamenting.'

He shuffled uncomfortably as the numbness radiated up one leg. But they were listening. Sullen, but he had them. 'If you show this to them, if you set the example by going inside for the night, I am better able to control it, because you are family. I need you to show them how to grieve well.'

The sister was watching him sceptically.

'Cold,' he muttered to himself, and drew his coat closer around him. He looked up hopefully now. 'We have sent him off well, yes?'

Toogernuppertootenner drew a long breath. 'No good, none of it.' She looked down, down at her long fingers resting on the ground between her crossed legs. 'Tell you what, mister. I can maybe ask them people to go sleep inside now, if you like'—she raised her intonation on that last word and it charmed him—'if you promise you won't lock us in.'

The Commandant thought about her proposal. There was no mad rush to do what needed to be done: it was more a matter of ensuring it was done in stealth. 'You are a capable negotiator,' he smiled. 'I will give you that. Very well.'

They left it there for the moment, and allowed the sounds of the night to fill the space between them. Again, that feeling the Commandant often had in the night: that they were an isolated point of light in a great dark world; that there was them, and nothing else but sea and rock, and that time didn't exist, or if it did it only worked at the wearying of human bodies.

'When are you planning on leaving us?'

Her face took on an inscrutable quality. 'Wind gettin up tomorrow. Think we go early, eh.'

Early. He turned the idea over in his mind. This woman was formidable but she was incapable of guile. 'Very well. What assistance can I offer you?'

She shrugged. 'Don't need nothin. You lot oughta stay in bed.'

The Great Hall

It is cool inside the great hall. The air is heavy and still: it does not carry an admixture of insects and fine grit. It carries nothing but aroma. Not the sea and its ever-rotting burden, but something clean and old and scholarly.

The people are gone. The living ones, at least. There are no students, no teachers, no researchers or ordinary gawkers. Just the long silence that admits the clocking of his footfalls. Such a beautiful time to be there. He has a sense that he is floating rather than walking, but the clocking persists.

He gazes down at the marble floor—how could he be walking? He senses he is aloft, up around the balustrades of the mezzanines. There is a sugary delight in his veins and his lungs draw deeply from the cool sweet air and it fuels him like he is a living furnace, and he feels a great rippling strength in his muscles and a delicious anticipation in his mind. For this place must surely be the repository of all he has striven for.

Level with him and soaring through the vault is the giant skeleton of a whale, hung from cables in mid-air. Other whales fly beside it like Valkyries, headed to a decisive battle never to be fought. Their jaws are wired to grimace, fins splayed down as though a wingbeat has taken place synchronously among the cetacean flock.

Below them on the floor marches an army of terrestrial creatures: oxen, bison, yak and buffalo. A mammoth, an ordinary cow and, out at the flanks towards the walls, the graceful sprinters of the cervids: gazelle, elk, caribou and deer.

Greedily he gulps in the vast room: it must be, he thinks, the same one his grandfather led him through when he was a small boy. He held that giant thumb then, peered in awe around his trouser legs to behold the curiosities in the cabinets.

He sees it all again now, but this time as its master, all timidity banished. He belongs, and he is welcome. He sees the galleries, the pillars and the intermediate ceilings. The clerestory and the skylights above, the geometrics of the mosaic tiling and the honeyed glow of the timbers warm and varnished. So great is the block of air the space holds that it is hazy towards its far end, where the incoming light is picked up in beams and the whales are swimming in it, in leagues of faintly clouded seawater.

But now he is descending, just slowly, and he is down, down on the gleaming floor. The spaces are cramped, made into a maze by the marching animals and by rows and rows of display cases, each a rectangular block of glass panes with thin timber frames, inviting him to peer in. Bones in perfect rows, descending in size like the hammers of a piano. Daguerreotypes, amphorae, crystals and seashells and scorpions. Butterflies exquisitely pinned so they flutter above their white card backdrop. Eggs of a hundred kinds, with cards that say plain things such as *gull*, *serpent* and *shark*. A stone sarcophagus, lid ajar. A slender bark canoe, balanced on a beam high above the animals. The head of a man, his mouth half open in mid-speech, scalp and skull quartered to reveal the snaking canyons of the brain. His eyes pleading *end this*.

Unseen currents pull him deeper into the collections.

In an open-fronted box, presented at the centre of a purple velvet shroud, the dried mass of an intestine, sliced to reveal the tangles of a tapeworm. A crowd of jars, each a foot and half tall, the cylindrical glass distorting the contents: buttery yellow shapes like blobs of lard. He peers, he squints, and in his belly the horror grows. They are foetuses, arranged in ways that suggest the curator was engaged in a sour joke: hands clasped over genitals, eyes pressed angrily shut and bulbous, swollen foreheads wedging the cylinders like cork stoppers. They match each other, choreographed into a chorus line of wickedly prancing demons. The one at the head of the display is wrapped in a spiral of its own umbilical cord, the striated coils of it wafting bloody threads into the preserving fluid.

He has lost control of his tour now, and he knows that none of this is real. But the realisation is of no comfort because he cannot escape it. The dream is not done with him and it will not release him until certain things have been seen.

The amulets he had confiscated, hand-sized bundles of animal skin that bulge with secret contents, there under dim light on alienating glass, a square card standing off at a discreet distance, cursive describing them. It is the cards that are accusing him, he now thinks. He snatches at them but his hand bashes uselessly against the glass pane.

And here are the spears he had taken in Van Diemen's Land. The stones he took and derided as the dumb fruit of primitive thought: now he sees their complex edges and their varied uses. A child's skull, turned away from him so that it is a smooth orb, centrally punctured by a bullet hole that would admit a thumb. An entire adult skeleton, forlornly downcast, feet on a small wooden block that speaks of crucifixion, or its aftermath as the arms hang limply. There is an iron ring beneath the jaw, resting on the clavicles. Secured by a bolt.

Behind him, the foetuses are stirring just a little, bobbing in their fluid. They anticipate fresh horrors. He cannot look back at them.

Now a shelf stretches away from him and into the gloom beneath the low ceiling formed by a mezzanine. The entire edifice of the museum has shrunk into this tunnel of narrowed vision. He can't focus, he can't focus…

And now he can and there are objects arranged along the shelf.

Heads.

Mannalargenna, arranged on a bower of his own ribs. Nobie. Noura, King William, Heedeweek, Moulteheerlargenna. A voice in him begins to plead, *these ones are not dead, they're not dead*, but he understands the sequence now. Andromache, Hector, Kitty, Pillah. These are not skulls and they are not preserved in any way. They are sentient human heads, fully fleshed and racked in agony and no matter where he looks along their assembled row, they watch him with eyes beyond pity or hatred or sorrow or supplication. The eyes are far away, ever distant and unconcerned with his presence, observing him as one might observe the struggles of ant.

And further along the row the skin on the heads is becoming paler, leaching to greys and parchment whites, sickly pink like rotted fruit, and he realises now that these are their own heads: his and fellows'. The Overseer, burnt by sun and wind to shades of brick dust. The Coxswain and the Sergeant. The Surgeon, adipose and bulging above his cleanly severed throat. The Catechist, twisted against his own tendons and splitting ripely at his scars, a fragment of clavicle suspended from the stranding muscles of his throat. The Storekeeper, eyes closed and mouth slightly ajar: humble and good and stone dead. Lastly, as the dread surges to meet it, his own head: caught in a desperate cry of alarm, eyes wide open and fixed upon some terrible vision that his murdered self can see and his dreaming self can only await.

And as he recoils he is spinning and tumbling, the floor and the great vaults alternating and the speed of the rotations increasing, and to strike any surface at this speed would mean certain death and still the centre of the revolutions is the shelf and the objects piled upon it and *one cannot die in a dream* he tells himself defiantly but he is no longer sure of it.

He slams—against what he cannot tell—and his body makes an almighty bang and then he ricochets through open air and dust and light and slams again and there is another great percussion when it happens, and then another and another, and he is separating from himself now, separating from the dream and dragging himself into the dim world of his room.

He felt sure there was banging but it had stopped. He was exhausted, caught in a tangle of sheets and greased with a pallid sweat that stank of guilt. Momentary silence, then the banging again.

The door.

'Wait,' he called weakly but the banging went on. 'Wait!'

A lamp. Trousers, a shirt. As he fumbled the boots onto his feet the banging resumed and he made a long groan of frustration and weariness. His fingers were shaky with it, his breath feathery. He swung open the door and there was the Surgeon, fist raised to hammer it again.

'It's the Catechist,' he said grimly. 'You must come at once.'

The Asp and the Catechist

The scream reached him when he was halfway there.

He had let the Surgeon go on ahead while he comported himself. Stepping out into the damp and the dark, he felt like the night had become indefinite and that everything now would have to be negotiated in shadow.

There was a prickling over his back and his forehead, and his legs were not entirely stable.

He tried to place the voice that had screamed. An adult reduced by agony to the piteous wail of a suffering child. The scream diminished now into weeping, and the weeping sounded like the voice of the Catechist, but broken. There was nothing he could imagine that would reduce a man of such arrogance to scream that way.

A crowd of the natives had gathered around the hospital building. Far from sharing in his shock, or showing evidence of any distress, they were talking and laughing animatedly. Some were dancing, and he had an ugly sense that the screaming was music to them. A boy was excitedly pointing at the stonework down low, near where the doorway steps met the edge of the path. *Lookit, sir!* There was a great splatter of blood there, visible in the lamplight against the silver rocks and staining the grasses below. He looked at it in puzzlement: it was clear that nobody had bled there because the blood had not fallen vertically. It appeared to have sprayed sidelong from the doorway.

He ignored the lad and addressed the nearest adult, a woman named Narrukker. 'What happened here?' he demanded, pointing at the blood.

She nodded in the direction of the interior. 'Surgeon fella,' she said, strangely jubilant. 'He done for the preacher.'

There would be no further explanation from them. He was on his own: they parted as he came through and when a new round of screams emanated from inside they began to jump about again, heedless of his presence. As he placed a foot on the doorstep the complete understanding came to him: they hated the man with the entirety of their souls.

He threw the door open. The Catechist was on a stretcher in the centre of the room, his bare feet facing the door. He was otherwise clothed, but the left sleeve of his shirt had been ripped upwards so that it hung in strips to either side of his exposed arm.

So much, so much for the Commandant to take in. The man's chin pointed way back; the skin of his throat mottled scarlet. He was groaning at the ceiling, his massive right hand gripping the side of the stretcher with a contortive power that had bent the supporting timber.

His left arm was turned slightly outward so the diverging veins of his forearm faced upwards. The forearm rested in a pile of bloodstained towels. A ligature of stout cloth had been fastened around his biceps and in the wide centre of the forearm, where a lag's tattoo might lie, a deep slice of flesh had been cut out, exposing the fat and sinews beneath his skin. The excision was the length and width of a finger, and at least half as deep.

The Surgeon stood off to one side, bent over a bench. He did not look up at the Commandant's entry: a range of bottles and flasks of varying sizes stood on the surface before him, along with something so wildly out of place that the Commandant's heart skipped a beat: a set of teeth, grinning evilly at him. They were the Catechist's, removed to protect him from himself.

'What in God's name…?'

The Surgeon met his gaze. 'Snakebite. Over at his house.' He was rummaging among his glassware. 'Lord knows what happened. He was under the floor or something.'

The Commandant understood that the excised flesh was where the bite had been—the surface of the arm surrounding it was bruised and swollen, blue-black and shining as if it might burst. The man rocked his head from side to side, breath coming and going in groans and sobs. There was dark vomit down one cheek and a pool of it splattered on the flagstones beneath him. Blood flowed in bright creeks from the wound, spreading on the cloths.

There would be no sleep, not now.

The Surgeon was pouring fluid from a brown glass bottle into a smaller flask. He averted his face slightly as though the liquid gave off noxious fumes. When he was done, he recorked the brown bottle. He took another and poured its contents into a flask, which he held up and sniffed.

'How long ago?'

'An hour or so. Least, that's when they found him. Delirious. As florid as his average sermon, actually. Poison's moving fast.'

He frowned. 'That lad, Whelk. Tangled up in it somehow. Think our preacher might've been roughing him up when it happened.'

The Commandant nodded at the flask in the Surgeon's hand. 'What's that?'

The Surgeon looked at the flask then tipped it into his mouth, swallowed and sighed loudly. 'Brandy. Settles the nerves.'

The Commandant regarded him with open disgust. 'Why is there blood outside?'

'I bled him,' replied the Surgeon, as though the answer was hopelessly obvious. 'Two full quarts. No effect whatsoever.'

'Can you not—' The Commandant held his temper. 'Could you not have disposed of the blood less theatrically?'

The Surgeon shrugged. 'I suppose so. I'll keep it in mind.' He turned now towards the prone form of the Catechist. He rested his hands on the man's chest, the stance that broadcast his uncertainty. He turned and took the brandy bottle from the bench and tried to pour it down the Catechist's throat: the man had enough strength left to turn his head and spit between his groans, so that it trickled down his cheek. Then the fluid caught in his gullet and he coughed a fine spray into the air that flickered golden in the lamplight. The Surgeon pinched the man's nostrils and watched until the mouth gasped open again, then shoved the neck of the bottle in and shook it. The brandy sloshed in the bottle until returning bubbles indicated that the Catechist had finally swallowed.

The Surgeon held the bottle up to the light and examined it. 'Third of a pint,' he said to himself. 'Have to do.' When he saw the scepticism on the Commandant's face he added, 'Aids the circulation.' He turned back to the bench and replaced the bottle. Now he had the smaller flask in his hand, the one he had been filling from the brown bottle.

'Help, please,' he muttered. The Commandant stepped forward, hands pointed helplessly.

'Hold his feet down. Don't breathe in.'

The Catechist's whole body clenched: he appeared to know what was coming. He opened his mouth and bared his helpless gums and a long, strangled sound issued from his throat that sounded like *No*.

'Brave now, my friend,' murmured the Surgeon. He looked once over the length of the man's body and, satisfied with the grip that the Commandant had on the ankles, he took hold of the wrist below the wound and poured the contents of the flask onto the exposed flesh. As the Catechist screamed and writhed once again, the smell struck the Commandant and his eyes blurred with tears.

Ammonia.

He imagined it burning at the delicate tissues that the Surgeon had exposed, fizzing and corroding, eating at the good tissue along with the poisoned. The three of them were racked by coughing as the Catechist thrashed beneath their hands. The flask was knocked clear and smashed on the floor.

The Catechist's coughing turned to wheezing, then his breath ceased to rebound and became faint. The Surgeon threw him a sharp look. 'He's out. Vile old creature—I'd thought him tougher.' He turned his back again and rested both hands on the bench, drumming his fingers.

He sighed. 'So little written on this. The great elapids…a neurotoxin…more potent in the spring and early summer. The animal is only beginning to feed, you see: been dormant, poison stored up, stored up for months. Can deliver a tremendous dose at once, tremendous shock to the system. Miracle he's still with us.'

He ran a hand through his thick hair and propped the other

one on a hip, deep in thought. A decision apparently made, he turned his back and rummaged among the receptacles again. When he turned around he was holding two heavy tumblers of brandy.

'Come,' he said. 'Let us take in the weather and consider all this.'

'But he…'

'He's not going anywhere.' The Surgeon shrugged. 'We've either got him or we've lost him.' He proffered one of the glasses and the Commandant took it. The Surgeon raised his own glass mischievously. 'A toast, gentlemen. The King!' He took a quick sip, strode past and opened the door. When the Commandant followed, he found the Surgeon seated on the doorstep. Beyond him the dark world awaited dawn.

The residents had all moved off. The hill to the east loomed darker than the night sky and a swell in King William Bay made a rushing sound under the wind to the north of them. The Surgeon had his drink cupped in both hands between his knees. 'Those visitors,' he began slowly, 'took a dim view of our chaplain in there.'

The Commandant considered this but did not respond.

'Did you notice?' He looked around, fixed the Commandant with a peculiar stare. 'They made it fairly clear that they recognised him.'

'It might not be wise to set too much store by that lot,' the Commandant replied calmly.

'Yes, but'—the Surgeon put the glass on the ground at his feet now—'a thing I've noticed about this place is the wanderers that pass through. This island, that island…some distant past on the mainland…Not all of them are necessarily who they say they are. You must have noticed it?'

The Commandant poked a dubious lip.

'This one,' the Surgeon continued, indicating over his shoulder and back into the dark interior of the room. 'You really think he's who he says he is?'

'A Catechist? Why yes, I've seen the letters.'

'And were they beyond the ability of a skilled forger?'

The Commandant snorted. 'I deal with volumes of correspondence in a month that would fill lifetimes for other men. I know the signs of inauthenticity.'

'Wouldn't we both say he preaches as though he's possessed?'

The Commandant considered this for a moment. 'Wouldn't that tend to the conclusion that he *is* who he says he is? A fairground huckster couldn't summon that kind of ardour.'

'Mm. Perhaps.' He swirled the glass, drank from it. 'But I'll go further: do you ever think it odd that you had all these people brought here to resettle them, to create a home for them, but those of us given responsibility for them are all in transit to something else?'

The Commandant shrugged irritably. He was too tired for this. 'I don't follow.'

'I'll speak frankly, then. This is a nest of liars and all of us are lying.'

The Commandant glared at him.

'No one else can hear us. Your prestige is undimmed. But consider: *he* is not who he says he is. His wife is party to his depravities, whatever they may be. She may look like blood pudding but she is the shrewdest woman I ever met. Now I do not spare myself: as I've said to you, I am here to handle as many bodies as I can so as to secure myself a teaching position. I will leave here with the greatest of alacrity the moment I can do so, and the welfare of these natives is of no concern to me beyond a practical interest in what works upon them and what does not.' He paused, sipped. 'And that's just *us!* The men in London and in Sydney who decide these things are no more interested in the fate of this place and its inhabitants than they are in the tribes of the Amazon. A colony outside of a colony; a troublesome addendum.'

'I saved an entire *people…*' sighed the Commandant. This was just nonsense, piled upon tragedy and shock.

'Did you?' chuckled the Surgeon. 'I've delivered more autopsies than infants. Anyway, you're assuming everyone shares your interest in saving them. Who asked you to do it?'

The Commandant spoke through gritted teeth. 'The Governor welcomed my approach. Funded me…equipped me to go out and find these people and bring them in.' He suddenly thought he might fall asleep in the middle of the sentence.

'Yes, but that's different from *asking* you to do it. You came to him, he saw the expediency in it, he agreed. Didn't want a slaughter on his watch, and you presented a neat solution.' The Surgeon regarded him with open scorn. 'I will suggest this to you. You will reject it, of course. But you, like me, are here to advance yourself. Saviour, diplomat, maker of a new society… you already have half an eye to the next horizon, do you not? If they live and prosper, it was through your agency. If they die out, you were there, cradling them through their passage into extinction. Really, there is no outcome here that can fail to advance your prospects. Which is more—'

'How *dare* you!'

'—than one can say for the natives.' There was no sign on the Surgeon's face that the Commandant's outrage concerned him.

'You are an inferior physician,' the Commandant grunted as he stood. 'And your incompetence has brought you to your natural level, an inferior posting. I care not for your idle opinions.'

'Ah,' smiled the Surgeon. 'But you *do* care. The opinions of others are *everything* to you.'

'Very well, then.' He stopped in the motion of opening the door. 'Since you're so well informed: what would you have done differently?'

There was a moment in which the Commandant thought the Surgeon had no answer, and it satisfied him deeply. But the caustic smile returned.

'I would not have made promises I had no intention of keeping.'

For a time there was only the night-thumping wallabies and the dull roar of the sea. A knot of fury inside the Commandant drove him to go inside and slam the door on this, even as exhaustion pinned him where he stood.

'Now,' the Surgeon continued brightly, 'speaking of prospects, let us go and have another tilt at the chaplain, shall we?' He got up, took his glass and pushed past. The Commandant remained there on the doorstep a moment longer. His eyes strained in the dark to make out the expanses of grass to the east and the west of him, the flimsy pickets of the barracks and the scraggling margins of the bush. He knew he was searching and he cursed himself for doing it. Somewhere out there…

A thin outcrop of she-oak saplings near the stockyards, a place he knew to be shady in the daylight. A shape that broke the regular striping of the pale young trees. There. The black dog, looking back at him. He took a dozen steps out into the night and squinted.

The collar was gone.

~

The Surgeon had again taken up the bottle of ammonia. From a fine timber box, he produced a hypodermic and screwed a long needle into it. This he left on the bench, lying there like a promise of violence while he arranged a metal canister and a small ceramic bowl beside it.

The Catechist was stirring only slightly, no longer delirious but unresponsive. He opened and closed his mouth, making a clacking noise. The Surgeon listened, took a sponge and dunked it in a jug of water. He pushed the sponge into the Catechist's mouth and squeezed it. Then he waved the canister under the ruined nose; seeing no effect, he took the bowl and a spatula and began to smear a dark brown paste on the Catechist's hands. It looked futile to the Commandant: more than that, it looked ridiculous.

'What are you doing?'

'Poultice. Mustard, some other herbs. Alleviates internal congestion. The venom has a coagulant effect, so it may'—he rubbed vigorously at the hands—'it may just…'

Still, the Catechist lay insensible. The Surgeon frowned and stepped around to the soles of his feet, bumping the Commandant out of the way as he did so. Here he repeated the process. Here, again, there was no result. The stench of mustard filled the air as the ammonia dissipated.

The Surgeon went on massaging the feet, making thick squelching noises with the paste. The Catechist only grunted faintly. His face had gone a deathly white. The Surgeon squeezed the feet a little more, then slapped one of them lightly and walked to the bucket, where he washed the muck from his hands and dried them with a cloth. The Commandant was intrigued to see what would be the man's next move in this increasingly desperate charade, but to his disappointment the Surgeon wandered over to the desk in the corner and returned with a book. He settled himself in a chair on the far side of the Catechist's prone form, took spectacles from his trouser pocket and opened the book.

'You're going to *read*?'

The Surgeon ostentatiously placed a finger between the pages and closed the book. 'Up to him what happens next. I can no more drive events than you can. So, it's Ovid for the time being.' He made half a motion to pick the book up again but stopped, a thoughtful look on his face. 'The past is ravenous, is it not?'

The Commandant had stopped listening. He was thinking about snakes. Despite all the sightings—the tiger snakes and the fatter ones that lived around the dam, the tiny thin ones that the children picked up unafraid—he had not had cause to record an instance of snakebite since he'd taken charge of the settlement; nor had he read of one in any of the reports from the men who'd had command before him. Trugernana had stood on a snake at Green Island a month ago, but miraculously the thing hadn't bitten her. The bullock driver—Moffat?—had complained often of seeing them cross his path. *If one of them stings the animal sir I may become trapped under the load*…but no; no bite.

The Surgeon droned on, oblivious. 'History devours everything behind us, leaves it in husks. And sometimes'—his eyes widened and he sat forward in the chair—'sometimes, it rears right up and takes a bite out of the present.'

Disinterment

The dawn came eventually and the Commandant felt it as a flood of mercy amid the raucous disputes of the crows and currawongs. Never in all his days had he woken to the gentle lilt of birdsong; in the London of his youth it was hawkers and night-men and here, for as long as he could recall, it was these profane creatures: Irishmen with feathers. Today he welcomed even these.

It felt like weeks since the funeral: it had been nine hours. The Surgeon was nodding off in his chair, and the patient remained as he had been for hours: hovering at the border of unbeing. The Commandant climbed wearily from his chair and slipped away: he had other business to attend to.

The sickly flotsam of the night washed over him, the dream in him still despite the grotesque intervening reality of the Catechist's ordeal. He ambled homeward, waiting for reason to re-establish itself, and soon it did: he remembered the importance of the day. The visitors. The grave. He dressed hurriedly and did not bother to shave his whiskers, just shoved a hat on, pushed his arms through a coat and rushed from the house.

There was little sign of activity around the natives' terrace. Old Heedeweek was there again, boiling a pot of water in the blue smoke of a reluctant fire. He looked up, waved in the direction of the beach at Lillie's Bay, and returned to poking the twigs. The Commandant hurried on towards the wide bay to the south and soon he saw the departing backs of the visitors, meandering over the rises that bordered the coast. Their vessel had been drawn up on the sand, the mast tilted at an angle as the hull rested on one side.

He watched them receding into the distance, belongings draped over shoulders and, in one case, slung between two of them. They seemed forlorn, alone with each other, and for the first time the Commandant saw them as mournful, not merely as mourners. He regretted much of this episode, and now he regretted having treated them so officiously. On the other hand, he thought, they were gone—and without trouble. *Excellent*.

He detoured off the beach track to the smaller trail that led to his customary lookout above Lillie's Beach. Get this done and then sleep, he told himself. The geese honked out of his way as he walked, powder grey against the straw-green tussocks. The sun was rising behind the hill: its light had touched the peaks of Hummock Island out at sea, but the bay and the boat and the people below him were still softened in pastels. One could only keep trying. Persevere with the Lord's work and endure the slings and arrows.

They had the boat in the shallows now. People were wading through the drifts of dead seagrass and climbing aboard, rocking it from beam to beam. The bags and bundles were passed over the gunwale and when all was done and settled, they unfurled their sail. Toogernuppertootenner was right: the early brush of the breeze on the water promised a day of gales. *Another* day of gales. Near his feet the finches were working over the seeds on the grasses, visible only by the startling blaze of red through their eyes.

The last of the visitors, a young man the Commandant hadn't noticed, stood waist-deep in the shallows, holding his arms high as people do when the chill of the water makes them reluctant. At a signal from one of the women he gave the hull a shove and heaved himself aboard. The boom swung into trim, the sails filled and they were underway.

Relief overtook him. He turned his back on them and started out for the settlement.

~

The sergeant met him at the door of the barracks.

A short man, hard-bitten. The Commandant felt the contempt emanating from him, a distaste he made no effort to conceal. Something a military man might feel for a civilian. *It'll be me in the breach when your peace-mongering fails.*

'I have them ready,' he said. 'As you asked.'

'Good. Go ahead.'

The sergeant led him through the building and out a back door. There, in a tiny parade ground, stood an assembled company of men, half-uniformed. They carried shovels, a pick-axe, a pinch bar. Two of them bore a wooden crate, slung between them by rope handles, and in it he could see a long flensing knife, a bundle of muslin and a smaller, square box made of light timber. If they understood the nature of their task, they showed no sign.

'What of the natives?' asked the Commandant.

'I have a separate detail taking them up past the Stony Castle for a hunting expedition. Up to the grasstree plains. They are most excited to go. Sir.'

'All of them?'

'Cep the young lad, the…Whelk, sir. He's still in his bed after the matter with the chaplain.'

'Very well.' He'd forgotten to find out about that aspect of the night's drama. He'd have to check on the boy when this was done. He took the watch from his pocket. 'And when will the rest of them be heading off?'

'Already sent the detail over to the huts. If you allow for their arsing about, sorry sir, be gone in ten minutes or so.'

And so they waited there, awkwardly slouched about as the morning warmed and the wind picked up. The Commandant had brought his journal and pen, and he took the opportunity to bring his notes up to date: they were a week behind. But as soon as he had begun writing, the sergeant's shadow fell across the page.

'Yes?'

'Just wondering, sir. The chaplain. How does he fare?'

The Commandant made a show of lying his pen on the page. 'He—er—he shows no sign of recovery. I'm afraid it doesn't look good.'

'Be fascinatin for the Surgeon, I'm sure.'

The Commandant looked him square in the eye. Was he goading him? There was no trace of insolence there, no clue to his intent. He examined the watch again.

'Perhaps we might move off?'

The sergeant raised his chin in the direction of the soldiers and they stood and lifted their various loads again. As they filed out and over the flat ground towards the cemetery, the Commandant couldn't help but look back over his shoulder. There, out in the distance, he could make out the ant specks of the departing natives, headed northeast on the grass towards the hunting grounds beyond the great boulder known as Stony Castle. They were a mile or more away, surrounded by the swirling dark motes of their dogs, whose excited barking carried all the way back. He wondered if *that* dog was among them: he hoped it was. The settlement was plunged in an unnatural silence. The flies were up now, and the men whose hands were occupied had to snuff at them with their breath to shoo them away. When the Commandant reached the cemetery gate his sleeves were damp with the sweat from his armpits. The backs of his hands were slick with it, the tiny hairs standing up to find the breeze. He took the timber gate in his hands and swung it open for the soldiers to follow. As they passed through in a rich stew of human smell he looked out into the field, at the graves in their rows. He held the gate in his hands and thought again, briefly, of the dog. The place looked so much less forbidding in this light; the idea of the dog as some kind of harbinger seemed foolish.

To an unfamiliar eye it would be difficult to find the grave that one sought. The symmetry of the rows resembled something surveyed for construction, though the burials could have randomly quilted the hillside and it wouldn't have mattered. The grass was flattened in a wide circle around Mannalargenna's grave by the previous night's mourners. He looked down at it and frowned: there were stones there after all. The diggers must have missed them. He took a young corporal by the arm and pointed them out.

'Go back and fetch a barrow, and get those—see? There...and

there, and those ones—over to the pile for the Storekeeper's wall, will you?' The lad turned mutely back the way they had come.

'How long, you think? Sir,' asked the sergeant, looking north in the direction of the boulder. He splashed water from a flask onto the back of his neck.

'Two hours to get up there, two there and two back. No rush.'

One of the corporals set his shovel in the earth and began to heft it out, and another started work on the opposite side. The tools rang as they stabbed at the ground. Sweat shone on the workers and pooled and dripped and, as they threw the dirt behind them, it blew back and swirled around them. Before long the fine sand had encrusted the sheen on their arms and faces and they were coated in it. One of them stopped to screw the grit out of his eyes with his fingers.

The Commandant urged them on, and they made piles of dirt behind them. The wildflowers that had been left on the grave, tied in schoolhouse string, were buried. When the soldiers were puffing loudly and one of them stopped to examine the blisters on his hands, the sergeant stood them down and another two took over. The Commandant watched one of the first two recovering his breath: a mere lad, and yet the deadened look in his eyes was already unmistakable.

The sun kept climbing and the heat built. The wind was gusty enough to dry sweat but it was a cruel northerly, a pestilent air that carried flies. After an hour the Surgeon wandered over in shirtsleeves, looking cool beneath his hat. 'How goes it?'

The Commandant felt all of the heat and frustration of the morning issuing from his collar like steam. 'Don't you have a patient to attend to?'

A wry smile. 'Well, yes. But he's in no hurry. Fiddly business from here on, I suspect. Must discuss an approach when you're, er, done here.' He leaned over the pit and looked in. 'Do you know what you'll require from me?'

He had made no attempt at discretion, and did not lower his voice. The Commandant glanced at the sergeant and the nearby soldiers and hissed at him.

'Just have a…a bowl and the necessary packing. And *shut up about it.*'

'Mm-hm.' A grating smile and he was gone, ambling away over the field. The soldiers resumed their labours, stopping at intervals to pick up rocks and hurl them aside. The grave seemed to be full of rocks. The Commandant had seen the pile that the gravediggers had removed in the afternoon—how did this place generate more and more rocks, in clean paddocks and garden beds, and now graves? The only thing these fields produced in abundance, aside from tussocks, was limestone. Every time the soldiers thrust again with their tools, there was a ringing sound and they'd have to scrabble with their hands to remove yet another pot-sized chunk of the damned stuff. It was slowing them down and draining their strength.

It was a relief, then, when one of the shovels struck timber. The man wielding it, older than the others and burnt pink by the fierce sun, stood in the hole with his legs propped wide. As he breathed heavily from the exertion, he suddenly burst into a violent fit of coughing and gagging, and leaned over the side of the pit to vomit on the heap he had made. When he was done, he drew a forearm across his mouth and looked up sheepishly at the sergeant.

'Pardon sir,' he muttered. 'Swallered a fly.'

The others—the Commandant among them—crowded around the top of the grave to see in. The soldier looked up, uncertain. The foul puddle that had issued from his guts lay hot in the sun beside him; he caught a whiff of it and carefully ladled a spadeful of dirt over it.

The sergeant pointed at the sliver of exposed wood. 'Scrape it back,' he said, and the soldier drew the blade horizontally. He worked the shovel back and forth until the four-inch planks of the coffin's lid were exposed, then rested the long handle across his waist while all of them peered down. The timber looked new where it had been scraped.

'Jump out o there, George,' said the sergeant.

He nodded to the Commandant, who took the pinch bar from where it had been left on the grass. As he placed his hands on both sides of the excavation he looked around himself at the exhausted soldiers and their sergeant, at the heaps of rocky earth disturbed now for the second time in all of eternity, and the fierce sky and the hills and the scrub and…there.

The black dog, perched regally on a nearby grave mound, paws forward and pointed at them all, head up and alert. Watching.

One of the soldiers sat beside the wheelbarrow, and on the wheelbarrow there lay a rifle. The timber stock faced them and the muzzle was directed out towards the empty ground of the hills. The Commandant looked at the black metal of the barrel, hot in the sun, and looked again at the dog. The soldier looked back at him, sullen yet compliant. It would only take a word to make it happen.

He cursed under his breath and picked his way down into the grave, to where the soldier had been standing. Once he occupied the same position, with his feet either side of the edges of the coffin, the lip of the grave was six inches over his head and a sharp angle of shade covered his lower body and the bottom of the hole. It was cooler in there. He was about to prise at the timber but stopped and looked up again at the sergeant.

'Pass me the, er...'—he gesticulated—'would you?'

The sergeant looked where the Commandant was pointing. He picked up the flensing knife by the blade and offered the handle to the Commandant in the grave. The Commandant felt a sudden wave of reluctance, a dawning revulsion at the trespass.

The sergeant had sensed it. 'Sir?'

They locked eyes for a moment, then the Commandant wiped the sweat from his forehead, took up the bar and drove it into the thin gap between the coffin timbers. He prised them apart: there was a squeak, then a loud crack as the planking gave way. He bent low and took the edge of the splintered plank in his hand and heaved at it. With another cracking noise it came free completely. He lifted the fragment and pointed it skyward: a pair of hands from above took it from him.

At first the Commandant did not understand what he was seeing in the long strip he had exposed. He took the edge of the next plank and tore that one away also, tossed it carelessly upwards. He had not breathed. He looked up at the faces crowded around the rim of the grave and saw the same confusion on them as well.

Two downward thrusts with his boot and he'd removed a third plank.

The coffin was empty.

The Visitors Depart

The Commandant ran out of air on the way to the lookout above Lillie's Beach.

He stopped, bent down and rested his hands on his knees. His body heaved up and down with ragged breaths. The flies caught up with him and he swished angrily at them as he looked down and waited for the burning in his lungs to subside.

He tried to think clearly. He and the Surgeon had been with Toogernuppertootenner the entire time when the body was in the storehouse for the post-mortem. There was a brief period after that when everyone on the settlement was at the evening meal ahead of the funeral…in theory it was an opportunity, but he felt sure all of the newcomers were accounted for during those hours. The funeral itself? Impossible.

His breathing had slowed, and he spat hot saliva on the grass, wiped it from his chin with his sleeve. He started running again, and felt the burning return as the ground rose towards his lookout. He was spent. He slowed to a walk and snatched the watch from his waistcoat pocket: midday.

They had done it overnight. They had gone and dug him up: he could not imagine how, or how many of them it had taken to get down to the coffin, remove the body and repack the grave without detection, but they had done it.

And now he remembered the load he had watched them carrying across the field at dawn. The last of the great Vandemonian chiefs. Did they understand nothing at all? They had robbed generations of the opportunity to study him, to reflect upon what had been lost. In death, he was the property of empire, and by no measure was he theirs. Damn them!

He reached the crown of the little hill and looked out over the water. Away in the south he could see the angry masses of the granite peaks, the low slump of Green Island and the cone of Chappell on the windblown sea. And there between them he saw the sail he'd watched unfurling that very morning.

The damned thing was whispering to him that he had not been careful enough.

How the Catechist Got Bit

In the days before the death of Mannalargenna, the Storekeeper had noticed a change in Whelk. He'd become even less social among the older people. He went to them with food, sat attentively when they sang or told stories and he had done his part at the funeral—he was dutiful, the Storekeeper thought—but it was a struggle. He no longer sought their gossip and recollections.

The Storekeeper struggled to bracket the time in his mind: it was possible that all of this dated from the death of Pipi, and that it was simply more noticeable now.

The crescents had grown halfway up his thumbnails, and their colour was fading. He wondered if the same deep ache had cast rings in his bones, or pebbles in his organs. Would his body one day cough them up when the grief had moved through him? And where would it go then, when it had passed out the ends of his fingers and evaporated into the world?

He was lonely, tired of his thoughts just swirling and eddying to nowhere, with nobody to help him sort them into useful and useless. He feared he had lost some important plank of restraint, or common sense.

A day came when he opened the store and immediately felt sure there were voices speaking to him from beneath the floor. He lowered himself to his knees and placed both his palms on the dry boards. He turned his ear to the timber and strained to hear what it was they wanted from him. He could smell the floor's wax, and he could see objects that had rolled away under the furniture—a potato, a ball of string—but the voices were eluding him, and that was the position he was in when his wife—of all the times!—barged into the store and saw him there, his arse in the air and his ear on the floor, and she briefly beheld him with a look of confusion and walked out again.

It was, he later recalled, the moment when his doubts began to crystallise. There was no retrieving his marriage.

The boy was a balm, though he came with his own worries. He would sidle into the store in the morning among the daily tide of people and their needs and position himself in a corner, or among the stacks, and if he was bored or there was work at hand, he would quietly take up a broom or a cloth or a pen. He had become a competent writer and his addition was sharp enough. And then, when the work was done and the shop was quiet, he would talk, because he trusted the Storekeeper.

So it was, in small increments, in detours and digressions and tears and rage, that the Storekeeper came to know the story of how he had found Whelk on his doorstep, and of the Catechist's snakebite.

~

It was the day of Mannalargenna's death, which explained why everyone else was unaware of it. The day that ended with the boy on their doorstep. His battered face, the blood matted in his hair.

Whelk had been in class with the other children in the late afternoon when the sounds of mourning were just beginning to rend the air. He was nursing a mouse in his cupped hands. He should have been more careful, he told the Storekeeper, but the man leading the class that day was an old convict, just filling time. Not so watchful, Whelk assumed—wrongly, because before he knew it the old lag had him by the ear. He swung him to the front of the room and stood him there and demanded: *Show us what you have, child.*

This was not how the old teachers were supposed to be, Whelk explained. It was a surprise. Whelk clasped his hands in front of him, his upper body curved protectively over them—a position he demonstrated to the Storekeeper—and endured the torment of hanging from his ear without reaching up.

The teacher struck him lightly over the back of the head. *Your hands, child. Open them.* But even then Whelk resisted, so the old lag wrenched the fingers open: and there was the tiny silver mouse, nosing the air delicately.

It fell when the fingers opened and scuttled a confused circle on the floor at their feet. Whelk ducked to retrieve it but the old man took hold of him by his neck. The class did not make a sound, according to Whelk: they sat there stunned.

The lag was wild now and he threw them a furious look down a pointed finger, then dragged Whelk out and over the paddock to the Catechist's door.

Whelk tensed his whole body; he tried to wriggle free; he tried scouring his feet into the ground. Nothing slowed his inexorable progress. He pulled at the teacher's trouser leg, even thought to bite the man but wasn't vicious enough to do it, not even in such extremity.

The Storekeeper felt the dread rising in him. He remembered Pipi, and he knew where the boy's story was heading: across the Catechist's garden, up the cut-stone steps and across the narrow porch. The teacher knocked and the two of them stood awkwardly together, waiting for a response. He knocked again, harder, and again there was no answer. So he pointed that finger between Whelk's eyes again and muttered, *ye stay exac'ly right there boy an don' ye move a muscle till the preacher come.*

The Storekeeper knew the next bit, because he'd been passing by after sundown and had spotted the small figure there. Seeing it was Whelk, he came closer. The boy was bent over, peering down to the left of the stairs and the loose brick, the telltale loss of the mortar around it.

'Whelk?' He kept his voice soft, not wanting to frighten him. Whelk looked around and saw him near the foot of the stairs. The boy's face was wary, his eyes suspicious.

'What's happening, boy?'

The tears had left streaks down his face. There was no good reason why a child should be here, on this doorstep after dark, as the wind moaned around the building and the other children washed and prepared for the funeral. This was the bitter lesson of Pipi's disappearance.

'Nothin sir.'

The Storekeeper took a step closer, stooping to make himself smaller. He eyed the first step but did not set a foot on it. 'Don't have to call me sir. You know that.'

'Please sir I am fine and well thank you sir.'

The Storekeeper had bent lower still and rested both hands

on his thighs, above his knees. He cocked his head, took his hat off and squatted. 'You in trouble?'

'Nossir.'

'Why ye here, then?'

'Sleepin here now'days sir.' Whelk's eyes darted. He was lacing and unlacing his fingers, as though trying to keep control of his twitching body.

'Aye, but why you on the doorstep?'

Whelk did not answer. The Storekeeper watched him a little longer; then, resigned to receiving no further response, he stood, grunting a little with the effort. 'You can come by the store, lad. Talk to me, talk to my wife.' He tried smiling. 'You know she likes you.'

There were heavy steps coming down the hallway of the house. Whelk looked back at the door, and looked again at the Storekeeper. His face was stricken with panic. 'Yessir.'

'Evenin to ye, boy.' He replaced his hat and walked a few steps backwards so that he could watch Whelk before he turned away. A whimpering sound escaped the boy: the door opened and the Catechist's wife stood there, her great bustle curtained with an apron. Her face was pink and shiny, as though she had been exerting herself. She looked out towards the Storekeeper, then down at Whelk and her hand went unconsciously to the comb on the left side of her head.

Then she clamped a hand on the back of Whelk's neck and heaved him inside.

~

In the afternoon the Storekeeper worked again at his wall and the boy came back to continue his story. The bottle had begun its gentle whispering: a break would be nice. Just a dram, nothing excessive. He was trying to clench himself against it, muttering to himself; the sight of Whelk, his slow, distracted amble and the crust of dried blood above his swollen eye, offered him a way to push the clock into another hour.

So he took up a small hammer and chipped at the points in the wall that displeased him, and the boy resumed his story.

Behind the door, at the foot of the gloomy hallway, the woman had looked him over. He knew she hated him, Whelk said, but differently to the Catechist's hate. *What was the difference?* the Storekeeper asked. Hers was like he had done something wrong, Whelk replied. Something terrible and *personal* to her. He could not understand any more than that.

He'd explained to her that he had been told to come. 'By whom?' she asked him, and the Storekeeper could imagine her face at that moment, cold and firm as new liver.

'By the teacher, ma'am. Said I got to see the Caterrist.'

'Look up at me when you address me, child.'

'Gotta come to the Caterrist ma'am. For he said I misumbehaved.'

Whelk imitated her making a *tsk* sound with her tongue and her teeth, then she had him by the collar of his shirt, the good one he had been told to wear for services and funerals. She brought him up close to her round pink face. She smelled of soap. 'You think I don't see?' she said, and in Whelk's repetition of it, it was a hiss.

He couldn't help staring at her cheeks. 'She got hairs there,' he said and for a moment the Storekeeper felt the boy's mischief bubble up.

'Think I don't know what goes on?' she'd said, and she took

the handle of the door to the first room, flung it open and threw Whelk inside. 'Think I'm blind, do ye?' The door slammed behind him. 'I see it *all*, boy.'

Each of these words from the Catechist's wife seemed to have burnt itself into Whelk's mind: the Storekeeper had no doubt it was verbatim. And his description of the room seemed even more indelible. It was the same room as always, he said. The one he had heard called the Spare Room.

As he picked up stones and deposited them in the Storekeeper's wall, Whelk itemised the things in the room, as if each was a witness to what had happened and could be interrogated to verify his story. An iron bed, new rust on the frame. A plain blanket, itchy. A crucifix high above the pillow, nailed there in the exact centre of the wall. A mat next to the bed, but floorboards showing all around it. The window nailed shut and a curtain tacked to the frame so that no light showed. A cupboard, locked. A bedside table with a Bible and lamp. An arrangement of dried flowers, dead flies in it, cobwebs. To the Storekeeper it sounded like a room arranged to smother every trace of living things.

Whelk had stood there, perfectly still in the centre of the room, for what must have seemed an eternity. He heard the Catechist's wife in the scullery, the weight shifting on her small feet. He dared not touch the bed; eventually he lay down on the floor with his head angled into the corner by the fireplace. Here a low cupboard door met the floorboards: the firewood hatch. He looked at the little door, listened again and, hearing nothing, tugged it open. It smelled like the ground, he said. Cool air came up from under the house. There were gaps inside the cupboard where the boards had rotted and fallen in, leaving a ragged inch or two of blackness. He reached in and felt the floorboards spring under his palm, rotten soft. It was dark in there, but as he looked down his arm into the gap, he could see facing him the corresponding cupboard door that led outside, edges coated in cobwebs and swollen into its frame.

But why were you looking in there? the Storekeeper asked at this point, and Whelk answered, *because I knew she was there*. Then he said that he had put a mouse in there. The Storekeeper was confused: 'she' was a mouse? There was no firewood in the cupboard. The Storekeeper knew this because it was his responsibility to deliver the firewood to all the houses and huts, and he had never delivered there.

The Catechist took his time. Whelk perched gingerly on the edge of the bed and folded his hands in his lap. He prayed it wouldn't hurt, that he would black out. The Storekeeper was surprised that Whelk would pray, and pray sincerely, but then he thought about what the boy was asking for. Blackness and silence—even forever—in preference to an hour of what the Catechist would bring.

Now and then, Whelk said, he passed the time by standing up and carefully smoothing the cover on the bed until it was perfect. He counted how many times he did this. He sat again, his back to the door. And when the heavy thuds came, he did not move. Nor did he move when the door of the house was opened, nor the door of the room. *Dry sounds*, he called them. Breath, the movement of clothing. Then the ringing of iron keys, the crunch of the lock. More metal noise as the key ring dropped onto the bedside table.

The Catechist had been at the funeral: Whelk could not have known this because he'd been waiting by the door while the procession took place, out of sight across the settlement. He couldn't have known of the Catechist's humiliation and his fury. When he opened the door and came in, Whelk did not look. The Storekeeper asked him why, and he could only shrug. Maybe he'd come to the end of manners. He sat there, he said, and stared as hard as he could at the timber boards of the wall. The Catechist stopped behind him: the footsteps told him so. He felt the bed move as the man threw his coat over the frame.

He concentrated fiercely. Chips in the paint, tiny shreds of cobweb.

'Why do you not look at me?' the Catechist said.

Whelk stared even harder. Brush marks. Specks of something brown, making dotted lines.

'*You will look at me.*' Louder this time, Whelk said. The Storekeeper knew the nature of the man, enough to picture the forces competing in him.

Terrify the child. Exult in it. Don't be overheard.

Whelk said he started tracing the column of nail heads in the timber, tried to imagine the frame beneath it. He could smell the man, he said, and he smelled like something that had died long ago.

The first blow came from nowhere. Not a word, not a movement. It connected with his ear and there was a noise like something dropped and smashed and he found himself on the floor beside the bed, pushed against the wall looking at the piece of timber that covered where the floorboards met the wall. He knew there was a name for this but he could not recall it.

He struggled to explain the next part, and the Storekeeper was reluctant to press him. He had tried to rise but everything was thick and heavy. The whole house was leaning to one side. The Catechist had ripped his clenched fists open, searching for the mouse, and Whelk saw the Catechist's clothes for the first time: a black waistcoat, a shirt, black trousers. He stood on one foot, holding the end of the bed frame for balance while he removed a shoe.

Whelk fell silent. The Storekeeper placed a series of monkey skulls so that they lodged neatly against each other in the centre of the wall, and thought about the Catechist's rage. He understood what had happened at the funeral. Speeches about God were the Catechist's job, not the Commandant's, and he had smouldered with fury at having been excluded. He needed to take it out on someone.

The Catechist had taken the shoe by its toe-end and the square block of the heel came down. The blow was so loud in his head, Whelk said—and he raised a hand to the swollen split above his eye—that he felt sure the Catechist's wife would come running. Then the Catechist had him by the ankle and was dragging him out from beside the bed. He saw that he was leaving blood as he went. When he had him clear by the end of the bed, he let go and stood over Whelk's legs for a moment.

He was doing this, Whelk said, and he mimicked the man breathing hard, hands on his hips. *And he said I was gunna meet the devil hisself.*

Fingers down the front of his coat, unbuttoning it. Whelk was miming the Catechist now, shaking himself out of it, throwing it. *He kicked me then.* And he acted out the kick. *He rolled up his sleeves.*

The boy was struggling—it was evident across his battered face—and the Storekeeper wanted him to stop, but the story was a tide now and it would not be held back. The old man had swung the belt free of his trousers and whipped it down. The buckle tore through Whelk's shirt and into the flesh of his stomach. It hurt, he said, indicating on his shirt where the belt had struck. Another blow *missed me, hit the bed.* The Catechist drew the belt up again to strike a third time, the brass of the buckle ringing on the iron bed frame.

As he did so, Whelk slid between his feet. He managed to get halfway under the Catechist, who looked down on him in surprise. The Storekeeper imagined the fringe of silver hair overhanging the silhouette of his head against the ceiling, a demon in a boiling sky.

A change, a turning. He drove further back between the legs, and now his feet were touching the corner of the room and *that was it*, he said: he could retreat no further.

Make it quick make it quick.

And then he had the idea about the firewood door.

The Catechist stooped forward, gathering the belt into loops again. He raised it, eyes down *like he was chopping wood*. But Whelk was faster. He had the knob of the small door in his fist and he flung it open and jammed both his feet inside. *Din know if I'd fit*, he said, but it was clear he had no other option.

His feet found the outer door and he kicked it. The Catechist was coming for him. *Thought he gonna hit me again*. But the Catechist was on his haunches, *laughin and waitin*.

'What was he doing?' The Storekeeper could not understand.

Guess he thought I was stuck. Whelk shrugged. *Din know I was kickin out the back.*

The Catechist put the belt down beside his knee. Whelk kicked again, harder. He heard the door give way, felt the air. He pushed at the floor, trying to will himself backwards into the cavity. The Catechist was smiling now, and he reached a hand (*big as my head*) towards Whelk's hair.

So I bit him.

'You what?'

Got his hand, the meat bit here—he indicated between his thumb and first finger—*an I bit him, hard as I could*. The Catechist had grunted and clenched his teeth, then driven his other fist into Whelk's head.

The punch stopped him; it pushed him further back, too, and now his knee caught the outside of the house. *An then I knew I could get all the way outside.*

A look of puzzlement settled over his features. 'What is it?' the Storekeeper asked, and Whelk replied, *I din know what she was going to do*, and before the Storekeeper could ask him who *she* was, he was off again. The Catechist had pulled back his bleeding hand, and reached with the other one, all the way to his armpit, to pull Whelk back inside the room. But Whelk had the outside wall against his knee now. He levered back—*it was easy then*—and fell into the garden bed.

An I knew he was gonna come after me, an he did.

The bitten hand, bloodied and torn, came first. Then a forearm in a sleeve, an elbow. The upper arm, the other hand. And slowly, his silver hair appeared, and then the Catechist's face, which Whelk had neither the words nor the skill at mimicry to convey.

The Storekeeper had seen the man angry, but even then he'd been fortified by arrogance. He thought of him now—wounded, furious and humiliated, wedged in the position that Whelk described—and the face he imagined was graven like God's judgment upon a whole city full of sinners, mad and eternal. Eyes that were not the eyes of a teacher, of an adult, of a man, of anyone at all. Eyes from some other world.

The Catechist was trying to push himself through, Whelk realised, and he was too big. *He was makin noises, showin his teeth*. He swung the free arm at Whelk, who had to shrink back into the garden to avoid it.

Listening to him, the Storekeeper couldn't understand why the Catechist had tried to force himself through the hatch. Perhaps it seemed a good idea at first, if he had managed to catch hold of Whelk as he squeezed out. But why did he follow? All he had to do was go back into the room and take the key and let himself out. Whelk might get a start on him, but he couldn't hide forever.

Whelk had deposited a load of stone in the Storekeeper's wall, and now he was dusting his hands. The sun found his bruises and the Storekeeper felt a terrible pity for him. But his expression was changing, his confidence growing. The hint of a smile appeared.

Then he gone backwards.

Something stopped the Catechist. *Like he got a big fright.* His face registered shock, new pain. He drew the arm back into the hatch, back into the rest of his body, which now began to thrash madly. Suddenly the other arm came free and hung down. Whelk smiled unexpectedly, recalling his own confusion—*I didn't understand what*—as the Storekeeper, too, struggled to keep up.

The big female tiger snake had come free with the arm, coiled around it.

The preacher screamed, Whelk said, and slammed the arm against the house and the snake dropped with a thud to the garden. It swirled, inches from Whelk's feet, briefly revealing its pale underside, then poured itself in a vertical line up the brickwork.

She nose goin like this—he wavered his hand left and right—*an I thought she goin back to him to get him again.* But it seemed the snake had veered away and disappeared into the wall.

The Storekeeper saw now that Whelk had known of the snake in its lair for a long time. So had Pipi. All those mice, and the frogs and lizards. Whelk had taken over the feeding, but he'd never seen the snake until now, finally, stretched out to her great fluid length—and it was a source of wonder to him.

That suspended moment must have stopped time: the two of them fixed on the departing snake. For the Storekeeper, it harked to the reflex, the swift glance every time he picked up a rock, or a crate, or a length of firewood. Waiting, half-expecting the time when there would be a pile of scaly coils underneath. The whip of instinct: which of them was faster.

Whelk had been left looking up at the Catechist's arm, hanging limply from the hatch. There were scratches from where the timbers had gouged at him as he forced his way through. But that wasn't all, and the Storekeeper understood now. Halfway down his forearm, and hard to discern in the darkness, there was a tiny smear of blood. Something glistening around it.

With his head also jammed in the hatchway, the Catechist had apparently tried licking at the bite and spitting. But when he dropped the arm again Whelk watched it oozing a little more. The damaged face must have appeared even more catastrophic now that he was wrecked and marooned in that impossible position. Whelk stood, weak and trembling. *I knew he was stuck an I din know what to do.*

Long minutes must have passed like that. The Catechist began to dribble, and the dribble made a string down to the garden. The word *Get*...came out of him; Whelk was unsure if he meant *get away* or *get help*, because the word *come out all spitty*. Around this time, Whelk had remembered that he was himself in pain, and that the world was still tilted. He quietly stepped out of the garden bed, and the last thing he saw was the hanging man convulsing and vomiting a torrent of shredded food and blood.

The thing he didn't understand as he turned and ran, Whelk said, was how the missus hadn't heard the whole thing. *It was loud*, he said, *and the Caterrist were makin horrible noises*. The Storekeeper wondered, too, though he kept his thoughts to himself. Either the woman had trained herself to hear nothing for so long that she could no longer hear at all, or…Or she had heard all too well.

At any rate, the boy had got himself across the hundred yards of grass before the pain and the lost blood overcame him. It was nothing but good luck that the Storekeeper was still awake and heard the thud on his doorstep as Whelk collapsed there. The wind was still whipping freely through the settlement, though the night had deepened. He lifted the limp form while his wife cradled the bleeding head, and they turned back towards the warmth of their home.

And the Storekeeper, preoccupied by this discovery on his front step in the dead of night, did not look out across the grass. Had he done so, he would have seen the Catechist's house: the dim light of a lamp behind the curtains of the front window falling on the brickwork by the steps. And there, at the cavity by the chimney-base, he would have seen the hanging head and arm of the Catechist, and the distinctive form of his wife. Motionless and alert, silhouetted on the curtain above.

The Treatment Takes Effect

The Commandant sent for his writing materials and brought his journal up to date. He would have preferred to work alone in the comfort of his own office, but the Surgeon had insisted that they keep watch over the Catechist together.

The funeral still burned in his memory; the melancholy theatre of the torches and the rain, the faces in the procession and the mournful hymns. This: this was what he could achieve with the natives, no matter the Surgeon's cynicism. But first he knew he must describe the women and their wailing, the cold shock of beholding the body. His distress? He deliberated, and eventually chose to include mention of it. It reflected well on his humanity: a compassionate man brought low by bitter circumstance.

Otherwise, these were functional matters in the main, easy enough to relate for posterity. But then the going became harder. How to explain the deep ambivalence among his officers, even as they saw the grief of the natives? Should he transcribe his eulogy into the journal, or should it stand separately? Should he report that Mannalargenna had gone to his death believing he had been betrayed; deceived into leading his people to their doom? And how to explain the disappearance of the body?

He wrote all of it out as objectively as he was able. He wrote of the arduous work of disinterring the coffin, making sure to present it as *a necessary check upon the burial, given various misgivings I had regarding the intentions of the natives.* Yes. This enabled him to explain the theft of the chief's corpse as *the confirmation of my worst fears regarding the character of the straitsmen's wives.*

His ruminations were interrupted by a knock at the door. The Catechist's wife, demanding to be admitted. She had dressed herself as though for a Sunday, in an elaborate white dress, her hair tied up under a bonnet. Ridiculously, she had carried a parasol over the short journey between her house and the hospital. Her face was pinker than usual, her mouth more tightly pursed, but other than those small signs she appeared to the Commandant to be well in control of her emotions.

The Commandant angled himself in the doorway so that her husband's body was not visible to her, and firmly refused her entry. She made no objection.

'Will he die?' she asked flatly.

The Commandant stepped forward, closed the door behind him and took her hands. He had a smile for these moments and he used it now. 'The Surgeon is doing all he can. Your husband is very fortunate that this happened to him within reach of excellent medical treatment.'

She snatched her hands away. 'I expect to be kept informed.'

Without another word, she stormed off towards her house in a thunderhead of skirts.

When he re-entered the room, the Commandant found that the Surgeon had made himself another drink. As he reclined with it and reached for his book, a bout of spasms contorted the Catechist's body with such violence it appeared he would slide off the stretcher. The Surgeon got up reluctantly to straighten him, then resumed his seat. The room returned to uneasy calm.

The Commandant thought it through once more. No one had specifically asked him to anatomise the chief. He had sickened and died between mail runs, so swiftly that there was no opportunity for the collectors to make their bids. He had months on his side. By the time the news was received at Home that a great leader had passed (a man whose like would never be seen again) and by the time those requests made their way to the settlement by return passage—by the time all of that had occurred, he would have had months to negotiate with the women of the outer islands to retrieve the remains.

All of this could be recovered. He sighed, and pressed his fingertips to his mouth. Why confess to his own negligence? He took the corner of the page in his fingers, hesitated just briefly, then tore it from the notebook. When it had come free in his hand, he stood and took a taper from beside the lamp, lit it and set it to the edge of the paper.

The Surgeon glanced up, raised his brows at the sight of the billowing flame in the Commandant's hand, and looked down again at his book. The Commandant waited until the little fire had nearly reached his fingers then dropped the burning page and stood on it.

~

When the faint smell of smoke had cleared, the Surgeon stood and walked a slow lap around the Catechist. He laid a hand on the man's chest, tapped his cheek with two fingers, and bent over to peer carefully at the excision in his forearm.

The Commandant watched him. 'Waiting for him to die now?'

'Well.' The Surgeon straightened, unconcerned. 'Either that, or for the treatment to take effect.' He picked up the hypodermic from his work table and laid it on the Catechist's chest, untied the ligature from his arm and draped it momentarily from his own mouth. Next, he took up a scalpel and closely examined the pale flesh where the wound was.

He indicated the Catechist's ankles. 'Would you mind?'

The Commandant took up his position again, leaning on the feet. He could feel no energy in them now, and expected no resistance, whatever it was that the Surgeon planned to do.

The Surgeon was so close to the wound that his nose nearly touched it. He squinted into it, then poked the scalpel in until its bladed end disappeared. As he prodded, the blood ran freely again and he mopped at it with towels already blotched.

The Commandant clutched the limp ankles but there was no reflexive response to the blade. At a nod from the Surgeon, he let go and stood back.

Once the Surgeon had made a puncture at one end of the large wound, he swapped the scalpel for the syringe. Driving the needle deep into the cut he had made, he held it there with two fingers stabilising it. Grimacing, he took the plunger in his other fist and drove it down with a faint pneumatic squeak; waited, then withdrew the needle.

The Commandant did not know what he was expecting,

and for a long time nothing happened. Perhaps, he thought, the Surgeon had finally killed him.

In the stillness the sudden violence of the Catechist's reaction was all the more shocking. He reared up off the stretcher and sucked a desperate breath out of the room. His gums were bloody and bared in a snarl, his good eye demonically misaligned into the field of the dead eye. His tongue bulged from a dark toothless cavern, racked with agony, and the light made crevasses and shadowed valleys on the skin of his face. It was a sight the Commandant would revisit in times of stress and fatigue for the rest of his days.

The Commandant, who presumed God's hand in everything that happened, could not see a trace of divine process in this. As the man gnawed at the air he was a phantasm, a vent from some infernal hole in the world. Though his organs might still function, embalmed in the Surgeon's noxious fluid, the Catechist was more in hell than in the room. His tortured head swung in a great arc above the stretcher, trailing a groan, then slammed down with a sickening hollow thud on the table beneath him. It lifted again, bleeding, and again he slammed it down. His body convulsed on its side, bouncing as if dropped from a hangman's rope. Then it was still.

Silence blanketed the room. The Commandant stood exactly as he had been standing, hands uselessly primed in the air, but now he stood at the feet of a corpse. The Surgeon had reared back and was pressed at his waist against the bench behind him. The bottles and flasks arrayed on the bench had all fallen; some smashed, others de-capped and spilling, mixing into foul-smelling brews on the timber surface.

Into the thick stillness came the tiny tinkling sound of a phial rolling over the benchtop. It reached the lip of the bench and the two men eyed it as it slowed, and tipped, and toppled. It caught a thin fierce ray of sunlight as it fell through the air; then it smashed on the granite flags.

~

My Dear Sirs,
It is my melancholy duty to inform you that on the sixth inst. our esteemed Catechist passed away due to medical complications arising from a serpent's bite, viz. *the Tiger Snake of these islands. The asp in question is common here and widely feared, being given a wide berth at all times by the natives. It appears a gravid female had taken up residence in the floorboards of the Catechist's home, unbeknown to anyone, and upon him reaching into a firewood hatch beside the hearth in a front room of the dwelling, his left arm had come into contact with the creature and thence been bitten.*

The man suffered no little distress as a result. I am informed that he had been bled of approximately four pints before my arrival at his bedside. The Surgeon had incised the wound to a considerable extent, seeking to resect the corrupted area of flesh (located upon the medial surface of the left lower arm, distally of the cubitus) but without effect. He then proceeded to administer brandy by mouth, applied topical poultices of ground mustard seed and, in light of the Catechist's continued deterioration, finally administered intravenous ammonia. It was shortly after this treatment that the patient awoke very suddenly from the comatose state into which he had lapsed: the great shock of which caused him to suffer a likely coronary episode from which he could not recover.

It seems advisable in the unusual circumstances of this matter that a post-mortem examination be undertaken, to facilitate a complete understanding of the sequence of bodily events that precipitated death. Our Surgeon has delegated the task to our acting mortician: I have stepped in to advise him of the required dissections and specimen retentions.

The man is of course in good grace with the Lord and will be buried with full ceremony in consecrated ground beside our chapel. To this end the natives have been taught divers hymns and requia, the opportunity of performing which ought ensure the occasion will be saved from complete abjection. His wife, I note in passing, is being cared for by the women of the settlement.

More pressingly, it is my duty to request of you a new candidate to join the settlement in the role of Catechist. As I have urged upon your office many times in the past, this Settlement stands or falls upon the quality of its religious instruction. Therefore, we seek the highest quality candidate you are disposed to provide, whether from within the colony or from Home. Such a candidate would be a man of fortitude, patience and an indefatigable ardour to convey the glory of the Scriptures to the remaining natives of Van Diemen's Land.

I ask that this request be furnished with the utmost haste, and I remain—

Your most humble and obedient servant.

The Coins in the Trees

The second day of February dawned heavy and thick, the outlined clouds of a thunderstorm snagged by the top of the hill.

Mannalargenna's funeral and the Catechist's gruesome end had marked the start of the summer; these were its final weeks. A sloop lay at anchor in the bay north of the settlement, rigging reflected in the glossy sea. Its longboat had been pulled up on the beach, leaving a track in the low-tide flats. The footprints from the boat led into the grasses, to the mouth of the narrow path that tunnelled through the tangled scrub. The path intersected the furrow scarred in the ground where the man and his bullock toiled from waterhole to tank, as though roped slaves had hauled an ancient ship through the bush.

Across the furrow and out on the open ground, the grass was nibbled short by the wallabies and scattered with their droppings. The warm air, pressed under the cumulus, was thick and damp. The painted buildings reflected the sun in its dying intensity before the coming storm. And there, milling in the cleared ground between the walls, was the party that had come in the sloop.

~

The introductions were still underway as the Storekeeper sidled up to the back of the little crowd. A man stood at the centre of the gathering, making a speech.

He was thin and stooped, an old scarecrow draped in black. The words that came from his mouth were the same platitudes the previous Catechist had used: words that filled space and had no meaning. *Damnation. Salvation.*

His face was obscured under a wide-brimmed black hat. *Penitence.* It made him a private man, along with his black cloak and black trousers. *Eternity.* It would be damnably hot in the hat and the robes. And then the dust would get to it all.

'It's a miracle,' the Storekeeper muttered, and someone looked around at him. 'Eight weeks and the mad bastard's been resurrected.'

There was no sign of a wife or children. The man had a black cloth bag with him, stuffed full. But just the one bag? The last Catechist arrived with a desk, with *crates* of books. Maybe that was all a preacher needed, a bag of books and some underalls. You could fashion a weapon against children with whatever happened to be lying about.

The mouth flapped open and shut, the teeth all yellow and pegged. A thin line of certainty when he (infrequently) closed it, and no hope of humour.

'Who sends these people?' the Storekeeper sighed aloud,

drawing glances of consternation. 'Where do they come from? Is there an endless army of these lunatics in Sydney?' There had been a moment, back in December, when the Storekeeper had watched the Commandant hurrying in and out of the hospital and had listened to screams on the wind that sounded like a wounded animal maddened by pain, and he had thought that might be the end of all of it. Something might replace it, replace *him*, and it might be a new start.

Gentle hands pushed him back away from the crowd and quiet voices soothed him.

He was still talking, this new preacher. *Contrition. Omniscience.* On and on. *Succour* and *Mercy*. They buried the old Catechist under a mulberry tree in the boneyard, in the clearly marked section for the white settlers where the graves had adornment, headstones, rails. The smith worked up a little fence of iron loops to box him in and the tussocks had started coming up on his grave now through the clods of sandy earth. His great lumbering ship of a wife had stood there scowling at the funeral, pink face set hard like the end of a bone. Not one solitary tear from her. She just gripped a hymnal in those dimpled knuckles and stared at the coffin as if it was her sacred covenant to make sure the old man stayed in the hole.

And now this new preacher stood here, every fibre of his black garb a grim promise. Nothing would change, and the holy lunatics would keep coming even when the sky went black and everything ended. A long line of them waited somewhere on a faraway beach, each with a black cloth bag in his right fist. Each one scowling at the back of the one in front.

Damnation.

He caught himself muttering again, and there was work to do. The suitcases and valises and crates were stacked neatly beside the door of the house and they needed loading onto the cart for transfer to the rowboat. His wife was leaving the settlement on the return journey of the boat that had brought the new hypocrite.

He lifted the luggage piece by piece and presently his wife came from the house, dressed in her finest clothes, and her eyes went from him, down there at the cart, to the Commandant, watching from his own balcony. Whatever she felt in her heart about this moment, about the two men, was not to be found on her face. She came down the steps and offered him her cheek. Then with the briefest squeeze of his hand, she climbed onto the cart and waited.

He wondered dumbly if there was something he should say. Did their marriage, despite its brevity, require some kind of eulogy? He looked up at her, willing to risk the first thing that entered his head, but her eyes were fixed on the tree line in the distance. The convict whipped the reins and the cart was drawn away.

~

A small party of lags did the work on the old Catechist's house. The floor of the front room was taken up and replaced, the firewood hatch bricked over. The day it was done, a convict stood by with a spade ready to dispatch the snake, but the only sign of the murderous reptile was a scatter of long shit in which could be seen the tiny bones of mice and lizards and frogs. Within days the new Catechist had moved a selection of the orphans into the long room.

Whelk had quietly settled himself back among the old people in the huts. His injuries had long since healed—the eardrum had been slow—but he was a different boy now. He lived in their company, absorbing their stories and the food they saved in their bowls. They loved him, and as there were fewer children now after the deaths and removals, they cherished him even more, and felt the urgency to give him their stories. It seemed to the Storekeeper, watching from his distance, to be a tolerable template for the endless nights and days.

For a week or so that was how it went, but soon enough Whelk was summoned, and quartered once again in the long room.

Outside of his sermons, the Catechist spoke only rarely, and when he did it was in a strange kind of Irish; not the musical speech that he heard among the lags but something more congealed. In passing one morning, in the store ordering trotters, the Catechist said he knew Whelk had told his story to the Storekeeper.

The Storekeeper's eyes must have betrayed him: the man leaned in and rested his forearms on the counter. 'They say he was there when the other fella was bit.'

The Storekeeper did not reply.

'That right?' With his hat clenched in his hands the man's hair was thin and white, his eyes so dark they might have been holes in his head, but for their watchful quality.

'Pays a man none to heed stories,' the Storekeeper said eventually.

'Hmm.' The Catechist smiled briskly. There was a smell about him, something like medicine, or liquor and smoke. 'I must ask the boy directly, then.'

~

The Governor's letter had arrived in the sloop with the new Catechist, among a great pile of other missives: invoices, supply orders, records, ledgers, requests for numbers and dates. Mundane things the Commandant could attend to for weeks before there came a need to report. But the Governor's letter stood out from the dun-coloured crowd. It was sealed with wax, the Governor's own private seal. They didn't waste their insignia on rejections, he felt sure. He had stifled his eagerness until the day's business was done, then retired to his study and poured a brandy. He found himself tugging at his waistcoat, smoothing his hair as he slid the knife under the seal.

My Dear Sir...

Would he use an aide-de-camp for this type of work? Was this His Excellency's own handwriting?

Moving fast, his eye understood the shape of the words on the page: only two paragraphs. The sinking feeling.

...funds sufficient to ensure adequate recompense

They were going to deny him yet again.

...despite your obvious capacity to fulfil such a role

It was political. It could only be political.

...regret that we must forestall upon any prospect of an appointment as Protector in the Port Phillip district.

The second paragraph dealt with the matter of the visit. Again it was clear from the shape that it was going to disappoint.

...a schedule which has precluded me engaging in such pleasurable travel as a voyage to inspect your settlement would

undoubtedly constitute. Please accept my deepest regrets for such disappointment as this may cause you, and be assured I will continue to examine opportunities to make amends over coming...

He slammed his palms flat on either side of the damned letter. A long breath hissed down his nose. They were toying with him. He could see now that he'd given them a warehouse for the natives: out of sight and mind on a mere trickle from Treasury. Their consciences were clean: they had stopped the killing, or at least slowed it and changed its form.

Why would they bother to visit? Why would they reward him with advancement, with a new assignment that reflected his rare achievements? He had been gullible: he was of greatest value to them exactly where he was.

There was a dull thud through the wall from outside: the cricket ball. These days would unfold forever.

~

The Storekeeper had taken the path behind the barracks and was concealed in the scrub halfway to the beach. He came here often, certain that he would not be observed. He set his tools down now and sat for a moment enjoying the morning sun, waiting for Whelk to arrive. Soon the boy wandered up, dumping the two heavy sacks at his feet. For a moment he just stood, resting a hand on the trunk of a she-oak, and looked at the Storekeeper.

'Doin some work here?' he asked eventually.

The Storekeeper didn't particularly want to talk about it, but Whelk was always an exception. 'Something I've been doing,' he said softly. 'I took the crate down there for you already. Just goin to finish this.'

He stood then, took a hammer and lined up the blade of his chisel horizontally against the trunk of the she-oak in front of him. It was an old tree, about a foot in diameter. Whelk studied him closely as he made an incision in the trunk at eye height: five swift blows, and he had driven the blade an inch into the tree. The dark brown chips of outer bark revealed first the blood-red live bark and then the bright terracotta of the timber. He put the tools down at his feet and rummaged in his pocket. There was a glint in his fingers as he pressed something into the cut he'd made.

'What's that?' asked Whelk.

'A coin,' he replied. 'Spanish dollar, I think.'

Whelk did not enquire further. He watched as the Storekeeper took up the hammer again and pounded at the edge of the coin until it had disappeared into the flesh of the tree. He stood back and assessed his work, and then he began to speak.

'I've been thinking,' he said, 'about how we make shells around ourselves to…to keep some of it out. Things that, if you could feel em entirely, they'd be too much: they'd take you to the bottom and you wouldn't be able to swim up, so the only way to endure is to shut some of it out. Much like how a man walks through a city or stands upon a stricken vessel in the breaking waves. He has to focus on the foot or two in front of him, or he'll be overwhelmed.'

He rubbed his thumb over the scar, which had begun to ooze sap.

'Rich man, he's got no trouble with this, nor any man of power. They make their decisions and set their horrors in motion and they do it by remaining insensible. It's when you hear the crying of the children or mothers wailing or the groans of dying men that you're paralysed. And what I see now is that I got no shell. No way of sealing my ears against it or lowering my gaze. I see all of it. And it is becoming too much.'

He stopped speaking because he was watching the boy look around himself at the forest. He had found one, two…three of the other trees with their scars; his head was swivelling, trying to take it in.

'If you could imagine every exile in a foreign land, or imagine being betrayed by the person you loved the most in all the world and having to accept that you never knew them. If these things could be stacked up, the human soul couldn't withstand it. That's why we're such practised deceivers, lad. Our capacity for joy is infinite. But our capacity for sorrow has a weight limit. Collapses on its axles like an overloaded cart if we take too much on.'

He saw the look on Whelk's face: the rush of words he may not have understood, but the meaning he'd clearly grasped.

'You're as wise as she was, my boy.' He produced a paper package from one of his pockets and unwrapped it. Inside was a small block of red sealing wax. He crumpled the paper back into the pocket and began to work the wax in his fingers. 'Cannot leave here and let it all vanish,' he said now. 'Can't just let the woods take over. It's all timber, all except my wall, and that's just limestone—melts in the rain, see? Buildings made of planks, graves with no headstones. Everything we did here is going to disappear.' He worked the wax with the pads of his thumbs as it softened. 'Can't just let it go back to grass when we're gone, because things have happened. The dead that are lyin in that paddock over there. Songs they took down with em…'

He pushed the wax into the wound in the tree, smoothing it with his fingers until the edge of the coin disappeared and the gouge was sealed. 'Commandant writes everything down.' He snorted. 'Well. Not everything.'

He looked around himself at the stripes of red wax that marked the trees: dozens of them, old and young, straight and angled, some fallen and drying in death. His eyes fell on Whelk.

'Coin grows into the tree, tree carries the coin. When it falls'—he gestured at one of the fallen ones—'it'll work its way into the ground and wait there. Everything works its way to the ground over time. All that's solid falls.'

Whelk was turning slowly where he stood, taking in all of the trees that carried the hidden coins. The currawongs speared through the swaying fronds of the she-oaks and the wide blue bay whispered somewhere out of sight. The Storekeeper was picking up his tools. There were tears on his long cheeks and they glittered in the perfect sun.

'Ready to go, then?'

Whelk nodded and they took a sack each, continuing down the path until it opened at the beach on the north side of the settlement. The light reflected so brightly off the sand that the Storekeeper had to squint to see Whelk beside the boat, bent over the gunwale and looking through the crate that the Storekeeper had put there overnight.

'It'll take em an hour or more to launch the longboat round the other side,' he said to the boy, 'so you got at least that long…'

'Mm.'

'There's a few days of water in that cask, but take it slow. And I got you this, what you wanted.' He produced from his pocket a brass compass. 'You know that big headland is Cape Frankland? Once you leave it, keep going northeast and you'll come to islands, and more islands—'

'I know.'

'—and once the islands are done you'll be on the mainland—'

'I know.'

'And after that, 's up to you how you get to Sydney.' He shrugged. 'I don't know how. Walk, I guess.'

'I can do it.' The boy was in a kind of daze. A state of great concentration or perhaps great emotion: the Storekeeper couldn't tell.

There was a movement at the top of the beach, a dark shape against the blinding sand. The dog, come once more to the beach where it had arrived. The Storekeeper watched as the boy stepped away from the boat and squatted on his haunches in the damp sand between tidelines. The dog approached across the beach, looking only at the boy, and for a moment the Storekeeper's heart leapt at the prospect that the dog might climb into the boat and go with him. But it stopped and sat, leaving a stretch of sand between them, and across it their eyes met.

When the boy stood again the dog did not move, but only watched him.

The Storekeeper helped Whelk load the two sacks in the bow, and he began to push the boat over the dry sand. The little mast was lying on the thwarts with a sail wrapped around it. A pair of oars lay beside it.

'Don't use the sail until you—'

'I know.'

They reached the shallows and the Storekeeper waded the boat further out as Whelk climbed aboard and settled himself. The water sparkled on his knees and his fists where they gripped the oars. The Storekeeper was up to his waist now and he leaned into the bow and shoved it so the boat and the boy slipped away from him and spun slowly to face north. The whole bay behind the boat was glassy: it was a perfect day to do it.

The Storekeeper returned to shore and stood beside the black dog, and he listened to the water running off his clothes in the stillness. The only other sound was the dipping of the oars as the boat drew away under the small power of the boy's rowing.

There would be an inquiry, he supposed; he doubted he had the mettle to stare them down. They would know it was him who had helped Whelk.

The little boat was already distant—a speck in the blue—and the boy's voice was faint and small. If that was what it was. The Storekeeper would never be certain whether he heard the final words, or whether it was the terns or the gulls, or just his imagination.

Afterword

The settlement at Pea Jacket Point struggled on for eleven years after the events depicted here.

Dozens more Aboriginal people died there, mainly from respiratory illnesses, including 107 people during the blighted two years between January 1837 and March 1839. Throughout, the inhabitants maintained their autonomy and actively opposed their exile on the island. They organised themselves politically around the Ben Lomond man Walter George Arthur, publishing Australia's first Aboriginal newspaper, the *Flinders Island Chronicle*, and draughting a remarkable petition to Queen Victoria in 1846: the first of its kind ever delivered to an English monarch by Indigenous subjects of the empire.

In 1847 the settlement, starved of funding and forgotten by the outside world, was quietly closed and its remaining forty-seven inhabitants shipped off to the abandoned settlement at Oyster Cove, Tasmania. There they languished in continued misery and obscurity, though they tried to maintain traditional practices such as hunting.

Eight of the ten children among them were removed separately to an orphanage: one of them, William Lanne, was shamefully mistreated by anatomists after his death. Truganini, often wrongly called the last of the Tasmanians, was renowned in colonial circles before her death in 1876. Her body was also desecrated by scientists. The Oyster Cove site was flooded and abandoned in 1874.

Tasmania's First Peoples live on. Today they are reclaiming their history and their languages, and continuing traditional practices such as mutton-birding and handcrafts.

~

Having secured his long-desired position as Chief Protector of Aborigines in Port Phillip in 1839, George Augustus Robinson left the Flinders Island settlement, never to return. He invested well and became wealthy, but estranged himself from his family. When his wife Maria died in 1848, he refused to pay for her headstone.

He left Australia forever in 1852, remarried the following year and travelled through Europe. Despite references in his correspondence to the memoir he believed would bring him fame, he never completed it. He remarked in a letter to one of his daughters, no doubt a stranger to him by then, that he seemed to have 'an evil genius for travelling'. He died on Home soil: in Somerset in 1866.

~

The site of the Wybalenna settlement was excavated and examined between 1971 and 1973 by University of Sydney archaeologists, and its story was told in a 1992 Tasmanian documentary, *Black Man's Houses*.

The graves of Mannalargenna and others were rendered invisible during the twentieth century, trampled by cattle. The ruins of the settlement still mark the grasses of Pea Jacket Point today.

~

The lands of the First Peoples of what is now called Tasmania—lutruwita or Trouwerner—were stolen: taken on the basis of false promises, without their consent. They have never been compensated.

Acknowledgments

Close to the site of this story, I have spent long and enjoyable hours with Ronald Wise, Gerard Walker and the families of Flinders and Cape Barren islands.

In the course of my research and writing across the three novels in this trilogy I was guided by Aunty Patsy Cameron and Aunty Maikutena Vicki-Laine Matson Green, and I acknowledge their rights as knowledge holders. I also wish to thank historians Grant Finlay, Nick Clements, Cassandra Pybus, Mark McKenna and Paul Daley—and Clive Tilsley of Fullers Hobart—for their reading and astute comments about Tasmanian history. Thanks also to Jack Latimore, Simon Barnard, Ben Walter, Melanie Ostell, Shane Howard, Adam Ford, Russell Jackson and Andrew Wrathall for a range of generous and ingenious contributions that in each case reflected both their expertise and the great people that they are. To the Sutherlands, thank you for the desperately needed solitude of Natty Muck.

Aunty Julie Janson stepped in at a crucial moment in the evolution of this manuscript; made sense and calmed the waters. I am enormously grateful.

To early readers Jo Canham, Bob Gott, Damien Newton Brown and Lia Hills, I remain amazed at your ability to see the flaws and strengths in the chaotic early stage of the manuscript. I have thanked you selfless souls before: no doubt, I will need to again.

At Text Publishing, I wish to thank Michael Heyward for

his immediate and sustained commitment to the idea of the three Furneaux novels; Jane Watkins for her professionalism and sage advice, and Mandy Brett—much more than my editor, my closest collaborator—for once again finding the gold in the rough (or whatever the right expression is…Mandy will know it). Thank you also to the teams at Text who do the important things I can't see, and to Jess Horrocks for her enigmatic, perfect cover design.

For readers interested in following the path of my own research into Wybalenna and the First Nations peoples of Tasmania, I recommend reading Plomley's *Weep in Silence* and *Friendly Mission* and Grant Finlay's *Good People Always Crackney in Heaven*, Cassandra Pybus's *Truganini*, Nicholas Clements and Henry Reynolds' *Tongerlongeter*, and Johnston and Rolls (eds), *Reading Robinson: Companion Essays to George Augustus Robinson's Friendly Mission*. Steve Thomas's documentary *Black Man's Houses* is also an excellent starting point in understanding the importance of the Wybalenna site.

The years of researching and writing this book were made all the more interesting by the times we were going through. My experience of those times was, if not easy, at least manageable, and I appreciate that wasn't the case for many writers. The love and support of my family, most especially my wife Lilly, made the difference. That love continues to mean the world to me.